A Detective Under Fire

H. R. F. Keating

A Detective Under Fire

MACMILLAN

First published 2002 by Macmillan
an imprint of Pan Macmillan Ltd
Pan Macmillan, 20 New Wharf Road, London N1 9RR
Basingstoke and Oxford
Associated companies throughout the world
www.panmacmillan.com

ISBN 1 4050 0107 0

1 3 5 7 9 8 6 4 2

A CIP catalogue record for this book is available from
the British Library.

Typeset by Intype London Ltd
Printed and bound in Great Britain by
Mackays of Chatham plc, Chatham, Kent

Chapter One

Detective Superintendent Harriet Martens, smart in uniform to the last button, stood that Thursday morning in March in the London office of Commander Boxall, head of the ultra-prestigious Maximum Crimes Squad, feeling flatly astonished. Just two minutes earlier the Boxer, as thanks to tales about his attitude to life, love and the criminal fraternity he was known far and wide in police circles, had abruptly risen from behind his desk and, without a word of explanation or apology had walked out.

Almost immediately through the room's partition wall she had heard him calling out a good-morning to members of his élite team next-door. Sharply curious to know what it could have been that had caused him to leave so suddenly when she had only just arrived to pay him the necessary courtesy visit at the start of the inquiry she had been brought down from Birchester to London to conduct, she had got to her feet and moved closer to the wall. And now she heard, loudly ringing out, a few words that sent through her a jolt of outrage.

What, she's arrived, has she, the dozy northern tart.

Immediately after her first reaction, she thought that whoever had shouted out those words had a pretty poor sense of geography.

All right, Birchester does lie some hundred miles north of London, but that hardly makes an officer of the Greater Birchester Police any sort of a northerner.

H. R. F. KEATING

All right, Birchester does lie some hundred miles north of London, but that hardly makes an officer of the Greater Birchester Police any sort of a northerner. Christ, how ignorant people are in the almighty metropolis about anywhere not within a few miles of their world. What's more, it isn't as if I'm Birchester born, or anything like it. Place of birth actually fifty miles south of London, child of an old Hampshire family, and educated, school and university, firmly in the south.

And, *dozy*.

We'll see who's dozy when I've completed this inquiry. Whatever difficulties arise from the curious way it's been set up.

Into her mind, as she stood there by the wall, there came a vivid picture of C.A.G.D. Anstruther, senior member of Her Majesty's Inspectorate of Constabulary, once a legendary chief constable, as she had seen him three days before in his room at the Home Office. Tall, thin almost to the point of fleshlessness, dressed that Sunday morning in tweed jacket, corduroy trousers and subdued check shirt with a soft green tie at its neck, a long face beneath scanty greying hair, eyes set in a sunburst of fine wrinkles.

Across his big, bare desk he had thrust for her to read a folded newspaper, the *Sunday Herald*, its Page One headline screaming BRIBERY IN MAXIMUM CRIMES SQUAD. Under that, almost as insistent, came the less strident, sneakier query *Tapes Reveal Tip of Iceberg?* with the by-line *Frank Parkins, Chief Crime Reporter*.

The Maximum Crimes Squad, she had thought then with a growing feeling of dismayed bewilderment. Set up hardly three years earlier to deal exclusively with crimes of major national and international importance. A highly prestigious team. The best, the very best. And

2

now an allegation like this. All right, it's the *Sunday Herald*, not exactly a paper of repute however much it's apparently flourishing. But still it would hardly print a story like this without some evidence.

And, yes, here it is, just beside a minor story about the plans for the so-called Euro Fence.

Thirteen tapes of disturbing evidence were handed to Scotland Yard yesterday ... The standard way for a paper to seem to keep its nose clean by passing evidence over to the police an hour or two before a story appears. Never mind how long that evidence has actually been in the paper's possession while it waited for the best time to break the story.

So can this be why ... More thoughts whirled through her head. Can this really be the reason why, well before dawn today, the Chief phoned me at home? Why I was told to go with all speed to Birchester Airport and get down to London, to report at the Home Office – on a Sunday, a Sunday – to Mr C.A.G.D. Anstruther. But why me? All right, an accusation in the press of this sort has obviously got to be investigated. But surely not by a mere detective superintendent. Any inquiry ought to be, must be, led by an assistant chief constable at the very least. The Maximum Crimes Squad, pick of the police in all Britain.

She finished reading and looked up.

'A bad business, sir. The much-vaunted Max, as the media call it. Horribly bad, even if what it says about *may be a scandal that goes much wider* turns out to be just a bit of puff. But— but what I don't quite understand is why I am here reading about it.'

C.A.G.D. Anstruther gave her a wintry smile.

'I rather counted on you asking me that, Superintendent. It gives me the opportunity to make matters altogether clear at the outset. You must have thought already that, if these *tip of the iceberg* allegations are to be investigated, as indeed they must be, then it requires action under Section 49 of the 1964 Police Act. There should be a stringent inquiry, led by the most highly regarded chief constable available. And I was ready late last night – they woke the Home Secretary, poor lady, with the earliest edition straight off the presses, and after her myself – to set about arranging just that.'

He paused, gripped the bridge of his long narrow nose between thumb and finger and slowly drew his hand downwards as if it would bring behind it an ordered series of thoughts.

'Yes,' he said.

For a moment he hesitated.

'But then it was represented to me,' he went on, 'by Lord Candover, the Minister of State, who, you'll know, looks after police affairs, that I should take into consideration the Maximum Crimes Squad's present task.'

He paused again.

'What I'm going to tell you,' he said, 'is strictly confidential. Thank goodness, there's no mention of it in the *Sunday Herald*. But the squad's sole task at present is a highly sensitive, large-scale investigation into what has come to be called people-smuggling.'

Ah, yes, Harriet registered. Sensitive, indeed. That little headline I noticed, the Euro Fence scheme, designed to check at the borders the mass illegal flow of immigrants into Europe. There's been plenty of controversy about it.

'Our information from Interpol, from the FBI and other sources,' Mr Anstruther went smoothly on, 'is that what were, until recently, a number of independent rackets have been subject to a series of take-overs and have ended as more or less one worldwide organization, run from Colombia where they've realized that trading in human beings is even more lucrative than trading in drugs. We believe their overall profits run now at something like sixteen billion pounds a year. Sixteen billion. The tentacles stretch from China, where there are links with the so-called snakeheads, on through Asia and then to the Middle East – poor devils in Iraq desperate to get out and willing to pay and pay – all the way to Mexicans still trying to cross the border into the States.'

He leant forward across the wide desk to add emphasis to what he was going to say.

'Now the Maximum Crimes Squad has been tasked with countering the British end of the whole business, this country being, as you know, the major destination for refugees as well as for deluded people hoping to find work here. Very well, it was pointed out to me that media comment on the squad being engaged in this task would risk its operations being dangerously hampered. So the suggestion is that an inquiry by an inconspicuous officer from some provincial force would meet the case. A matter of not rocking the boat should these allegations eventually prove to be confined, say, to the pair of low-ranking rotten apples the *Sunday Herald* does name.'

Harriet thought.

'I see that, sir. But isn't there a risk that an inquiry into what is after all an élite team, if it is conducted simply by an officer of my comparatively junior rank, would not have the – what shall I say? – the firepower to resolve the matter?'

'And it is for that reason, Superintendent, that,

5

when I came to consider which force to ask to second some officer, I chose Greater Birchester Police, and specifically yourself. You may not be aware that, thanks to more than a little media interest – all those stories about the *Hard Detective* – your name is not unknown at the Home Office. So, yes, though of course you will be working under some difficulties, considerable difficulties even, I am relying on you.'

He fell silent, directing at her a long, speculative look.

'Yes,' he said at last. 'Relying on you. Not necessarily, however, because of your much commented-on implacable attitude to all wrongdoing. I have had, I may say, access to your personal record, and from what I read there I suspect you will be able to bring to this inquiry a certain quality not every police officer possesses.'

Once again he sat in silence.

So, is he going to tell me what that quality is, Harriet asked herself.

He was. But what C.A.G.D. Anstruther eventually brought out with careful deliberation came as a complete surprise.

'You called the Maximum Crimes Squad just now an élite team, Miss Martens, and so it can be said to be. And as such, if any allegations of the seriousness of those the *Sunday Herald* hints at should arise about it, it would seem right to have them investigated at an equally high level. However, a team of that calibre has been ruled out. So . . .'

He came to a momentary halt, then offered her a diffident, wintry smile.

'You know, Miss Martens, I am conscious that in today's police service I myself am something of an

6

anachronism. Indeed, I shall be retiring altogether in a few months, and some new officer, with perhaps new ideas, will be occupying my chair. But, as someone who began in the police in very distant days, I am burdened – I think *burdened* is the word – with a set of attitudes that are now, I'm sure, frequently regarded as absurdly out of keeping with the times. I am, in short, a dinosaur. Or, perhaps I should call myself' – the smile flickered on to his face again – 'a gentleman. A gentleman, as you may say, of the old school.'

He let the description rest there for a moment.

'As such,' he went on, 'my notion of what constitutes an élite is possibly rather different from the usage which you, in speaking of the Maximum Crimes Squad, somewhat casually adopted a moment ago.'

Hint of criticism here, Harriet swiftly wondered. C.A.G.D. not someone to approve of *somewhat casually* doing or saying anything.

Again his small reticent smile.

'But, you know, I have a suspicion that, despite that casual reference, you may well share something of my feeling for what a true élite is. You have had, I saw from your P/R, a somewhat unusual upbringing for these days. A father, to begin with, who was a colonel in a distinguished infantry regiment. Then your education at an old-established girls' public school, followed by Cambridge. And a remarkably good degree there, if I may say so. In short, if I see myself as a gentleman – however little I make mention of it – then you, I believe, come from the same stable. I hesitate to say a *lady*, because that implies something rather different from what I have in mind, but the word will have to suffice.'

He leant forward abruptly across the gleaming

surface of his wide desk, and Harriet saw in his wrinkle-surrounded eyes a look of shrewdness that, in C.A.G.D. Anstruther's days as a detective like herself, must have sent a sudden shiver of apprehension through many a criminal on the opposite side of an interview-room table.

'That's why I am happy, Miss Martens, that as there has to be an inquiry into the top reaches of the Maximum Crimes Squad, you should be conducting it. I believe you will bring to it – what shall I say? – inherent qualities that both tell you what should be done and give you the determination to see that it is done.'

Harriet sat there for a moment, if not totally stunned, at least reduced to dumb silence.

Then a trickle of inward amusement, mingled with an almost solemn sense of pride, lifted her out of her inward-looking state.

So, she had thought, is this what I am? And is this why, of all the detective superintendents from one end of the country to the other, I am regarded as the one to be given this task? Because in Mr Anstruther's eyes I am a female gentleman.

Chapter Two

Commander Boxall had not stayed for long in the room next-door to his own from which Harriet had heard those mocking words *dozy northern tart*. But when he returned to his desk, where in the ashtray the squashed butts of three dark cigarillos still left Harriet inhaling their harsh smell, he went to his chair and slammed his massively broad frame down into it, stretching the seams of his dark flecked-tweed three-piece suit to straining point. The heavy gold watch-chain across his waistcoat gave a little jump.

Well, Harriet thought, after all he isn't called the Boxer for nothing. If this is the put-you-in-your-place way he chooses to go about things, it is. I'm not going to let it make any difference to me.

'Okay,' he said, after awarding her a bellicose glare for a second or two, 'you're welcome here at Persimmon House, Miss Martens, though Christ knows why we've been landed with you – bloody *Sunday Herald* storm in a piss-pot. Still, you're here, and we'll have to make the best of it. Haven't been able to offer you any accommodation in-house, of course. This place may be nicely out-of-the-way of any interference from my old comrades in the Met, but we're bloody cramped all the same.'

'That's all right, Commander,' Harriet replied,

9

carefully neutral. 'I've been allocated offices in an off-shoot place of the Met's at the Surrey Docks Business Park, over on the other side of the river at Rotherhithe. It's a fair way from here, of course. But I dare say I'll manage.'

Had she seen a tiny flicker of smugness on that fiercely hooked-nosed face at the mention of the distant Business Park? Had a few quick strings been pulled to put difficulties in the way of an investigation that, it was plain, the Boxer in no way welcomed? No telling. But . . .

'All right, but let me warn you, we can't let you park any cars at the back here. We need all the room we've got for ourselves. So when you come calling you'll have to find somewhere outside. And, you won't know this, but the whole Westbourne Grove area's parked bumper-to-bumper nowadays. Trendy Notting Hill types' trendy vehicles.'

'Well, I haven't actually brought a car down to London. I didn't like to deprive my husband. So, until I can get hold of what I'll need from the Met, the poor old taxpayer's going to have a pretty big bill for cabs.'

A momentary look of disappointment opposite? Hard to say. But nice to have shown I've no intention of being walked over.

'Sod the taxpayers. They're damn lucky to have me and my lads putting our thumbs firmly down on the people-smugglers until those weak-kneed politicians get their famous Euro Fence set up. But never mind that. What I'm not happy about at this moment is having two of my best lads unavailable. Bloody suspended. How long's that going to last for?'

'As long as it takes, Commander. And that will depend, as you must be aware, on how much co-operation I get from you. And every other member of your squad, senior or junior.'

'Oh, you'll get co-operation. I've got to give it. But take note. You'll get the co-operation you're entitled to, and no more. I won't have some sneaky bitch from God knows where poking their nose into what doesn't concern them. I've got an operation to run here, and a bloody important one. World-wide ramifications. Don't you forget that.'

'No, Commander, Mr Anstruther at the Home Office has fully explained to me the extent of your current operation, and I well appreciate its importance. But let me make it clear. I have been tasked with investigating the allegations made in the *Sunday Herald* three days ago, serious allegations backed, it appears, by tapes of apparently good evidential value. And I am going to do whatever's necessary to discover what substance there is in the doubts they raise, to ask whatever questions I see fit. And I shall expect answers. Full answers, and truthful ones.'

Commander Boxall, the Boxer, looked at her steadily and silently.

From the far side of the desk she caught a whiff of his after-shave, cutting through the room's permanent odour of rank tobacco smoke. By no means your common-or-garden Old Spice, something altogether classier, fine and astringent.

No. There's more to the Boxer than an excess of male ego. He hasn't got to where he is without superior qualities to that. A formidable opponent. If opponent he's going to be. As I think he is.

But now from him, abruptly, a climb-down.

'So, tell me, Superintendent, are you being properly looked after down here? Where are you staying? And your team? You brought some likely lads and lasses from Birchester, as well as this stinking awful March weather?'

A climb-down? Or an adroit shifting from dangerous ground? Plus another little jab in making the miserable weather outside something I'm supposed to have brought down with me, the dozy northern tart's unwelcome gift. And, damn it, as a matter of fact it was pleasantly warm for early March in Birchester yesterday.

But nothing to quarrel over in that. Keep challenges for when the going gets truly rough.

'Yes,' she answered, nice and smoothly, 'I'm getting some people from my own force. But it takes a little time to free good officers from their current responsibilities. As you'll know. However, the first two or three of them should be here this evening, and I'll be able to brief them first thing tomorrow. In the meantime, I might try and see one or the other of those two suspended DCs.'

'Oh, yes? Early bird, are we? Well, okay, if that's the way you are. They'll both be at home, or should be, hanging about instead of working for me. My Miss Mouse outside'll give you their addresses.'

'Miss Mouse?'

Harriet had not been able to stop herself asking the question. From the quick glance she had given the young woman in the Boxer's outer office there had seemed to be, true enough, a distinct mousiness in her appearance. A little plump creature with a small face and a pale pointed nose and, yes, mousy hair sleeked back to a wisp of a pony-tail. But surely *Mouse* can't really be her name?

The Boxer shot out a quick, and quickly furious, glance.

'Does it matter what I call the girl, miss? Her name's House, as a matter of fact. So ask Miss House, Miss House, for the addresses of those two. She'll give them to you, quick as a mou— She'll give them to you.'

He glared across his desk.

'I said *co-operation*,' he snapped. 'And that's what you'll get. Though I doubt if you'll have much joy from DC Frecker, or DC Underwood, come to that. They're both of them pretty cheesed-off with Mr Frank Parkins of the *Sunday Herald* and his damn lies.'

'So it's your view, sir, that even the accusation made against those two is just so much newspaper guess-work?'

'Yes, Superintendent, it is.'

Across the mess on the desk a straight look of defiance. The Boxer.

'There are those tapes, of course, Commander. Thirteen of them, I understand. I've not listened to them yet, but I'm supposed to be getting copies shortly. Perhaps, in view of what you've said, I'd better see the strength of those before I go any further. Have you heard them yet?'

'No, I haven't. But I don't expect they'll be worth much of my time when they are sent to me.'

'That would have to be a matter for your judgment. And mine.'

The Boxer's mouth set in a tight line. And then suddenly he smiled.

'They been looking after you properly, those people over at the Yard?' he asked. 'Found you some half-way decent hotel and all that?'

Well, well. The dozy northern tart's presence in

13

London acknowledged to be reasonable at last. Or is it? Is he just trying another tack? Still, a bit of conciliation from me, too, now. Made my point made, I think.

'Thanks for asking, sir. But I've managed actually to find a billet for myself, with an old London friend. In Ealing. She's an ex-Met officer, as a matter of fact, someone I've known since we trained together.'

'Ah, yes, you're ex-Met yourself, aren't you? Tell me, whatever made you go off up to the sticks?'

So, Mr Anstruther is not the only one to have got hold of information about me. The Boxer been indulging in a spot of careful reconnaissance? Into the enemy's forward positions? Looks pretty much like it.

But she smiled as she answered. If she had to strain to do so.

'Well, the Met's not the only force where you can have a decent career. But I mustn't keep you any longer, sir. What I'd like to do, if it's convenient, now that we've at least met, is to have a more informal discussion some time, perhaps over lunch.'

'I don't have time for long lunches, Miss Martens. I've got on my hands what's probably the most important investigation the country's ever had.'

But then another sudden friendly-seeming smile.

'Still, dare say I could manage a quick drink round the corner in the Duke of Norfolk. Phone me.'

Walking away from Persimmon House, icy rain flicking at her face, Harriet found she was thinking, not so much of the Boxer and his all-too-evident determination to put obstacles in her path, as of what she had felt the Sunday before as the afternoon plane had flown her back, almost shell-shocked, to Birchester.

What is this I've been tasked with, she had asked herself again and again. An inquiry of the utmost importance, no doubt about that. Corruption in the Maximum Crimes Squad. All right, it's not as big as the National Crime Squad with its large team of detectives from all over the country and at its head a director-general, no less. But the Max, she told herself recalling the long briefing C.A.G.D Anstruther had given her, is actually more important. Its every officer specially chosen, its targets often transcending national boundaries. If corruption exists in the Max, it's got to be rooted out. A cancer in the guts of the whole police service.

Yes, but, more than dealing with that, is what more that's been laid on my shoulders.

Why, after all, did C.A.G.D Anstruther choose me? Not because I really am the sole officer capable of this vital rooting-out. Damn it, there must be a hundred detective superintendents, more, whose records over the years make mine look nothing much. Yet Mr Anstruther, legendary C.A.G.D Anstruther, wanted me.

Was it, after all, because, if it all goes wrong, there'll be no great scandal? Because, if I am sent back to Birchester with a black mark against my name, not to be washed away till my retirement date, there won't be any too important repercussions? Because, if things go very badly wrong, I could be summarily got rid of without yelling and screaming from the media? That's possible. I suppose it is possible.

But no. Mr Anstruther chose me because he believed I was the one to press forward the inquiry, whatever the obstacles, till the whole truth comes to light. I know it was for that. He wasn't feeding me any boosting pap. I can't really say how or why I know he

15

wasn't. But I know it. Nor was he looking for any sort of patsy. He was looking for someone who could do this job, looking perhaps for the only person in the circumstances who can do it. However steel-spiked with difficulties it proves to be.

Yes, he chose me because of what he had fixed on from those few almost absurd details that told him what I am, what I have been from the day of my birth. From those details he had read of in my P/R, that record which, save in really exceptional circumstances, he should not have seen. Just as I should not have, ready to read in my bulging briefcase at this moment, copies of the personal records of all the officers of the Maximum Crimes Squad.

She had tried then, unsuccessfully, to repress a tiny amused smile.

He chose me because I am a gentleman. A female gentleman.

Then she had forced herself back into thoughts more to the point.

I've been told I can have the pick of the officers I want to assist me. From the Birchester force for the most part, of course, people I know about. But I've actually been given a free hand, with the proviso only that I limit my team to the smallest number I need.

A list. I could begin to make a list now. There's half an hour still till we land.

From her briefcase, squeezed up beside the confidential files she had been given, she pulled out a notepad. Out of the top pocket of her uniform jacket next she slipped the silver ballpoint she had been given for her twenty-first.

A name or two jotted down.

Harriet had been told that the offices she had been allocated at the Metropolitan Police out-station in the Surrey Docks Business Park were now available, so she had left Persimmon House aiming to get to her friend Rekha Pathak's flat with time to change out of the uniform she had felt she should wear for her formal meeting with the head of the Maximum Crimes Squad into ordinary working clothes.

Rekha Pathak had once, if only for some months, been Detective Sergeant Rekha Brown, Metropolitan Police. In the days when Met officers had not looked particularly kindly on either women or Asians, Rekha had decided that there was no career for her in the police, nor even one as the wife of PC Michael Brown. So divorce, reversion to her maiden name, of which she was proud, and a job in social services.

It had been at much the same time that Harriet herself had left the Met, having come to the conclusion that a woman police officer there was never going to be regarded as much more than, in a phrase her father often used, *a head cook and bottle-washer*. In Birchester, she had risen fast up the ladder. As had Rekha in the world of social work to the point where, now, her activities were confined to membership of numerous statutory bodies.

Harriet had kept up with her over the years, if largely with Christmas cards, safely confined to secular holly and robins on their way to a Brahmin. When, however, she had needed to be in London all day for any reason and her husband was otherwise occupied, she had on occasion taken up a standing invitation to spend the night in Ealing. In the way that happens with some friendships, she and Rekha had never found long intervening gaps had dissolved the rapport they had discovered in the gym and the lecture-rooms of the Peel Centre at Hendon.

Now in Ealing she helped herself, in Rekha's absence, to a quick early lunch from her fridge. Then she set out again making for the nearest Underground station, well wrapped against the chill, rain-flecked wind in her newish calf-length green coat, but with a scarf which she had always hated, a dreadful Paisley design, knotted under her chin in place of the round green hat, easily blown-off, that went so well with the coat.

She found the complicated journey to Rotherhithe and the Surrey Docks Business Centre even more frustratingly interminable than she had expected, and soon sharply regretted leaving the car back in Birchester for John to use. First she took the Central Line from Ealing Broadway to Liverpool Street, eighteen stops with delays, it seemed, at each one. Next came two stops only, after she had marched her way to the platform for the Metropolitan Line, that brought her to Whitechapel. And finally, after another tramp to another platform, there was the swoop under the river, three stops on the East London Line.

Coming out of Rotherhithe station, she had hoped to hail a taxi. But, it seemed, this was a part of the world where such things were almost non-existent. So eventually, with a frustrated sigh, she extracted her *A-Z* guide from her briefcase and, winding her wretched scarf over her head again, set off through the rain to find a long curling street, Timber Pond Road, somewhere along which she knew the Business Park was located.

Clutching the rapidly spattered *A-Z*, she trudged along counting the turnings, conscious that at every step her coat was getting more soaked, her scarf doing less and less to keep the wet out of her hair. She tried to make herself think about the name Timber Pond Road, reflecting, she guessed, Rotherhithe's now ended history as part of London's once-busy docks. But the fingers of cold wind poking at the back of her neck rapidly put to rout any such academic speculation. Some other day perhaps when this wet misery, somehow due she could not help thinking to the Boxer's malevolent determination to make her life difficult, had lifted. Surely weather as foul as this could not last for ever.

At long last she came in sight, towering up, of a large black-painted board, *Surrey Docks Business Park*. Underneath that heading, she saw as she approached, a series of little rectangles carrying the names and block numbers of the various enterprises the Park sheltered, firms no doubt accepting its remoteness in exchange for low rents. She glanced over them. Two theatre companies, neither of which she had heard of. What was evidently the place where a publishing concern – one she had heard of – stored books that had failed to sell. A curtain designer, whatever that was, and – this might be useful – *Billy's Diner*. And finally in the bottom left-hand corner, in very small letters, *Metropolitan Police*, with beneath *No Public Admittance*.

Trudging past blank-faced block after blank-faced block, none showing much sign of life, she at last located the place, part of Block 15. A rawly young uniformed officer was manning the small reception area.

'I've been expecting you, ma'am,' he said when Harriet had shown him her warrant card. 'You've been given a couple of vacant rooms on the first floor, but I think you'll find they've been fully equipped.'

'Good. But, tell me, what happens in the rest of the Met's share of the block?'

'It's a records store, ma'am. Mostly junk, in fact. But some of it's got a high security rating, so there has to be somebody on duty here. Any help I can give you, you've only to ring down and ask.'

'Right. Well, you can tell me one thing here and now. Billy's Diner? Will my team be able to eat there?'

'Oh, yes, ma'am. I go there myself. The food's all right—'

He stopped himself, and looked at her.

'Well, not quite senior officers mess, ma'am.'

'Oh, I'm not quite as fussy as that, Constable.'

A faint reddening appeared on cheeks which, she thought, scarcely needed to be shaved. And then, suddenly, a deeper blush.

'Oh, sorry. Sorry, ma'am, I clean forgot. A package has been delivered for you. They— They said urgent, ma'am.'

The tapes, Harriet thought at once. Copies of the evidence the *Sunday Herald* sent to Scotland Yard.

'Where is it?' she barked at the poor embarrassed youngster.

'Up— Upstairs, ma'am. I told them to leave it there.'

In less than a minute she had run up the stairs, found her set of offices – barely furnished but well-heated, thank goodness – and through the open door of the second room, bulky on the plain wooden desk, a large package.

Not waiting to take off her rain-soaked coat and only tossing aside her horrible Paisley scarf, she tugged off the white plastic bands round the box, and, opening it, saw, as she had expected, a bundle of tapes and a machine to play them on.

She slipped on its headphones, banged in Tape One and pressed *Play*.

Soon, however, she realized, not wholly to her surprise, that the bulk of their contents was pretty much useless. The long meandering chats DC Frecker and DC Underwood – called, she discovered, for fairly obvious reasons Pantsie – had had with a minor crook named Arnie Voles produced for almost all their length no more than idle talk. But, no doubt about it, there were occasional passages which pretty well substantiated Frank Parkins's case against the two of them. They certainly made nonsense of the Boxer's implied suggestion that his two detectives were probably doing no more than pursuing to the full their parts in the investigation of the many-tentacled people-smuggling racket.

DC Frecker, referred to once or twice as Freckles, could be heard suggesting to Voles that he should produce substantial amounts of cash. Why he could be made to do this was not absolutely clear. But, to Harriet's mind, it was plain enough that Voles must have been extorting money from illegal arrivals in London under threat of denouncing them to the Immigration Service, and that both Frecker and to a lesser extent Underwood were in turn extorting money from him.

The Boxer was probably perfectly aware that this was likely to have been the case. But plainly he was not going to allow any officer of his élite team, picked by himself, to suffer any penalty without making a fight of it. And the tapes' evidence was unclear enough perhaps to give him room for manoeuvre still.

Which made Harriet all the more determined at least to nail both men so that they stayed nailed.

But, she thought, as the final tape went rattling to its end and she put aside her notepad, if the evidence against those two suspended men is all that there is to the business, would the Boxer have taken the attitude towards me that he has? He might, of course. But isn't he doing more, a lot more, than just being a tiger fighting for its cubs, right or wrong? Why, really, is he so much opposed to me that he's gone to the length of pulling strings with friends in the Met in order to make my life difficult? And more. Hasn't he gone to the extent of talking to people he knows in the Greater Birchester Police? Going that far to find out everything he can about me?

So does he, in fact, know, or strongly suspect, that the hints of *a wider scandal* in the *Sunday Herald* may well be more than just guesswork? A lot more? And so does he see me as more than a mere irritant? Does he see me as the enemy, to be fought to a standstill with whatever weapons come to hand?

All right, on the tapes there's nothing, other than a few wild surmises, a few would-be knowing jokes, to give substance to Frank Parkins's hints about corruption at the squad's highest level. Yet Parkins has set down his hints. In cold print. So surely he knows something, however tenuous, with which to back them up? He must do.

And – the thought came suddenly – can it even possibly be that the Boxer himself is playing the same sort of dirty game that his Freckles and Pantsie were, if for infinitely higher stakes? Is that the reason for all the hostility? Or is it that just – *just*, for heaven's sake – he's protecting another officer high up in the Max?

Someone, of course, he directly appointed himself? And, if that's so, will I be able to get at whoever that is as surely as I'm determined I'm going to get at friends Pantsie and Freckles?

From her briefcase she hauled out, once more, the extra copy of the *Sunday Herald* she had purchased before taking the plane back to Birchester. Despite the efforts of the Monday papers to expand on Frank Parkins's story, it was still, she thought, her best source of information.

Once more she read over the now creased and smeared front page.

But, ponder as she would each word in the light of what she had just heard on the tapes, there was still no more to be got from it all than she had learnt on Sunday. Plain that Parkins had some inkling of something much graver that might lie ahead for the Max. Or plain at least that he wanted his readers to believe he had such information, if only to have them rush to buy next week's paper. But were his hints in point of fact no more than that? Cleverly used words to make it seem that there was something juicier to come? Revelations about, not two detective constables who had succumbed to greed, but about high-ups in the country's most prestigious police squad?

For the fourth, fifth or sixth time she scrutinized her list of the Maximum Crimes Squad personnel, down from *Commander Charles Boxall*, through the names of his senior officers, Detective Superintendent Quinton, second-in-command, Detective Chief Inspector Griffin, DI Browning, DI Phillips, DI Outhwaite, DI Mary Smith, even the file for the squad's former Number Two, Detective Superintendent Mallard dead of a heart attack almost as soon as the squad was formed. Down to the most junior recruit at detective-constable level she scrutinized each file, though she knew it was something of a futile process. But she felt really that if there was a name there that would prove eventually to be that of someone being paid by Pablo Grajales, the distant, powerful former drugs czar now in control of the more lucrative people-smuggling racket, no amount of looking would help her to pinpoint it now.

No, she thought, a better way at this time to get my nose into what's happening, rather than have long battling interviews with two cunning Detective Constables, will be to visit the offices of the *Sunday Herald* and talk to Frank Parkins.

She glanced over at the room's squarely flat window. Rain was streaming down it, and a thin pool of it had collected on the little strip of window-ledge at its foot.

Right, if I must go out into that, I must. But there's one thing I'm going to do first.

She picked up the phone on the bare wooden desk, found that it was connected and dialled the number she had for Scotland Yard's supply department. Yes, a car. I want a car delivered to me here. By tomorrow at the latest. And maybe in due course I shall need two or three other cars.

Chapter Three

Harriet had unthinkingly hoped to go to the *Sunday Herald* offices in one of the cabs she had told the Boxer she had every intention of using. But, coming out of blank-faced Block 15, she found that the rain had now turned into heavy sleet, whipped into a sort of mini-blizzard by a newly sharp east wind whistling up the river. And nowhere in sight along Timber Pond Road, as she sheltered under the scant protection of the tall black-painted locations board, was there any passing traffic, let alone a taxi plying for hire.

Not another human being even anywhere to be seen, apart from the man along there, or perhaps woman – difficult to make out under the hood of that jacket – hunched over a moped at the kerb, busy, despite this bloody sleet, having one of those long, long mobile chats people love to indulge in. Giving up at last, she set out on foot for the Underground again, noticing only that her distant companion in misery had evidently decided, too, not to stay any longer.

By the time she had found, a good way further along the south bank of the river, Herald House, a looming new building all glaring, flat-to-the-walls windows and heavy rectangular concrete pillars, she was feeling much more bedraggled than she cared to be. But there was little to be done about that, and, squaring her shoulders, she mounted the wide flight of steps and pushed her way determinedly through the building's hugely tall glass doors.

Yes, they said at Reception, Frank Parkins is in. They rang him, and, yes again, he would be happy to see Detective Superintendent Martens. 'Take the lift to the fourth floor. Mr Parkins will meet you.'

And there, waiting outside the lift in the savagely neutral building, was the *Sunday Herald* chief crime reporter. He was standing slouched against a coffee-machine, a faintly snide smile playing over his long face, giving a glimpse of twisted, tobacco-stained teeth. Suede jacket, blackish at the edges of the pockets, its collar lying not quite flat. Green trousers, heavily creased around the midriff. Striped tie, stringy from much wrenching up and down, hanging loosely from the unbuttoned shirt collar.

'Well,' he said, 'so this is the famous Hard Detective, cause of all that fuss up in Birchester the other day. Or am I wrong?'

So, here's another sharp-nose besides the Boxer, quick to flick up a name on a computer screen just as soon as the receptionist below had given it to him.

'Perfectly right,' she replied. 'Though it's your colleagues in the press that I blame for the *fuss*.'

'Do you? I thought you were wallowing in it. And are you down here in the Smoke now to wallow yet more?'

'I hope not. And I rather think you're the one creating fuss at the moment.'

'So you read the paper up there in the north, do you? You saw my little piece? Well, it's nice to know I've created some fuss, even though you seem to disapprove. But that can't be what's brought you down to these dangerous parts.'

'Mr Parkins,' Harriet cut in sharply, 'I would like, if I may, to have a word with you in private.'

'Ah, some dirty doings in Birchester? Come into my humble abode, quick as you like.'

He turned, opened a door with his name painted on it a few yards down the long featureless corridor and ushered her in.

The room was much as Harriet expected. A mess. Strongly smelling of cigarettes, despite the statutory notice fixed to the wall near the door, *This Is A Non-Smoking Area*. A desk, its computer, yes, in use, with three separate telephones beside it and as many untidy piles of papers as there had been scattered across the Boxer's desk at Persimmon House.

'Okay,' Frank Parkins said, 'plonk yourself down somewhere and tell me what it's all about.'

Harriet glanced round, saw a chair without a pile of old newspapers on it, and sat.

'Very well. But what I have to say will be in strict confidence.'

Frank Parkins's face broke into a twisted-teeth smile.

'Come on,' he said, '*in strict confidence*, to a crime reporter?'

'Mr Parkins, I said *in confidence*. Let me tell you, unless I'm absolutely sure what I'm going to say will not go beyond this room, I won't keep you one minute more.'

'Well, well, what a Hard Detective it is. But how can I convince you I can keep my fingers off my computer, if it's worth my while putting them there?'

'Oh, your word will do. Provided you're aware that

if you break it you'll never get anything more from me. And I might have a lot to say.'

Parkins grinned.

'You win.'

'Right. Then let me explain. I am here to see you, in fact, precisely because of the fuss you created last Sunday.'

Frank Parkins's eyebrows rose up.

'Yes,' Harriet went on. 'It has been decided at high level in the Home Office that your less substantiated allegations about the Maximum Crimes Squad should not receive the level of inquiry they may seem to warrant. The fact is that the Max has been tasked with investigating—'

'The worldwide people-smuggling racket.'

'How—' Harriet let that word escape before better thoughts intervened.

'I do keep my ears open, you know,' Parkins said. 'Things get about, even if no one will admit to them officially.'

Harriet cursed herself. It was more than confidential that the people-smuggling investigation had been given to the Max. It was secret, and it needed to be. The squad was not going up against a handful of British criminals, however high-powered. Their enemy was operating on a global scale. And the squad's involvement was something no newspaper reporter should write about. And now she had more or less confirmed what Parkins had guessed or gathered.

A moment's more thought and she saw she was over-reacting. Something on the scale of the fight against Pablo Grajales's shadowy worldwide enterprise could not be kept entirely secret. And, if anybody was to have acquired a hint of what was going on, then a crime reporter from a well-funded newspaper was likely to be that person. Sooner or later Frank Parkins would have picked up enough hints to have put two and two together. No doubt there were other journalists who had got hold of similar tags of knowledge.

'Very well,' she said, 'if you know that much, you will be aware, or you ought to be, that the squad's work is going to be unnecessarily hampered if it is subject at every moment to— Shall I say, press intrusion?' Here comes the crunch, she thought. If I'm to persuade this slavering news hound to tell me what lies behind his wider allegations, then I'll have to seem to put myself under an obligation to him so that he'll reciprocate in the hope of at some time in the future learning things from me things I strictly ought not even to hint at. 'However,' she went on cautiously, 'since you have learnt what the Max is doing and have not put it into print, I assume you can keep silent. If it's in your interests. So I'd be obliged now if you take care that nothing I tell you goes any further.'

'If what you tell me is worth keeping to myself, I'll do that. For a time at least. So, fire away.'

'Very well. The truth is that the inquiry into the evidence you handed in at the Yard last Saturday has been put into my hands alone. And this is something the powers-that-be are particularly anxious not to have become common knowledge. If it does, it would not be long before more people than you, Mr Parkins, will be asking why the inquiry is being conducted at such a discreetly low level. And then what the Max is at present engaged on would almost certainly come fully to light. Their targets in this country and in places abroad will be warned. And will take counter measures, counter measures that might even result in people losing their lives.'

'Okay, okay. You've made your point. So why exactly have you come to see me?'

'Very well. It's not, of course, about what DCs Frecker and Underwood have done. That's something that can be dealt with in two or three days. Suspensions turned into dismissals, and that'd be that. But in your piece last Sunday, Mr Parkins, you hinted at more corruption in the Max than what those two have done. *Tip of the iceberg*. That's what your headline writer said. All right, perhaps you haven't got evidence you can print to back that. But evidence of some sort you must have. And I want to know what that is. Or were you just playing with words to make yourself look bigger than you are?'

Frank Parkins gave another of his twisted-teeth grins.

'Clever lady, aren't you? You're saying that either I'll have to admit I'm a journalistic chancer who's got nothing worth anybody knowing, or that I'm so good at my trade that I've got hold of something it's my duty to pass on to you. That's where you think you've put me. But what if I don't choose to agree with either of your alternatives?'

'Then it's very likely you're laying yourself open to a charge of withholding evidence of a crime.'

Frank Parkins smiled.

'But that's a charge you won't be very anxious to bring, isn't it? Not if it means me standing in the dock in some Magistrates' Court somewhere and coming out with just what it is that the Max is investigating.'

Harriet thought for a moment.

'All right then, suppose I simply appeal to you as,

what shall we say, *a good citizen*? After all, it is actually your duty to give what evidence you have, however slight, to the proper authorities. In this case, to me.'

'Oh, come on. That's plain bullshit. Frankly I'm—'

One of the three phones on the desk shrilled out. With a faint shrug Parkins picked it up.

A peremptory squawk from the other end.

'But I've got someone with me.'

More squawking.

'Okay, okay, I'll come up.'

He banged down the receiver.

'Sorry. You'll have to wait to hear the rest of that. I shouldn't be very long.'

He left in a few rapid strides. The door staying wide in his wake.

Harriet looked at it. An idea slid into her mind.

Quietly she walked over, glanced out into the corridor, saw Frank Parkins vanishing into the lift.

For a long moment then she experienced the common enough reluctance to embark on any course where the outcome is altogether unclear. Almost a paralysis of the will. But, with a shake of her head, she pushed the feeling away. She had been given a task. Not to assess the evidence against a pair of lowly detective constables, but to find out whether corruption had spread high into the prestigious Maximum Crimes Squad. A way of advancing that task had by chance just been put in front of her. Right or wrong, daring or dangerous, that chance had to be taken.

She closed the door in one quick movement, turned and went round to the far side of Parkins's untidy desk.

And, yes, on his computer there was still her own hastily consulted mini-CV. So, with any luck, no password needed before she looked elsewhere in its files.

Rapidly she got to work, calling up whatever file-names looked likely to hold the material pointing to corruption in the higher reaches of the Max that Parkins was determined to keep from her. If there was, in fact, anything to be found.

Maximum, Max, Maxsquad, Boxall, Boxer, Corruption, Corrupt.

Yes, something coming up here.

But, no. No, damn it, here's a file under *Corrupt* all right. But a password needed to get into it. So, has Mr Parkins got something there about what he's found out? Something worthwhile? Or does the file relate to some sort of corruption elsewhere? It could do. There's always corruption about. No way of finding out. No way at all.

But he still may have a file, an openable file, with something for me.

Once more she began her tapping, trying now the names of each of the senior officers in the Max, as she remembered them, indelibly, from her reading of their personal records – Browning, Griffin, Outhwaite, Phillips, Quinton, Smith. But, again, nothing. Hurriedly she turned to less senior names under which Parkins might have recorded titbits of information he had got hold of. With no better results till she tried *Frecker, Underwood, Freckles, Pantsie.* Yes, screeds of stuff under the last two nick-names. But rapid scrolling revealed nothing more than what she already knew. *Voles, Arnie,* she typed. No luck. Then *Persimmon,* as a last wild try.

Once more, no good. And nowhere more to go that she could think of.

She sighed, and remembered she ought to get her own details back up on screen, wryly amused at their file-name, *Hardtec.*

Less hopefully she turned to the drawers of the desk itself. A scribbled reminder of a phone number with a significant name against it? Even a mysteriously sealed envelope?

Only thing for it, to search, and hope.

Ah, something.

A scrawled name on an untidy, papers-spilling file had caught her eye. *Candover.* Could there be somewhere here something about the Max? After all, Lord Candover is the Minister who, in fact, is responsible for me being down here in London.

Look, look.

The routine, familiar from a thousand spinnings of suspects' properties in her earlier days, came back to her intact. To her, or rather to her quick-moving, instinctive fingers. In little more than two minutes they had riffled through the cuttings-jammed file. *The Partying Peer – Move Up for Party-mad Candover – The Fourteenth Lord, A Profile – Minister's Police Brief – On the Fence with the Euro Fence – The Model and the Minister.*

But, if the search routine had come back intact, another buried instinct had atrophied.

She had not heard the door being opened.

'Well, well,' Frank Parkins said. 'The Hard Detective turning into – what? – the hard sneak-thief? The soft sneak-thief? Whichever.'

Damn.

All right, the danger there from the moment I began to hunt. And now I'm totally exposed. Right, make what I can of it nevertheless.

'If you will keep concealed evidence you're bound to hand over, what else can you expect but that I should take advantage of a chance that came my way?'

'Even by committing what is, you should know, a criminal offence?'

'Oh, come on, Mr Parkins. You know I'm not the first police officer ever to cut a corner. Something I dare say you yourself have done a good deal more often than most police officers, and with nothing like such good intentions.'

'Which doesn't actually make what you've been doing any less of an offence.'

'Oh, yes, I know what offence I was committing. I could quote you the sub-section of the Act. But, let me tell you, I'd cheerfully do it again, given the opportunity.'

'Well, you certainly won't get that. Now that I know what a senior police officer coming into my office is capable of, you can be sure no one like you will be allowed to stay alone in here for even half a minute.'

'I dare say we won't be. But don't start seeing yourself as whiter than white. You're not. Not by a long way. If you've come across me committing a minor breach of the law, let me remind you that you are committing a much more serious offence in keeping from me whatever evidence you have against some senior officer of the Maximum Crimes Squad.'

'But what if I haven't got any such evidence?'

'I think you have. Otherwise, why that plain hint last Sunday? You must have something to make that worth printing.'

Frank Parkins grinned.

'Perhaps I was just being a bit naughty. It's possible, isn't it? And, you know, it was actually that plain hint, as you called it, that had me summoned by my Editor just now to talk to our tame lawyer.'

'And what did you say? That those *words complained*

of, as the libel people put it, were true? Or that they were, as you yourself put it, just a piece of naughtiness?'

'Wouldn't you like to know?'

'Yes, I would. It's my duty to find out if the Maximum Crimes Squad is compromised. And I am going to carry out that duty, come what may.'

'Are you indeed? So have you got officers working with you who'll be rather better at burgling my office than your own not very efficient attempt?'

'Which means, does it, that a more efficient attempt would produce something worth finding?'

'Which may or may not mean that. But, let me warn you, now I'm alerted to the possibility I'm certainly going to see that precautions are put in force a good deal more effective than our present ones. So you can tell any amateur burglars on your pay-roll not to bother.'

'And what makes you think I've got *amateur burglars* at my disposal? Or is that just another of your wholly unsubstantiated allegations?'

'Hardly. You may not have managed as yet to recruit to whatever team you've brought with you officers with those particular skills. But I bet you could, without any trouble. I'm sure the Max, for instance, has its share of breaking-and-entering merchants, safe-crackers, forgers and heaven knows what. Though you'll hardly go looking for ones to help you there. Still, I dare say you've got your share of such fellows up in Birchester.'

Well, if we have, Harriet thought, I've taken bloody good care, dozy northern tart or not, to know nothing about them. And, if I'd got to know, I'd have made sure they never came under my orders. A swift look into

Parkins's computer is one thing, but wholesale burglary ought to be left to the security services, if anybody.

'You know, Mr Parkins,' she said, 'I don't think exchanging insults is getting us anywhere. No, let me put it to you, quite simply, once again. Have you got any evidence, however slight, of corruption of any sort in the higher reaches of the Maximum Crimes Squad? And, if you have, are you willing to tell me what it is, in terms as confidential as you like?'

'No dice.'

'I give you one last chance.'

Once more Frank Parkins favoured her with his humourless grin.

'Goodbye, Superintendent. Nice to have met you. Oh, and give my best to Commander Boxall when you try questioning him. If you ever manage to do that. A great one for putting spokes in wheels is the Boxer.'

Harriet turned to the door, reflecting that this nasty individual certainly knew a lot about senior police officers. But Frank Parkins had not finished.

'And remember,' he said as she stepped out, 'you owe me one.'

She turned.

'What if I do?'

'Oh, just that I never forget to call in a favour. Sooner or later.'

Blackly furious with herself, Harriet, emerging from the bleak new building, decided there was nothing more she could do until the officers she had asked for from Birchester had arrived.

Getting even a hint about the top echelon of the Max from Frank Parkins was plainly a dead-end.

No, she thought, the way forward now will have to be working from the bottom up, and hope that it gets me somewhere. What I'll have to do is question Freckles Frecker and Pantsie Underwood. Question them till they drop. But that's not something to be done without another officer by my side. Clever sods like those two will deny anything they say unless I can got them a hundred per cent tied up.

So that's for tomorrow. Now it's *Home, James*.

When she arrived at the Ealing flat, weary, wet and dispirited, she was delighted to find Rekha was at home.

'God, Harriet, you look like a dog coming out of the water. What have you been doing? It's not all that far from the Tube to here.'

'Oh, the wet. That's from tramping round south London. I wanted to see someone at the *Sunday Herald*, and I couldn't find a taxi at that Business Park place. I had to walk for miles.'

'My God. They should never have put you out there in deepest Rotherhithe. But come in, come in. Get rid of your things. I'll make you a decent drink. Unless you want a hot shower first.'

'You know, I'd like that. Wash away some of the frustration. I'm not best pleased with the good offices of the Metropolitan Police just now. I rather suspect, in fact, that putting me and my team all that way out there was something clever arranged on the old-boy network.'

'The Masons? I thought that was done with nowadays.'

'Well, I wouldn't be too sure of that. But, no, I think it was something more informal. My guess is that the famous Commander Boxall wanted to keep me out of his hair, and made a few calls.'

'The Boxer? Yes, that figures. He doesn't only fight with the fists that earned him that Queen's Gallantry Medal of his. He fights, as I remember even from my long-ago Met days, with any and every weapon that comes to hand. But whizz off and get under that shower now, or you'll be fighting a cold as well as the Boxer. We'll talk more over those drinks.'

'Yes, thanks, I'll do that. But, remember, I didn't tell you a thing last night about what I'm down here for.'

'No, no. And you're not going to tell me a thing now,' Rekha said with a grin. 'Goes without saying.'

So, a quarter of an hour later, with Harriet showered and wrapped in her thick dressing-gown and Rekha in her floating soft-blue sari, they began, whiskies in hand, discussing what had never been mentioned earlier.

'So,' Rekha said, 'the Boxer as tricky as ever? Is that what it amounts to? Or is there something more?'

'You're not saying you've actually heard something, after all these years out of the police? Something that might actually show he could be corrupt?'

'My dear, I was only a detective sergeant when the Met and I parted company. No, all I know about the Boxer now is pure gossip from other old Met friends, just his flash lifestyle and all. The Savile Row suits, the Scorpio car. But, tell, tell. Do you think it's really possible he could be taking some huge bribe from someone? The head of the élite Max?'

'God knows. I don't even have more than those hints in the *Sunday Herald* that anyone at the top in the Max is corrupt. And I got damn all out of Frank Parkins there when I went to see him this afternoon. Worse even, I made the appalling mistake, when he was called out of his office, of trying to find something on his computer to give me a lead, and when I couldn't find anything there I began going through his desk drawers. And— And he caught me in the act.'

'Oh, no. Whatever did you do? What happened?'

'Well, I sort of brazened it out. Told him he was committing an offence if he kept secret any evidence of wrongdoing.'

'And it worked?'

'Just about, I think. Only he had some nasty parting words for me.'

'Tell me, every syllable.'

'Okay, confession good for the soul. *You owe me*, he said. Only three syllables, in fact. But they were enough.'

'You're right. You could be in trouble yet. Do you think you're going to see the whole tale laid out in next week's *Herald*?'

'No. No, I don't imagine a creature as sly as my Mr Parkins will content himself with just that. No, I reckon at some stage soon he'll want to learn from me how much I've found out, and if I don't or won't tell him, then it'll be a formal complaint about my conduct.'

'Which might mean your inquiry coming to an abrupt end?'

'Yes. Yes, it could very well mean that. Defeat. All right, that in itself might be tolerable. Just. But I don't want to lose the fight because . . . Well, I was given this job at the particular insistence of a man I've come to have more than a little respect for.'

'You, having much respect for anybody. Doesn't sound like the DC Harriet Martens I used to know.'

'Come on, I wasn't that full of myself. Or was I? Don't answer. No, I'll tell you now who it is I'm talking about. Do you know anything of one of Her Majesty's Inspectors of Constabulary called – wait for it, cluster of classy initials – C.A.G.D. Anstruther?'

'Oh, yes, of course I do. Top-class chief constable before he went into the Inspectorate. Might have been a brother officer to all those family members of mine who for generations graced the police in every part of India, princely rule or British rule.'

'And do you know why he made me his personal choice to conduct this inquiry? It was because my father had been a Regular Army colonel and I had been to a top-ranking girls' public school and one of the older Cambridge colleges. In short he believed I was, though he didn't say it right out, a fully trustworthy female gentleman'

A broad grin appeared on Rekha's pale-brown, still flawless face.

'Well, there's something that really appeals to a high-class Brahmin lady'.

'Okay. So now you can understand how I'm hardly delighted with myself if right at the start, I've buggered up the whole inquiry'.

Chapter Four

'All right,' Harriet said to DS Watson, renowned throughout Greater Birchester Police for the way whatever his two large, flap-like red ears registered remained word for word in his head, 'we'll stop here.'

She peered once again at the *A–Z* guide on her lap.

'Yes, this is Tennyson Road. So Milton Road, where at Number 134 DC Frecker should be spending his days of suspension, is the next turning to the right. And, provided we're at the correct end of that long poetical street, we ought to be within two or three minutes walk of the place. Just as well. It looks as if the rain's about to come down once more.'

'Can't we go into Milton Road itself, ma'am? Drive along till we see Number 134?' Watson asked, looking up at the dark clouds moving sullenly across the sky.

'We could. But I don't want to give Frecker too much warning of our arrival, and a car pulling up just outside the house might well attract his attention, especially one as appallingly noisy as the pool at Scotland Yard was kind enough to provide us with.'

'Yes, like driving a tank.'

And, Harriet privately asked herself, have I been given it because someone has alerted the people at the pool that any hindrances put in my way will be gratefully received?

'Right, let's go,' she said, with a sigh.

Almost at once she saw she had chosen exactly the wrong end of poetical Milton Road. So it was not for ten wind-whipped minutes more, striding along past little almost identical houses one after another, that she was able to march up the broken-tiled, pale mauvish front path of Number 134 and press her gloved finger firmly on the bell-push for Flat 2.

Nothing in response to the long peal.

She rang again, at even greater length. Then at last a sullen voice issued from the entry-phone.

'Who's that? What d'yer want, this time of the morning, for God's sake?'

'Detective Superintendent Martens and Detective Sergeant Watson, to see DC Frecker.'

'Oh, sod—'

'No, Constable, you may be on suspension but you're still a police officer, and I am authorized to ask you questions. Open up.'

The entry-phone buzzer sounded.

Harriet pushed swiftly at the door. The two of them went thundering up the thinly-carpeted stairs. The door to DC Freckles Frecker's flat was, however, open and the man himself was standing just inside. A slight, scrawny figure, only just within the current regulation height for a police officer, he was dressed not in the just-out-of-bed shorts Harriet had half-expected, but in a grubby-looking shirt and yet grubbier jeans. A dead pale, unshaven face, paradoxically free of any trace of freckles.

'Come in then. Come in, if you've got to.'

The flat's sitting-room was no more inviting in appearance than its owner. A big, old television with, naturally, a satellite channel adventure film unreeling on its screen to an accompaniment of crackling gunfire. A two-seater sofa plonked down directly opposite, its covering greasy with much wear, its cushions flattened. One other small, villainously uncomfortable-looking armchair with the dull khaki waterproof jacket flung down on it barely covering a clutter of copies of the screaming headline *Sun*. A two-bar electric fire in front of the badly-painted, narrow iron mantelpiece seemed hardly to be combatting the ferocious cold from outside.

'Right,' Harriet snapped, 'let's have that telly off.'

For an instant it looked as if Freckles Frecker was going to object. But then, with a sly smile that seemed to say *No skin off my nose*, he went over and flicked the set into silence.

Harriet sat herself on the worn sofa, a little surprised to find no loose spring poking up at her. She nodded to DS Watson to take the place next to her. Frecker, not without an impudent glare, went over to the other chair and tossed the jacket and papers on it to the floor – to reveal a soiled white bra of ample size.

'Your girlfriend, wife?' she asked sharply, unable to remember what Frecker's personal record stated. 'She in the flat?'

'Nah. That's just something left here by someone yesterday.'

'Sergeant,' Harriet said, 'just have a look round the rest of the flat, will you?'

DS Watson got to his feet, disappeared.

'What's it to you, if there was someone?' Frecker said. 'Bleeding on suspension, ain't I? Got to do something, stuck in here all day.'

He gave Harriet a pointedly questioning look,

picked up the bra and put it on the window ledge behind his chair.

DS Watson came back in.

'Bedroom window open wide, ma'am,' he said. 'And a flat roof below.'

'Right. Thanks, Sergeant.'

She turned back to Frecker.

'What you do with yourself when you're off-duty is no concern of mine,' she said. 'But for your own sake, I wouldn't want whatever we have to say to one another to be overheard by an outsider. Or even by your wife, if you've got one.'

'Had one. But you know about police marriages. If it's the same where you come from.'

The words *dozy northern tart* ran like a quick thread then through Harriet's mind. She let them run out.

'Right. Let's get to the nub of this straight away. You've no doubt read what the *Sunday Herald* had to say about you and DC Underwood. Was it true?'

'Why should it be? Why should every fucker believe what a sod like that Frank Parkins says, and not believe me?'

'Because Frank Parkins had evidence that supports what he wrote.'

'Evidence? Some tapes? What's on them to prove I ever did anything more than pass the time of day with that toe-rag Arnie Voles?'

'Pass the time of day? I think you did rather more than that.'

'You do, do you? Well, I ain't quite so stupid as to do more than chat with a bugger like Voles.'

'I asked what exactly your relations were with Voles?'

'My relations? Well, he was in the immigration

racket, wasn't he? Small fry, not one of those people trying to bugger up the Euro Fence. But in it, right at the bottom, busy taking and taking from dozens of those poor sods what ain't got the right papers. And I'd been tailing him, hadn't I? Tailing, that's what the Boxer— That's why Commander Boxall picked me special for the Max, knew there wasn't no better tail in the whole Met.'

For a frail moment he puffed up his thin chest.

Harriet moved to put an end to that.

'So Voles was extorting money from those people,' she barked. 'And what were you doing? Extorting money from Voles in your turn. You and Underwood. And don't try to claim that didn't happen. I've listened to those tapes, all thirteen of them. So let me repeat just a few of the words I heard. *But, Freckles, I ain't got that sort of moolah*. That's Voles. And what comes next? *Freckles? Freckles? 'Detective Constable Frecker, sir' to you, you little piece of shit*. Remember saying that? Those very words. Bit stupid of you, wasn't it, to come the big boss over Voles? No wonder, he went spilling it all to Frank Parkins.'

She had squashed a momentary impulse to say *bit dozy of you*. Never descend to the level of people like Frecker.

'All right, that would've been stupid, if you like. But tapes can be faked, you know. That fucker Parkins, get hold of an actor, to imitate me. Didn't think of that, did you?'

'No, I didn't think of that. And do you know why? Because it's utter bloody nonsense. No, Frecker, you're there on those tapes. There, trying to get money from a small-time crook in exchange for not charging him.

And that's something you can't wriggle your way out of.'

For a long moment Freckles Frecker sat crouching forward in his villainous armchair, glaring with hatred.

But what he said next looked as if it might, just, be leading in the direction she wanted him to go.

'All right, maybe I was getting something out of a toe-rag. But what of it? It's done every day, always has been.'

'Oh, yes?'

A little grin shot out then.

'Well, p'raps they don't do things like that up from where you come from. But down here we know what to do with scum like Voles.'

Once again Harriet reined herself in, and simply sat in onward-pressing silence.

And restraint – Mr Anstruther would be proud of me, she thought – paid off.

'Anyhow,' Freckles said, less cockily, 'I ain't the only one, and I don't mean just Pantsie Underwood either. You must've got 'im on the tapes, too. 'Cos he was with me when we took those few quid off of Arnie Voles. Working together, weren't we? Been spinning that freeloader Reynolds Liebling's place, hadn't we, soon as he'd pissed off to the States?'

Reynolds Liebling, Harriet thought. The American who's currently the Max's chief target, Pablo Grajales's London man. And, yes, a freeloader, a party-goer, if I've remembered rightly.

But am I getting towards the top level of the Max now? *I ain't the only one and I don't mean just Pantsie Underwood either.* So who does he mean?

She pounced.

'All right, we know all about Underwood. But you're

talking about some other officer in the Max, aren't you?'

But it seemed she had gone too far.

Freckles settled into a glowering silence.

Is he cursing himself for even hinting about another Max officer? Does he know something about someone? Someone very much his senior? And is he suddenly afraid that any hint he has of something wrong there may in the end, if it can't be made to stand up, get him into even worse trouble than he's in already?

So has he suddenly become determined not to say another word?

All right, but two can play at the stay-silent game.

She sat perfectly still, her eyes unwaveringly fixed on Freckles, her expression totally neutral.

The battle raged in deadened silence. Beside her, she became aware of DS Watson's suppressed breathing.

But the battle did not rage for very long.

'Yeah, you don't know nothing, do you?'

Freckles paused for just an instant, seemed to gather himself up. And then the spate of words shot out.

'Ever think about all them fancy suits, that Scorpio motor, that gold watch on its big chain? Easy enough you making trouble for me and Pantsie, the likes of us. But what you going to do about them at the top? Untouchable, that what they are?'

'Are you telling me that Commander Boxall is accepting bribes?'

'Not what I said, is it? I didn't say nothing. No more than what's in front of your eyes, got the balls to look.'

'No. You're not saying more. But could you? Have

you ever had any evidence, no matter how slim, that Commander Boxall is corrupt? If you have it's your duty to tell me. Your duty to the police service you've taken an oath to.'

The Boxer. The Boxer himself corrupt? Can it be him? If so . . . Christ, it'd never entered my head. But . . . But in strict logic it could be so. It could.

But Frecker had been going on. She gave him her full attention.

'Yeah, well, what you think? If I'd got evidence – and I'd need to have pretty bloody good evidence, make an accusation like that, wouldn't I? – if I had got evidence, don't know what I'd do. Maybe go to you, or someone like you, and take it from there. Or maybe I'd think the Boxer's too good a detective to shop him like that. But it don't matter which I'd do. I ain't got any evidence. How could I have?'

'So what you've said, about your superior officer, is no more than simple malice? Is that it?'

'Make what you like of it, I don't care. You're going to put it in your report that me and Pantsie's guilty. So we're fucked whatever happens.'

Harriet rose to her feet. Beside her, DS Watson, large red ears filled no doubt to capacity, followed suit.

'Yes, Frecker,' she said. 'You've blotted your copy-book. You've admitted enough to me, and to DS Watson here. And you'll have to pay the consequences. I dare say your friend, DC Underwood, will prove to be in the same sort of mess. It'll be left to an officer from the Met to make the charge. But don't deceive yourself that it won't happen.'

She left then, hardly able to wait till she was opening the front door of the house before turning to Watson.

'The Boxer,' she said. 'You know, I think that nasty piece of work up there was in two minds about shopping him. I told you at my briefing this morning that this is what the inquiry is really about. Not about those two, but about finding if there is anybody at the top of the Max who's succumbed to Pablo Grajales and his billions. All right, we learnt nothing about that just now, nothing we can go further with. But Frecker did point the finger, and point it pretty directly to the very top.'

'You're right, ma'am. Nothing I heard indicated anything to a certainty. It all sounded to me more like what you said to him, just malice. So . . . So, what are you going to do now, if I may ask?'

'I'll tell you one thing. I'm not going to go haring over to Persimmon House to tackle Commander Boxall. He needs more careful handling than that. No, Sergeant, my list for this morning was, first, Frecker, then Underwood. And that's what we'll do.'

Pantsie Underwood looked absurdly unlike his nickname. Noticeably older than his friend, Freckles, tall and heftily built, he had something of the Sergeant Major about him, the high cheekbones of his slab of a face touched with florid red. He was dressed, not in the scrubby, just-out-of-bed clothes his co-accused had worn, but in a good blue serge suit, with a stripy police tie neatly knotted at his neck and black shoes glinting with polish. But, however different in appearance he was from Freckles Frecker, his manner shared something of his friend's truculence.

His wife had opened the door to their ring, but as soon as Pantsie had heard Harriet's name and rank he came lumbering out into the narrow entrance hall with its walls clustered with framed photographs of police groups in every kind of sporting gear.

'I've been expecting I'd have to see you,' he said blankly. 'You'd better come through.'

Then for the benefit of his wife, who had been murmuring in the background about *tea or coffee*, he said with a soft growl 'No. Nothing. This is official.'

Giving the room he had marched back into a rapid assessment, Harriet saw it was in much the same contrast to the room in Freckles' drab little flat as the two DCs were in appearance. Its three-piece suite looked as smartly shiny as if it had come from a local department store only the day before. There was, too, a great goggle-eyed TV, without so much as a speck of dust on its surfaces, and even the many framed certificates on the walls had evidently, too, been dusted every single day. Wall-to-wall carpeting and a long low radiator under the wide net-curtained window made it pleasantly warm after the bitter cold outside.

For a moment Harriet's mind flicked back to Freckles Frecker's chill, unwelcoming room of an hour or more earlier. Hadn't there been something a little wrong about it?

But, whatever that had been, she failed to put her finger on it. Perhaps it was just that she would have expected a flat where Freckles was, as he had said, *stuck in here all day*, to have harboured more of a fug. It had certainly not been in any way warm. But then Watson had found the bedroom window wide open, and perhaps the cold outside had invaded the whole place from there.

But no time now for idle speculation.

Taking in more clearly the array of certificates on

the walls, Harriet saw they were mostly for sporting triumphs. She thought now she might begin with a small bombshell for the man who had gained them. No harm in letting him know that, from his well-studied personal record, she knew more about him than he might expect.

'No certificates for opening safes, DC?' she said, sitting down on the glossy sofa and giving the array on the walls a more obvious inspection.

The question had all the disconcerting effect she had hoped for.

'Safes? Opening up safes? How— What d'you know about that?'

'I've had access to your P/R.'

'That's meant to be personal, private. That's what we've always been told.'

'So it is personal.' Now the stab. 'Until that right is forfeited. As yours has been.'

'Why's it been forfeited? What have I done to deserve that? Only had my name spread all over some stupid piece in some stupid paper.'

'Oh, no, DC. More than that. A great deal more. You have been accused by Frank Parkins, Chief Crime Reporter of the *Sunday Herald*, of taking a bribe from a common criminal not to proceed with a charge of—'

'But that's a damn lie.'

'I don't think so. I've listened to the tapes Arnie Voles made of conversations between him and yourself and DC Frecker, and from them it's perfectly clear you asked Voles for money, for quite a considerable sum.'

'Well, if you know so much and believe what's on those tapes, what are you here for? You've got your so-called evidence. What more do you want?'

'Right, to begin with, I'd like to know why you, and

I suppose Frecker too, started out on that course. I'm happy to tell you there's nothing on your P/R that indicates you're any sort of a bribe-taker. Of course, there may be things you've done and got away with. Your friend Frecker tells me that sort of thing is common practice.'

'What did he say that for?'

'I expect he was hoping to make his offence – his offence and yours – look less serious.'

'Well, I don't know about Freckles. One thing, though, I can say he's been straight ever since he joined the Max. I'm sure of that. And if there's nothing on my P/R saying I'm a taker, then it's true I never have been.'

He stood in silence for a long sullen moment. Then, with a visible effort, he took a deep breath.

'Anyhow,' he said, 'if people with shiny reputations up there can go a bit left-handed, then no shame to me and Freckles if in the end we tried to help ourselves on those lines too.'

'And that's your justification, is it?' Harriet said, feeling herself with a fishing-rod in her hands and something nibbling at the bait. 'That others are doing it? Others higher up in the Max than you and Frecker?'

'Well . . .'

'All right then, who precisely are you pointing the finger at?'

'I'm not pointing no finger. But— But . . .'

'But what, DC?'

He stood for a moment, plainly wrestling with some inner thought.

'All right then,' he broke out at last. 'Why don't you look for someone dressed up in all them fancy suits, running a Scorpio motor, gold watch on a chain?'

A quick side-glance reassured Harriet that flapping-eared DS Watson had taken full note of those particular words and would be able to reproduce them, verbatim.

But Underwood must not be let slip the hook now that it was firmly in his mouth. There was still more to be found out about what exactly had started the two of them thinking they could get away with demanding cash from Arnie Voles.

'And that is the full extent of your claim that officers senior to you are accepting bribes?' she said, biting out the words.

Underwood's slabby face took on a look of mutinous stubbornness.

'You asked,' he said, 'I told you what I could.'

'Very well. So now I'll put this to you. Perhaps it will help you to provide a better answer than you have managed to so far. You said Frecker was not on the take from the time he joined the Max until this recent episode. So why did he start when he did? Why did you?'

'I can't speak for Freckles, for DC Frecker. But, well, I've had expenses. There's that sofa you're sitting on. Six months with what they call *nothing to pay*. But at the end of six months there's a hell of a lot to pay, and I need the cash.'

'No, that's not a good enough answer. Why, I asked, did you and Frecker suddenly think it was somehow all right to break a rule you had both adhered to ever since the Max was formed. Why?'

A glare from the sergeant major eyes.

'Why, Underwood?'

No answer. No answer for several stubborn seconds. And then the answer came.

'All right, if you must know, Freckles and me got the idea we wouldn't be the only ones.'

'Oh, yes? And what precisely gave you that idea? Did it just come out of the blue? The pair of you suddenly thinking *Why shouldn't we make a bit of money?* Was that it? I hardly think so.'

She had to wait to see the result of her shot. But not for long.

'If you must know, it was a job we'd been on.'

'What job?'

The big man standing in front of her shifted his feet uneasily in their highly polished black shoes.

'I don't know if I should be telling you this,' he said. 'It was something a bit dicey. But not done off our own bat. On orders.'

'You can tell me anything. I've been extensively briefed about the Max, and all its activities.'

'All right, but don't think I won't say I was pressured if I'm put in the wrong over it.'

'I'll live with that. Never you mind.'

'Well then, a couple of months ago we were breaking into a flat belonging to someone called Reynolds Liebling.'

'I know all about Reynolds Liebling. And I can well see why the Max might feel it necessary to enter his flat, however illegally. Go on.'

'Well, I was there to do the safe. Since you've seen my record you'll know I was at school with a boy, who's now serving eight for burglary. Not the first stretch he's done. And in the days before I'd even thought of joining the police he taught me a hell of a lot about safes and how to get into them. Not that I ever took advantage.'

'Yes, yes. I know all that. As you surmised, it's all

in your P/R. But go on. You were in Reynolds Liebling's flat to get his safe open. Who else was with you? Frecker, I suppose.'

'Of course he was. He'd been tailing Liebling for weeks, seeing him go to all those posh parties, seeing him pick up a girl or two, take them back to the flat. So it was from what Freckles had seen that Mr Boxall knew Liebling was off back to the States. He'd watched him buy his tickets. Liebling was scared to use the phone in case it was tapped, as it was, of course. Then, with him off the scene, there wasn't much for Freckles to do, so Mr Boxall put him on to this task. That's all.'

'No, it is not. Who else did Commander Boxall task with entering the flat?'

Another moment of mutinous silence.

'Who else, I asked.'

'Well, it was DI Outhwaite.'

'Was it? Well, I know about Mr Outhwaite. A detective with an impressive record. Came to the Max from the Fraud Squad at the Yard.'

But . . . But hadn't there been something else in DI Outhwaite's file, something that, as I read it, just scratched at the surface of my mind. Some small thing not quite what I'd have expected. What was—

But no time for that now. Keep Underwood in my grasp. Don't let him slip away.

'So he was there in the flat, Mr Outhwaite, to assess whatever material he would find in the safe you had opened. Yes?'

'Yes. That was it. He had to look in the safe.'

'And what happened? Something must have given you and Frecker the idea that it was all right to go on the take?'

'Well, yes. I suppose it must have been . . . I don't

know. It was Freckles's idea really. But it was when the two of us were on our way back from the job that he told me he thought we could get cash out of Arnie Voles. We'd had dealings with him just a few days before, and Freckles said he was ripe for it.'

'All right, Frecker suddenly had his bright idea. But why just then? Was there something he'd seen or heard on that job that put the idea into his head?'

No reply.

'Come on, was there something? There must have been. What was it that Frecker had realized, or guessed, after you'd been on that expedition into Reynolds Liebling's flat?'

'I don't really know. All I know is Freckles had this idea. And it seemed okay at the time. So a couple of days later, when we happened to meet up with Arnie Voles, we put the squeeze on him. I needed the cash, badly. I told you that.'

'You did. And you went on needing the cash, I suppose, and milking Voles till you, the both of you, went a little too far and Voles talked to Frank Parkins. Is that it?'

'I suppose so.'

'All right. At least you've been honest about it now. That may do you some good in any disciplinary proceedings. If you keep your mouth shut. So, I'll leave you for the time being, though I warn you this won't be the last occasion you and I may have things to say to each other.'

Chapter Five

'Sounds like you're on to something, ma'am,' Sergeant Watson said, as with an engine-roar that made the wretched pool car shudder from one end to the other, he started it up. 'The two of them both pointing the finger in the same direction, even using much the same words.'

'I don't think so,' Harriet said.

'You don't think so? But— But, ma'am, it's all there surely. Both of them happening to say almost the same thing. Who was it they were describing, ma'am? Was it really Commander Boxall? Or is it someone else you've met?'

'Oh, yes, it's Commander Boxall that Frecker was hinting at. But think of the words Underwood used in describing him.'

'The words, ma'am?'

'Yes. Repeat them to me, Sergeant.'

DS Watson sat silently for a moment in the juddering car. Then he spoke.

'*All them fancy suits, running a Scorpio motor, gold watch on a chain.*'

He turned to Harriet.

'That's as clear a description as you're likely to get,' he said. 'And Frecker used much the same words.'

'But he didn't use much the same words, Sergeant.

57

He used the very same words, bar a meaningless adjec-
tive or two. He directed our attention to those three
things, the suits, the car and the gold pocket watch, in
the precise order that Underwood produced them just
now. And, if you think about it, you'll remember that
when Underwood launched into that stuff about *people
with shiny reputations* he stood there in silence for
a moment and then actually took in a breath before
launching into his set piece. His set piece, Sergeant.
No, all that was a put-up job. Underwood had learnt
his part, most probably at Frecker's teaching. He's
clever in his way, Frecker. He must have thought he
would draw my attention away from himself and
Underwood by sending me to look at one particular
person at the top of the Max. In fact, at Commander
Boxall himself. They were both describing him. If a
little too clearly. But Underwood isn't as clever as his
partner. He repeated what he'd learnt by rote. The
same objects in the same order.'

'Oh, damn it, yes. Yes, ma'am, you're right.'

But I was as near damn-it wrong about something
else, Harriet thought. Until I realized what trick
Frecker was trying, I had seriously wondered whether
the man in the Max who was being paid from Columbia
was the Boxer himself. Right, he's not corrupt, I know
that now. But I also know he's clearly determined to
frustrate my inquiry, and by using whatever under-
hand methods he happens to hit on.

'I hope so anyhow. Because they very nearly sent
me off nicely on a totally false trail.'

'So . . . So you reckon there's nothing in those hints
about the tip of an iceberg in that story in the *Sunday
Herald*?'

'Oh, there may yet be, Sergeant. After all, that's

why we're down here: to find out if those hints in the *Sunday Herald* have any substance to them. And that's what I'm going to do.'

'But for the present we're left back at square one?'

'If you must use that wretched cliché, yes. You're right, we are back at the beginning.'

They drove off in gloomy silence.

It was only after they had turned off the busy Old Kent Road on to Rotherhithe New Road towards the end of their journey that Harriet, shifting round in her uncomfortable seat when they were halted at a red light, just caught sight in the wing-mirror beside her of a motor-cyclist or perhaps moped rider who in the otherwise deserted street was coming to an inexplicable halt some hundred yards to their rear.

But it was not until they were nearing Timber Pond Road and the comforting prospect of their well-heated offices that something stirred in her mind. Not quite knowing why she did so, she wriggled round and looked out of the car's back window.

And saw some hundred yards back a moped rider wrapped in a sleet-whitened hooded jacket.

'Sergeant,' she said, 'I find this a little difficult to believe, but I think we're being followed. A man on a moped.'

Watson looked in his mirror.

'I see him, ma'am. And, yes, he does seem to be keeping a steady distance behind us. Had you spotted him earlier?'

'I think so. Right then, a little evasive action, please. Not too much. Enough to make sure he is on our tail. If he is, let him catch up. I'd very much like a good look at him.'

Watson suddenly swung right into a side street.

Harriet, hunching down so that she could see as much as possible in the wing-mirror, waited to see what would happen.

And, just at the moment she had expected, allowing time for the man on the moped to overshoot, wheel round and take their same side road, into the mirror came that familiar figure.

'He's there,' Watson said.

'Yes, but too far back to get a look at him. Try another sharp turn when you can.'

Watson left it to the very last second and then, with a squeal of tyres that imperilled the old car, took the next turning at speed.

But now, when the moped rider appeared in Harriet's mirror again, he simply came to a halt as soon as he must have seen them.

'He certainly knows what he's about,' Watson commented.

'You're right, Sergeant. All we can do now, I think, is make our way back to the Business Park and let him see us get there. If he clocks that Block 15 is our final destination, it's no great matter.'

Then, as Watson twisted and turned to get back to Timber Pond Road, she began to think that perhaps, after all, the presence behind them of the moped rider was not something to be so lightly dismissed.

All right, we're being followed. I'm being followed. No doubt about that now. But the question is: why? Here am I, a senior police officer, wearing civilian clothes, down from Birchester on what you might call a secret mission. Or at least one that hasn't been given any publicity of any sort. And someone has taken into their head to track—

She broke off. A sudden new thought.

Yes, someone is tracking me. But it's not just today. Even when I set out from the Business Park yesterday to go to the *Sunday Herald* there was a man on a moped further down the road who started off as soon as I had made up my mind not to wait any longer for a cab. So is this the same man behind us now?

She bent down and peered into the wing mirror.

Yes, it certainly could be. Impossible to be sure with that drab coat he's got on. But there's something about the way he's crouched over that machine that seems familiar.

Right, why is someone so interested in my movements that they've been following me, possibly day and night? The press? It could be, I suppose. It's at least not wholly impossible that Frank Parkins let slip to one of his rival colleagues that this detective superintendent from Birchester, the once-notorious Hard Detective, no less, is on duty down in London. Not wholly impossible, but not very likely either. I can't see Frank Parkins letting slip anything. But nor, knowing what he knows about me already, can I see him needing to have me followed.

So who? And what? What can this moped man be hoping to gain?

Then an ugly idea.

All right, I'm investigating possible corruption in the Maximum Crimes Squad, and no one, on Lord Candover's suggestion, is supposed to know that. But if there's been some leak, either through Frank Parkins or in some other way, then is it possible that Pablo Grajales back in Colombia can have got to hear about me? And has ordered action to be taken?

And, if Grajales knows about me, what might he have ordered to be done? Eliminate the nuisance? It's not inconceivable. He must have casually had eliminated dozens of awkward individuals as he accumulated all those billions. Dozens? Say, hundreds. So why not one more? Why not me?

She shrugged.

No answer worth having to be sorted out from all the possibilities and half-possibilities. No, it's wait and see. But watch out. Yes, that certainly.

They drove into the Business Park and headed for Block 15.

Harriet did not even bother to look in the wing mirror while they did so. The clever man on the moped was not going to let himself be seen close up as easily as that.

'When we've been back a little while,' she said to Watson, however. 'Say time enough for you to get yourself a cup of tea, take a quiet look outside. See if our chap's anywhere about. Get as good a sight of him as you can.'

'Ma'am.'

But before Watson had reported a total lack of success Harriet found herself wrestling with a whole new complication.

As soon as she had got to her desk she had seen, prominent on its neatly kept surface, a letter. A letter, she found when she ripped open the envelope, that was entirely unexpected.

Mrs Althea Raven, chairman of Sunday Herald Properties. And an invitation to lunch.

Now what the hell is this about?

A consequence of that disastrous business in Frank Parkins's office? Well, no, not really likely. If the *Sunday Herald* is going to take some sort of legal action against me, its chairman wouldn't invite me to lunch.

She took another look at the sheet with the *Sunday Herald* logo at its head.

Lunch at the Groucho Club. Smart as can be. And, yes, tomorrow. Not exactly plenty of time to say another day will be more convenient. Bloody high-handed, in fact.

So what will that high-handed lady want to talk to me about as the so-called glitterati of the literary and journalistic worlds go wandering past the table?

No idea.

Can't think of anything remotely arising from that encounter with Frank Parkins which there could be to discuss, except for what it was I did. And that surely has been accounted for. *You owe me.* So, can it be that the *Sunday Herald* is desperate to find something to stiffen up the allegations it made? And that its chairman has decided to wring something out of me?

Fantasy surely. Purest fantasy.

Then what else? Only one way to find out, of course. Go.

Tomorrow, Saturday. The Groucho probably much less occupied on a Saturday lunchtime. That the reason Mrs Althea Raven has chosen tomorrow? A very private chat? But what about? What about, for heaven's sake? And, come to think, it's almost certain to be about something that matters a good deal, at least to the chairman of Sunday Herald Properties. Because Saturday is the day when all the really big boys of the world of commerce, and the big girls of course, should be down at their country homes. But Mrs Althea Raven – *Althea* a pretty upper-class forename – has decided to forfeit her relaxing weekend in order to meet Detective Superintendent Martens, Greater Birchester Police.

Damn it all, I've more than half a mind after all to

say *Detective Superintendent Harriet Martens regrets she is unable* . . .

But, no. No, this may be some sort of a lead for me. Perhaps, unlikely though it seems, there has been a conference at the *Sunday Herald* – another conference with their tame barrister – and a decision has been taken to tell me what neither Frank Parkins's computer nor his desk drawers revealed. To tell me just what it is he knows.

It was while she talked to Rekha Pathak that evening that Harriet began to realize she was not after all at the beginning of it all. Starting to satisfy Rekha's teasing curiosity by recounting the events of her day it came to her that there was one thing still well in play. Surely something may come out of my mysterious invitation to lunch with Mrs Althea Raven. Then, as she came to talk about her two interviews of the morning and what she had deduced from that twice repeated *fancy suits, Scorpio motor, gold watch*, she realized something else.

With Watson in the car, she had seen that trick as something sly Freckles had cooked up. But could it not have been cooked up by someone a good deal cleverer than Freckles?

'Do you know,' she said to Rekha, 'I believe this whole clever piece of misdirection was actually planted on me, not by sharp Freckles Frecker, but by— Guess who?'

'By our old friend the Boxer, naturally,' Rekha chimed in. 'Typical of the man. The prince of double-dealers. All very fine when he's catching out criminals, but not so good when it's you who's his target.'

'But the more I think about it, the more I'm sure that, yes, it all was a Boxer ploy.'

Then a new thought.

'But, listen Rekha, what am I going to do about it, if we are right? I'm damned if I'm going to go about pretending all the time that I've fallen for it and am suspecting the Boxer himself, while he sits there grinning smugly and thinking I won't cause him any more trouble. And in the meanwhile he'll be hoping quietly to find out himself who's corrupt in his precious squad – if there is anybody – and will deal with them. And no one then ever gets to hear that the great Boxer recruited a bad apple.'

'You certainly mustn't let him get away with it, I agree. But what I'd do in your place is let him go on believing, for a little at least, that his secret's safe from you. Then, when you explode it, he'll be all the more caught out.'

'Yes. You know, I think I might just do that. It'll at least show him, when the time comes, that he tangled with someone a little more of his calibre than a dozy northern tart.'

'Okay. But you shouldn't let that pretty little description rankle with you. You go on about it quite enough as it is.'

'No, I know. But I would just love to prove whoever said it totally wrong.'

'Oh, you will. You will. I'm sure of that.'

But will I? The thought lodged itself in Harriet's head. All very well for Rekha to be optimistic on my behalf, but she's not up against the facts of it all.

'But tell me more about Freckles Frecker,' Rekha went bouncing on. 'I'm fascinated by dodgy characters of his sort.'

Harriet, who was in any case determined not to tell Rekha about the man on the moped and, especially, about her nightmarish darts of fear over who might have set him on her track, swiftly embarked on an account of Freckles tossing the old copies of the *Sun* off his chair to reveal that large size bra.

'So ace detective Harriet Martens deduced that whoever had worn it could not have left without that very necessary support, and so was still on the premises?'

'No, not exactly. It turned out, when my Sergeant made a search, that the lady had scarpered through the bedroom window, supported or unsupported. And, when I asked Freckles about her, he told me it was none of my business if he entertained himself while he was on suspension.'

And it was at that moment that one more idea came to her.

The woman who had left that flat in such a hurry, no doubt just as she herself had rung at the front door, did not have to have been a one-night stand. She was, in fact, more likely to be a regular girlfriend. A girlfriend who for some reason didn't want to be found in the flat – jealous husband? – but who knew she would be coming back, and so was willing to be out and about with her great big breasts flopping up and down.

And if that's so, isn't it possible Frecker has told her, whoever she is, more than he strictly should have done? For instance, the good news that his income was increasing and that she would benefit. More even? Had he told her why he had thought it was all right to go on the take again? Told her he had the blessing – no doubt not specifically given – someone in the Max a lot senior to himself who was doing the same thing, if on a much larger scale?

Harriet stopped herself then and made a mental note. All right to discuss the inquiry in light-hearted terms with her old friend and former Met colleague. But there came a point where she ought to call a halt.

So it was in the privacy of her room later that she used her mobile to call the dilapidated dockside hotel, once home to seamen between ships, where the members of her team had been accommodated. She tasked WDC Lambert and DC Higham, both of whom she had selected for her team because they were skilled in surveillance, with keeping watch on Freckles Frecker's flat.

'You'll see, like as not,' she told WDC Lambert, 'a woman with a large bust coming out of the place. You'd better be there good and early, say at 5.30, though you may, of course, have a long wait. But I don't want her missed. Find out where she goes and, if you can, just who she is.'

At shortly before 6.30 next morning she was woken, not by her travel alarm, but by her mobile's warbling.

'Martens,' she answered blurrily.

'It's Lambert, ma'am. We've sussed her.'

'Already?'

'Yes, ma'am.'

'Right. Who is she? Name? Address? No need to give me *Occupation*. I can take a pretty good guess at that.'

'With respect, ma'am, I don't think you can.'

'What? What is this?'

'Ma'am, the woman in question is Police Constable Phyllis Witherspoon.'

For an instant Harriet thought this must be some sort of a joke. But no junior officer was ever first to embark on a joke with her.

'She's a policewoman? Frecker has a girlfriend who's in the Met?'

'Yes, ma'am. She came out of Frecker's flat, with him, at just before 05.45 hours – you were right about the big bra, ma'am – and while he rode off on his bike she took a brisk walk to the police station a quarter of a mile away. We made discreet inquiries there and found WPC Witherspoon had just reported for duty at the start of her relief. Or, rather, at the start of a double shift. They're pretty short-handed, flu and all sorts, and I gathered that Witherspoon will end up manning a desk in the radio room till 2100 hours tonight.'

'Right. You've done a good job. I'd like to see you outside her nick there at half past eight tonight. But take the rest of the day off, you've earnt it.'

Mrs Althea Raven proved to be a lady of forty, or a little more. Beautifully cut blonde hair, although the hairdresser had clearly been forbidden to conceal its first streaks of grey. Equally, although something had been done to smooth away the sharp frown lines across the forehead and the spider-web of wrinkles beginning to show themselves round the eyes, plainly nothing in the way of cosmetic surgery had been done. As to the lady's clothes, Harriet, who paid only moderate attention to fashion, noted merely that a good deal of money must have been spent on the dove-grey suit and the softly draped dusty-pink blouse, open at the throat to reveal a necklace of what had to be diamonds however unostentatiously set. A quick downward glance took in fine, thin-heeled black shoes.

Soon enough she learnt more about her. Barely had the two of them been led to a discreet corner table than, with altogether unusual promptness, a white-shirted waiter appeared.

'Madam, the courgette flowers as usual? And for your guest?'

Harriet had barely had time to glance at the menu card she had been offered.

'I'll have what you're having,' she said to Mrs Raven. 'If that's all right.'

Then she thought *Christ, what the hell will a courgette flower taste like?*

'I generally drink just Vittel water, the only tolerable sort,' Mrs Raven went on. 'But, if you would like wine, do say.'

And be, if only to the slightest degree, beholden?

'No, no. Water will suit me very well. I've got a lot to do this afternoon.'

The waiter vanished.

'You're certainly a believer in getting down to work,' Mrs Raven stated. 'You've been in London for only – what is it? – two or three days?'

'When the work's important, yes, of course I get down to it without delay,' Harriet answered, noting that the company chairman opposite her, being given such flattering service, had plainly done her homework. Or had it done for her.

Mrs Raven gave her a sharp glance across the little table with its heavy white cloth and array of cutlery.

'I'd like to tell you something about the *Sunday*

Herald, and about myself,' she said, to Harriet's immediate surprise.

'Yes?'

Mrs Raven paused for one moment.

'I wonder what, as a police officer from the North of England,' she went on, 'you think someone like myself does with her time. Just sit in a large office, go to an occasional board meeting, receive rather large twice-yearly dividends?'

'No,' Harriet answered, grabbing the chance, 'you're not altogether right about me. I'm an officer of the Greater Birchester Police, as a matter of fact. So not, of course, from the North.'

And by no means a dozy northern tart, she let herself think with an edge of savagery. Nor am I ready to sit here and be lectured as if I was some sort of uncivilized ignoramus.

'I see I've been misinformed,' Mrs Raven came smoothly back. 'However, I would like to tell you what it is that I actually do. What, in fact, the *Sunday Herald* aims to do. We're a paper with high ambitions, you know. Ambitions to serve the public, to play our full part in the life of the nation.'

And not at all, of course, to make a great deal of money, Harriet added in the privacy of her mind.

But what's this statement of high principle leading to? Surely not to warning me off her territory in some way. Frank Parkins has done as much of that as necessary.

But Mrs Raven, brushing aside the waiter who had re-appeared with a broad basket of large pieces of various breads, was in unstoppable spate. A credo being set forth.

'No, I may have become company chairman

because my late father-in-law – He was Lord Creel, you know – owned the paper, among a good many other concerns. But when he died and it was suggested I take over, I didn't see myself as simply a representative of the family, a figurehead. No, I saw I had been given an opportunity. People despised the paper then as *one of the populars*. But I saw it as something different, as a popular voice responding, even though it hardly knew it was doing so, to the needs of the people. And our present circulation shows I was right.'

She paused to allow the rebuffed waiter to offer Harriet the breads. Harriet took the first piece that came to hand, something brown and seeds-dotted.

Lord Creel's daughter-in-law went steamingly on.

'You'll say that merely responding to the mass of people you hope will buy your paper is the worst sort of profit-making. But you're wrong. You know where the power in this country lies nowadays? Not among the aristocracy I married into, I can tell you that. Nor does it lie with the great multinational corporations, however often the clever-clever commentators tell you that it does. And it's certainly not with the politicians. All they're doing when they put an Act of Parliament on to the statute books is responding to the wishes and desires of the mass of the people. No, the days of élitism, of any sort, are over. Or, if you will, the only élite today is the common people.'

A gulp for breath now, if a well-managed one.

Harriet had just time to think.

Why am I being bombarded with all this? What on earth is she— And will I be able to recall enough of it all when I talk on the phone to John tonight to ask him whether there's any sense in it? Let alone remember to tell him the Groucho dining-room has walls of solidly unbroken purple, and a clashing red carpet underfoot?

'But I saw,' Mrs Raven was hammering on again, 'the potentiality of the paper. I saw that nowadays a newspaper exists, or ought to exist, to present the people with the news, the real news about things that affect them directly, things that go straight to their hearts. To say the things they want to hear. To be the voice of the people.'

She halted then and allowed the attentive waiter to present her with her plate on which, in a thin lake of tomato-coloured sauce, there rested a pair of deep-fried courgette flowers. Harriet, as the waiter put a similar plate in front of her, decided they resembled nothing so much as a pair of herby batter-covered mini-truncheons.

'That's very interesting,' she said to Mrs Raven, struggling to see how she could wriggle that anodyne response into a question that might elicit something to the point.

But Mrs Raven had launched into speech once more.

'And that is what a newspaper in these times should be doing. Look, at the so-called broadsheets. Yes, they have their reviews of terrible little plays at obscure little theatres and even more esoteric classical concerts. But what really are they full of these days? Exactly the same sort of news that we print, the human interest stories. They've had to copy us, had to. Alongside those high-flown reviews, what do they have? Reviews of the sort of thing our critics write about, the pop concerts, the blockbuster movies. Because that's what culture is nowadays. Thank goodness, people began to realize not all that long ago that *culture* doesn't mean art films from France. It means anything. Popular culture. So we at the paper can give the people what they want to read about, the profiles of stars, of singers. I tell you, I made sure right from the start that the sort of arts coverage the paper used to have, self-indulgent imitations of the big Sundays, went straight out of the window.'

A pause for breath, but not one long enough for Harriet to put in her pennyworth. Not that, she thought, I've really got a pennyworth, or even a ha'penny worth to put in.

'Do you read the *Sunday Herald*?' its chairman jabbed out next, leaning sharply forward across her untouched plate. 'Of course, you've had to read last Sunday's issue. But did you read us before? I very much doubt, from what I've heard of you, that you would have done.'

She sat there glaring.

And Harriet in her head took note of that *from what I've heard of you*. So the Boxer's not the only one who's decided it's necessary to find out as much as they can about me.

She produced some sort of answer to the jabbed-out question.

'Oh, yes. I see the *Sunday Herald*. From time to time. You've had reports about crimes in Birchester, though usually tucked away on an inside page. But, yes, I know what the paper's like.'

She lifted to her lips a piece of courgette – apparently you got the courgette itself behind the flower. Not truncheon-hard, rather the opposite.

And once again asked herself where all this was leading. And got an instant answer.

'Your investigation,' Mrs Raven snapped out.

Then she leant forward over her plate, so far untouched.

'Perhaps it's time we came to your present activities, some of which you saw fit to conduct last Thursday in my paper's offices.'

But she gave Harriet no time to defend her intrusion into the blankly soulless corridors of Herald House.

'You know why you were chosen to lead this inquiry of yours, don't you?' she asked, voice steely.

The question, coming as it had, out of the blue, knocked Harriet into temporary silence.

Can I answer, she asked herself, that, yes, I do know why. Say *It is because C.A.G.D. Anstruther, of Her Majesty's Inspectorate of Constabulary, particularly selected me?* Or can I even say, but of course I absolutely cannot, *It's because I'm a female gentleman?*

'I'll tell you why, since you seem unable to answer for yourself. It's because it is intended that the inquiry gets nowhere. That's why a woman police officer from somewhere in the Nor-Well, from Birchester, if you will – was entrusted with the task. If there is any corruption in the higher reaches of the Maximum Crimes Squad, then the people responsible for setting up that organization in the first place will want to make quite sure no blame attaches to them. And that any action that may have to be taken is taken so quietly that the general public never gets to know.'

Can I put her right? How can I put her right?

Harriet was given no time to frame an answer.

'And this is why, if there is something that has gone badly wrong, it is going to be brought to light by someone who can't be muzzled. By the *Sunday Herald* in short. So, Miss Martens, let me give you a piece of advice. Spend a little time busily working away in those dingy offices they've hustled you into. What is it? Block 15, at the Surrey Docks Business Park. Then, as soon as you think you've been there long enough, produce a report saying there's no question of corruption among the senior officers of the Maximum Crimes Squad. And then go home to— To Birchester.'

So now I know, Harriet said to herself. Now I know why I'm sitting at this table in the smart-smart Groucho Club, looking at most of my two deep-fried, flower-topped courgettes swimming in their red sauce.

She took a deep breath.

'Mrs Raven,' she answered, weight in every syllable, 'let me say that you are wrong. Wrong about why I was chosen for this investigation. Wrong about what sort of police officer I am. Wrong about the mighty power of the paper you own. Wrong, I dare say, in your whole conception of what is and is not an élite in this country. And finally wrong in having asked me to lunch here today.'

She pushed back her heavy chair, put her two hands squarely on the white tablecloth and pushed herself to her feet.

Her gesture was only a little spoilt by her failure to remember exactly where in this strange-to-her purple-walled room the exit was. So the momentary delay did allow Mrs Raven something of a come-back.

'Very well,' she said, her voice chill, 'if you are really determined to leave, let me say my car is waiting just outside and my man will drive you to where you wish to go. To Rotherhithe or wherever.'

Harriet, spotting the way-out at last, remembered that when she had arrived there had been a long gleaming limo parked in full illegality just outside, a uniformed chauffeur at the wheel.

Right, she thought, making her way down the club's narrow stairway, I'll give myself the pleasure of walking right past it, taking the Tube back to Rotherhithe and there getting myself the lunch which I've mostly missed in the democratic warmth of Billy's Diner.

But I wish I had managed actually to taste one of the flowers at the end of the courgettes.

Chapter Six

'If I didn't know better,' Harriet said to WDC Lambert, as she stood hunched up from the icy rain in her old neutral brown padded jacket, 'I'd have said street-walker and no doubt about it.'

Across on the other side of the road in the light of the lamp just inside the police station's side entrance there had stepped a tall figure, generous bosom in a glaring orange tee-shirt thrusting aside an unbuttoned black plastic mac, skin-tight jeans tightly embracing long, long legs. A woman as unlike the female constables Harriet had known in her Met days as could be.

'Just what I thought myself, ma'am, when we tailed her first thing this morning. But it's Witherspoon all right.'

'Off we go then.'

There was no traffic at that moment along the shiny rain-slicked surface of the road. In half a minute they were across and advancing towards their target as she set off at a good pace in the direction of Freckles Frecker's flat.

'PC Witherspoon?'

She swung round, a look of puzzlement, even of alarm, on her big, broad-browed face, its lips gashed with orange as bright as the thrust-forward tee-shirt below, the eyebrows two solid black arcs above wide baby-blue eyes.

'Who are you? I'm off-duty. If you—'

But Harriet had her warrant card under those blue eyes.

'Detective Superintendent Martens and Detective Constable Lambert.'

Any response? Has Frecker been telling her about his troubles, the investigation? And, yes. A look, gradually taking on substance, of wary obstinacy.

'We need to speak to you. In connection with the inquiry I am conducting into allegations in the *Sunday Herald* newspaper concerning corruption in the Maximum Crimes Squad.'

'That got nothing to do with me.'

'I think it has, Constable. Am I going to take you back into the station? Or are we going to find somewhere nearby, out of this weather, where we can talk?'

A moment of calculation. But only one possible answer.

'There's a little caff just round the corner here. No one much goes in there this time of the evening. Stinking awful coffee. But you'll have to put up with that, won't you?'

Harriet let the jab of spite go unrebuked.

Two minutes later the three of them were sitting at a narrow pinkish plastic-topped table with cups of coffee in front of them. Herself and Lambert on the inner side, the big PC on the outer.

Unthinkingly stirring the grey liquid in front of her, Harriet saw that an oily slick had instantly spread over its whole surface. *A greasy spoon*, she thought. Well, I never expected to see such a factual illustration of that.

But she had more pressing business.

'Right. It was you, wasn't it, who left Freckles Frecker's flat by the back bedroom window when we called there yesterday?'

'I never—'

Then a better attempt, but still a twisting bid for escape.

'Who— Who is this Freckles Whatever you talking about?'

'No, that won't do. You came out of that house a few minutes before 5.45 a.m. today. You were seen going into the nick back there, and were identified as Police Constable GN 348 Phyllis Witherspoon. You are DC Frecker's girlfriend. Tell me now, why did you go scrambling out of the back window there yesterday when we rang at the front door?'

For a long moment she sat glaring in front of her. But then she did produce an answer.

'Freckles said I'd better hop it. That's why.'

'All right. But why did he think you should disappear like that?'

'I dunno. 'Spose he thought I'd loose off about something he didn't want you to know.'

'I see. So what is it that you know and DC Frecker would rather I didn't get to hear about?'

'God knows. Freckles tells me lots of things, but I reckon half of 'em are lies.'

'He tells you a lot, does he? About things you must have a pretty good idea he wouldn't want the officer investigating corruption in the Maximum Crimes Squad to learn, I dare say. So now is there anything – aren't there a good many things? – you ought to be telling me?'

'Why should I?'

'Because, as you very well know, it is an offence to withhold information about a criminal act.'

PC Witherspoon sat there on the other side of the pinkish table. Thoughts, plain to be seen, scrolling rapidly through her mind.

Then she straightened up an inch.

'All right, I'll tell you about me and Detective Constable Freckles Frecker.'

And Harriet, at the way the girl had pronounced Freckles' rank, began to think that her wait in the rain and cold opposite the police station might prove to have been worth it.

'That's what we want to hear about,' she said, less intimidatingly.

'Okay. Well, I met Freckles when I was on foot-patrol one day, six months ago more or less. The cheeky bugger fancied me. Well, a lot of blokes do. Got what they like, haven't I?'

She urged her splendid bosom forward by a quarter of an inch.

'Go on,' Harriet said, a touch sharply.

'Yeah, well, he came right up to me there in the street. *Oh, Constable, Constable, could you help me?* And, right away, out it come, the sort of help he needed. But I wasn't much impressed. He's not exactly a hunk, you know. Bony as all hell, in fact, and don't I know it. Knees and elbows dig in something terrible. But you know what he looks like. You've seen him, haven't you?'

'Yes,' said Harriet, 'I know what DC Frecker looks like.'

Quite enough bed-talk.

'Yeah, well, that's the point, you see. I wouldn't have given him the time of day, not for a moment, in the ordinary way. But he told me straight away he was a fellow officer, a DC in the Max. That's what did it for me. Elite squad, what they say about the Max, ain't it? And I know what being in an élite squad means. I know all about the police. My dad was a Sergeant in the Met, 'fore he retired. And his dad, back in the old days, was Special Branch. Just an ordinary sergeant, but a Special all the same. So I thought . . .'

She lapsed into silence.

So that accounts for this unlikely-looking constable, Harriet thought. Family tradition. Despite the full-sail bright orange tee-shirt, the orange-gashed lips, the whole street-walker appearance, she is cast in a mould. A mould that could lead – unlikely, unlikely – even to the very top.

But enough idle imagining. What I've got to learn from this policewoman street-walker is whether Freckles Frecker told her anything worthwhile.

'Yes? What did you think?'

The sharp question was enough to pierce the girl's reverie.

'Yeah, well, I thought then, never mind what this bloke who's come up to me looks like, if he's in the Max he ought to be— Well, something. He ought to have that little bit extra.'

'I know what you mean.'

'But when it come to it, he just didn't. Didn't have nothing any chap I'd met hadn't got. And that's what, after a week or so, made it all go what they call pear-shaped.'

'But you stayed with him?'

'Yeah. I didn't ought to of. Ought to have chucked him soon as I cottoned on he weren't really no élite detective, in the Max or not. But I didn't. I'm a bit of a lazy cow, tell you the truth. Then when we were having a row, row an' a half really, I did let him know just what I thought of him. And what did he do? Right in the middle of it he asks me, the weather bloody cold like it's been all winter, if I'd like to go off for a week to the West Indies.'

Ah, yes. Just what I thought. Frecker suddenly able to offer a big unexpected treat. So can I learn now just why he felt able to use Arnie Voles as his milch-cow? And others, too, perhaps?

'Did that surprise you, a sudden offer of something like that?'

'I'll say it did. I mean, Freckles ain't exactly mean, I'll say that for him, but it was always plain he never had that much cash to throw around.'

'And then all of a sudden it seemed that he did? Did you ask him how that had come about?'

''Course I did. I wasn't going to let a piss-artist like Freckles put one over on me. Wanted to know whether that cash he said he had was real, didn't I?'

'Right. You asked him then, did you, how he'd suddenly got enough for a holiday for two in the West Indies? And what did he tell you?'

The big girl opposite looked down at the untouched cup of sludgy coffee in front of her.

'Said he'd got his claws into a piece of shit called Arnie Voles, feller at the bottom end of the people-smuggling racket. Said he could get the odd five hundred out of him whenever he wanted.'

'And what did you think of that, knowing he was an officer in the Max?'

PC Witherspoon sat for a little, considering.

'Yeah,' she said at last. 'Yeah, I mean, right, I didn't think too much of Freckles by that time. But from things he'd said, every now and again, I knew he was sort of proud of being recruited to the Max. Specially as it was the Boxer himself who wanted him. You know who I mean by the Boxer?'

'I do.'

'So, yeah, I was sort of surprised by Freckles saying he was doing that. I mean, he was sort of betraying the Max, weren't he?'

'He was. So what did you say to him when you realized what he'd begun to get himself into?'

Opposite, a blush spread for a moment over the broad-browed, orange-lipsticked face.

'I s'pose you think I ought to of told him what a shit I thought he was? But, well, I didn't. It's not every day a girl gets the chance of a holiday in the sun, all paid for. And when we'd come back, well, he'd spent the money on me, hadn't he? I couldn't just walk out on him.'

'No, I see you would have felt you had to square your account. But did you ever ask him afterwards why he had suddenly gone back on – what? – on his loyalty to the Boxer?'

'Yeah. Matter o' fact, I did. One night in bed. A couple o' nights 'fore you come ringing at the bell.'

'And . . .?'

'An' he said something about if others could do it, why couldn't he.'

'Others? What others? Did you ask him what he meant by that?'

'Yeah, I did. Had to, didn't I? But I didn't get no answer, not a proper answer. He brought something out in a sort of mutter, like he was really a bit ashamed. And after that, all I got out of him was mutter. Or worse.'

'So he told you nothing in effect? Nothing?'

'Yeah. Told me to shut up. Said he wanted his beauty sleep. Turned over in the bed. An' it wasn't even as if we'd done it. Not like Freckles, that weren't. Always ready to go at it like a bleeding rabbit.'

Harriet felt she had come to a blank wall, every bit as final as the back Freckles Frecker had turned to the big girl opposite.

'All right,' she said, with an inward sigh. 'you can go on your merry way now. And thank you for being as frank as you were.'

'No bother.'

And, swaying her full figure provocatively, whether in innocence or not, out into the murky street she went.

Harriet looked down at the coffee in front of her, now not only oily but stone-cold.

'Do you want yours? Or another?' she asked WDC Lambert.

'No. No, ma'am. But— Ma'am, I think while we've been in here there's been someone outside watching us. I didn't like to say anything, not while you had Witherspooon on the run like that, but I really did think there was someone.'

'There still?'

Lambert carefully turned her head.

'No, ma'am. Gone. Or not where he was before, certainly.'

'You're sure he was watching? Watching us?'

'It looked like it, it really did. And there's no one else in here to have been watching.'

'Right, we'll go out and have a look-see. Take it quietly, though.'

Harriet paid for the three untouched coffees and

then, pretending to be deep in conversation, the two of them made their way out.

But, though she stood there for some time in the still coldly falling rain, making belief to be pulling up the hood of her padded coat and adjusting it, she saw no one who was not plainly going about their ordinary business.

'Right, whoever he was, he's gone now. You're sure it was a man?'

'Oh, yes. Quite sure.'

'Description?'

'He was keeping himself well into the shadows, ma'am. All I can say is he wasn't very tall.'

'All right. You did well to spot him.'

The man on the moped, Harriet thought. And is he . . .? Can he really be a man employed, however remotely, by kill-and-think-nothing Pablo Grajales?

Chapter Seven

Harriet, heading for Rekha's flat and all the time aware that the darkness and the sleety rain made it almost impossible to spot any pursuing moped rider, decided her next step must be to see DC Underwood, Pantsie, again. If she could succeed in getting out of him who it was his friend Freckles had meant when he had said to his bedmate WPC Witherspoon *if others could do it*, then her way forward might be there for the taking. Certainly there was little hope of getting out of Freckles himself what he had even given up his sexual pleasure to keep silent about. So, back to Ealing she drove.

In the morning, a hasty breakfast grabbed, she went straight round to the nearest newsagent's to get the new *Sunday Herald*. A quick flick through its pages, heavy with photographs, mostly of partly naked young women – Voice of the public, Mrs Raven? – convinced her that Frank Parkins had not been able to produce any valid follow-up to his first story about corruption in the Max. More of a relief was that there was nothing about a senior police officer rifling a desk in mighty Herald House. But perhaps there had not been time to get that story into devastating shape? Or perhaps something worse was in store?

And all the while as she skimmed the columns,

there was a darker thought about the advice Mrs Raven had given her at that threatening lunch at the Groucho. Advice? Or had it been an order? Do nothing more than go through the motions.

All right, I did reply, emphatically enough, that I'd no intention of doing any such thing. But is Mrs Raven going to leave matters there, that arrogant offer of a ride back to unthinkable Rotherhithe in her enormous limousine rejected? No telling.

The drive across London to the Business Centre with very little traffic this early on Sunday was apparently free of any following spy. No doubt because anyone tailing could not risk staying unobserved. So she arrived all set to pick up her pair of ears, Sergeant Watson, and tackle Pantsie Underwood once more. But fate decided differently.

As she stepped into the outer office, Detective Sergeant Adah Zaborski shot up from her computer.

'Ma'am, can I have a word? Urgent, I think.'

Darkly Jewish Adah Zaborski was a star. Possessed of a remarkable head for figures – she had, though she kept very quiet about it, a mathematics Ph.D – on more than one occasion she had brought the Greater Birchester Police fraud squad successes no one had thought possible. Harriet knew she had been lucky to get her seconded now. But, anticipating that the inquiry would involve detecting some large bribe ingeniously disguised, she had pressed hard.

Though in Birchester her path had seldom crossed DS Zaborski's, she had come to feel an odd, unaccountable sense of kinship with her. Perhaps it was because her faint Polish accent, stemming from her refugee origins, combined with that mysterious ability with figures, had made her something of a misfit in the police world.

Once, when talking about her at home, John, struck by her forename, had pulled down from his overflowing bookshelves a battered, spineless childhood volume, *The Complete Book of Fortune*. From its chapter 'The Meanings of Names' he had read out, *Adah: Clear-minded, a good friend and a fierce enemy*. Ever afterwards Adah had become something of a talisman for them both, Harriet bringing back tales of her financial triumphs like so many record salmon pulled from the stream, John joking that their mistakes in everyday life were from lack of *clear-mindedness*.

That last was a quality, Harriet thought now, which, if *The Complete Book of Fortune* had it right, might be doubly and trebly needed in the hunt for whoever at the top of the élite Max was in the pay of Pablo Grajales. If there was anyone who was.

So she had no hesitation in taking Adah straight into the privacy of her office.

'Right,' she said, closing the door behind her. 'Sit yourself down, and tell.'

'Well, ma'am, you know I've begun to get figures from Sergeant Downey back in Birchester who's hacking into places down here that strictly he shouldn't be.'

'My orders.'

And some little victories, she thought, for the dozy northern tart over London clever-dicks.

'Yes, ma'am. So, as you instructed, I've been looking at the bank transactions of the senior officers in the Maximum Crimes Squad, checking for any unaccountable large credit payments. Not that I expected to find anything like that. A much more likely indication of a bribe having been received is when there are regular outgoings suddenly terminated when the expenses incurred are being paid from some other, successfully hidden fund.'

'Okay, figures expert, and you've found one of them doing this? That's what you want to tell me?'

'No, ma'am. You don't get a lucky break like that so easily. I haven't even had all the figures from Sergeant Downey yet. It takes time to get them. No, what I've found is something much simpler. Even worryingly so.'

'Well, what?'

'Just an hour ago Sergeant Downey, clocking up overtime no doubt at a fearsome cost, sent me the first figures from Detective Superintendent Quinton's account. And right away this is what came to light. Just over a month ago the sum of £217,520 and 74 pence was paid in. Now, on that particular day that sum was the exact equivalent of half a million US dollars, less the regular bank transfer charge.'

Quinton, Harriet thought. The Number Two of the Max. Christ, has it really gone as high as that? Grajales must be . . . But perhaps this'll be something explicable after all.

'Are you telling me this is bribe money?' she snapped out at Sgt Zaborski. 'No other explanation possible?'

'Well, ma'am, the money was almost immediately paid out again.'

'Paid out?'

'Yes, ma'am. It's a not unusual procedure when bribe money, or any other dubious sum, is paid into an account that might eventually be seen under a magistrate's order. You get the money out of a visible account and into somewhere else as quickly as possible, and hope that, if months later an investigation gets under way, people like me don't go through the figures as far back as that one swift transaction.'

'But in this instance you've been on to the figures before this transaction – two hundred thousand plus, did you say? – was buried away?'

'Yes, ma'am. Thanks to you getting Sergeant Downey on to the job as quickly as you did.'

'So the question is, yes, where did Mr Quinton put that hefty sum?'

'We can't say, ma'am. Not yet. Sergeant Downey has been trying to locate it elsewhere. But he has to be very careful when what he's doing is absolutely against the rules.'

'I know, I know. Oddly enough, I was learning about a similar piece of corner-cutting, by officers of the Max, just yesterday, a little breaking-and-entering. Justified, I thought then. Much as Sergeant Downey's activities are justified now.'

'Yes, ma'am.'

But Adah Zaborski had answered with just the whisper of a sigh.

Harriet wished she could share the qualms the sigh had expressed. But she knew she could not. There were times when to achieve ends that mattered something inadmissible had to be allowed with the means.

'So when will Sergeant Downey have a result?' she asked. 'This may be it, you know. Will he have anything today?'

'No, ma'am. Not on a Sunday. There'll be some computers he'll need to access that won't be available.'

'Monday then? Will he find out then?'

'It's possible, ma'am. But I can't guarantee it.'

'Right, Sergeant,' she said. 'Even without Sergeant

Downey's extra inquiries, Mr Quinton must be our prime suspect now. Before this morning's out I'm going to have a talk with him. With the advantage of my not being expected. Or, rather, of our not being expected, because I want you to come with me.'

She saw then the tiny, resistant look that appeared on Adah Zaborski's face.

'Oh, yes, Sergeant,' she said. 'I know you'd much rather be sitting here sailing away above us all, communing with your computer in your own private heaven. But if I'm going to be asking Mr Quinton about his finances, I want you there at my elbow.'

At once she rang Persimmon House and found, not much to her surprise, that the Boxer gave his 'Miss Mouse' no weekends off.

So, speaking with someone in a position to see and hear a great deal of what went on in Persimmon House, she took care to call her, first, by her proper surname and soon after 'Mary'.

But when she asked whether Detective Superintendent Quinton was in his office little Mary Mouse sounded almost shocked.

'Oh, no, not on a Sunday morning,' she gabbled out. 'Mr Quinton never comes in till the afternoon on a Sunday. He insisted on that when he joined the squad. Never on a Sunday morning, except in absolute emergencies. He's a Roman Catholic, you know, and I think he goes to some special service at Westminster Cathedral, with some special sort of singing, I think.'

'What time is that?'

She had, inadvertently, shot out her question almost with the ferocity the Boxer might have used. And she achieved the same result. Fluster.

Think of something quickly to put myself back on a good footing.

'But Commander Boxall, is he in on Sunday mornings?'

After all the Boxer had said, loftily, that he could manage *a quick drink in the Duke of Norfolk sometime.* All right, let's ask if this quieter Sunday might be the time.

'Oh, yes, Commander Boxall is always in on Sundays. Unless things are very quiet. And they're not now, you know. We pulled in one of their high-up agents yesterday.'

The note of simple pride. Miss Mouse, detective.

'That's good news. Very. So, perhaps this would be a good moment to ask if today would be the time for the informal meeting Commander Boxall's promised me.'

'To ask Mr Boxall? Now?'

'That's it. You know, I think he'd be pretty pleased to give me half an hour or so, after he's just had such a triumph.'

'Oh, yes, yes. Yes, he would be in a good— Yes, I'll ring through straight away and ask.'

And, it was *yes.*

'Mr Boxall will be happy to meet you at one fifteen. But he says not at the Duke of Norfolk, but at the Earl of Lonsdale. It's just a little further along Westbourne Grove, on the opposite side.'

Then a gulp of hesitation. And a rapid embarrassed rush of words.

'Sorry. But Mr Boxall said to me he wouldn't wait for even a minute if you were late.'

The Boxer said that, did he? But I bet it wasn't

meant to be passed on. One slight success for the sometimes devious northern tart.

She put the phone down.

Luckily, DC Higham was able to find out fairly quickly what time Sung Mass took place at Westminster Cathedral, and it seemed that Detective Superintendent Quinton would almost certainly be back at his flat in Chester Square, not very far from the cathedral, by eleven. Time then to tackle him there, and afterwards to hurry over to Westbourne Grove and the Earl of Lonsdale.

I might have something very interesting for my friend, the Boxer, by then. I really might.

As the doors of the lift in the tall, white-painted house in Chester Square smoothly parted, Harriet, waiting on the second-floor landing, stepped forward and introduced herself and Detective Sergeant Zaborski.

Maurice Quinton looked down at them both, his large high-bridged Roman nose pointed in inquiry, cold blue eyes fixedly neutral. Tall, aged – his personal record had told Harriet – thirty-four, dressed in a well-cut dark grey suit, white shirt thin-striped in grey, discreet blue tie, he might have been a quietly prosperous, still youthful stockbroker or a set-on-his-path youngish Foreign Office man. But he was, she knew, a police officer with a string of successes to his name, marked out from his first day in the service for high things.

Yet had the ambition that must have driven him also led him to seize some hinted-at opportunity of reaching the heights, not in the police, but in some other way? It would do no harm, for instance, for an early-retired senior police officer seeking a seat in Parliament to have at his disposal something of a small fortune. And there were other paths to power that with money in the bank would be all the easier to climb.

'The Sabbath calm, Miss Martens?' he said now. 'Commander Boxall has told me why you are up in London, and I've been expecting you to want to talk. But hardly at this hour, or indeed at this place.'

'If you know why I am *down* in London,' she said, quick to replace Quinton's *up* with a corrective view of where the pinnacle of the British Isles is, 'then you must have realized my inquiries ought to be pursued with immediate vigour.'

A sudden smile then, if a somewhat bleak one, on the narrow face looking down at her.

'Why, yes, Miss Martens, I was perhaps not giving your task its due weight. Won't you come in? You and, was it, DS Zaborski?'

He unlocked the heavy front door of the flat, led them into a long hallway, carpeted by what looked like a Persian runner, and then on into a room that Harriet immediately recognized as a *drawing-room*, so similar was it to the one in her father's house in Hampshire, if more obviously a bachelor's lair, and furnished, too, with rather more distinction.

Tall windows, elaborately draped in silky green, looked out on to the trees of the narrow strip of Chester Square. A walnut side-table stood between them, with on it a scent-drifting camellia plant in a deep bowl of Chinese porcelain, facing a similar piece that Harriet could think of only as an escritoire. On the walls there were a dozen or more dim landscapes in heavy dulled gold frames as well as three or four little gilt-backed chairs. A pair of rigid-looking, high-backed sofas in wood-inlay completed the room's furniture with, making the long room clearly a bachelor's one, a tall armchair in solidly comfortable saddle-brown leather. Near to it the marble mantelpiece displayed a row of ruby-red and emerald-green goblets, softly reflected in the silvered glass of a large, ornately bordered mirror. No fire in the grate below, concealed as it was by an antique fire-screen, but the whole big room was kept warm by large old-fashioned iron radiators.

So warm indeed that Harriet soon became uncomfortably aware she had not been invited to take off her long coat.

From in front of the elegant, but workmanlike, escritoire Quinton took hold of a heavy little captain's chair and twirled it round in a single easy gesture that did not even cause the round leather cushion on it to slide off. He sat himself down, crossed one leg carelessly over the knee of the other, and indicated to Harriet and Adah that they should occupy the nearer one of the two high-backed sofas.

'Well, Miss Martens,' he said, 'how can I help you?'

'I'm here to ask for your insights, Mr Quinton,' she answered, approaching with careful caution the real object of the encounter. 'I don't need to tell you how seriously the Home Office is taking the story in the *Sunday Herald* of a week ago and that reference to the scandal going *much wider*. I interviewed that man Frank Parkins last week in the hope of finding out what evidence he might have. Needless to say, I got nowhere. And his piece in today's paper didn't advance his claim, for all its hints and innuendoes.'

'I dare say you're right,' Quinton said. 'I don't read the *Sunday Herald* myself.'

Not even when it might have something in it

hinting the second-in-command of the Max is possibly corrupt? Well, perhaps not much to be deduced from that, either way.

'No,' she went on quickly, 'if Parkins does know something, it's very likely not backed as yet by any hard evidence. But if there is anything at all that could at some future date be supported by evidence, I want to find that before he does.'

'I suppose you would. It would be quite a feather in your cap.'

Harriet was on the point of denying that she was driven by any such personal motive. But then she thought *Oh, yes, talk of a feather in a cap, what I might have expected from you, Mr Ambitious Quinton.* And she held her tongue.

'So,' she said, 'can you tell me if there has been anything that has – what shall I say? – caused you a flicker of disturbance about any of your immediate colleagues, either before or after that first *Sunday Herald* report?'

No trace, of course, of any sort of dismay on the fine-drawn face opposite, lit as it was by such light as came through the room's tall windows on this darkly overcast, rain-threatening day.

'A flicker of disturbance? No. No, I don't think I have felt that, Miss Martens. Perhaps I don't know my immediate colleagues as intimately as you may know yours.'

Seeing him glance then at Adah Zaborski, sitting silent and attentive beside her, Harriet absorbed the message. Some senior officers might be hail-fellow-well-met with their colleagues, senior and junior, but Maurice Quinton saw himself as made of different stuff, aloof and aloft.

'A pity,' she said. 'I had hoped you might have noticed something perhaps about one or another of the senior members of the Maximum Crimes Squad that would give me something to work on, however fruitlessly in the end.'

'I have not. Rightly or wrongly, I don't care to pry into other people's private lives.'

A cold rebuke. But one that might provide all the same a way forward.

'Yes,' she said. 'That's not something one likes doing. But I've been tasked with finding out whether there is any reason to believe any officer in the Maximum Crimes Squad, particularly any senior one, has been compromised by these world-scale people-smugglers. And I have to pry, as you put it, in order to do that. To pry into every aspect of those senior officers' lives, however little I may like doing it.'

She paused. Then jumped in.

'So, Mr Quinton, I come, for instance, to the point of asking you directly whether there have recently been any unduly large sums paid into your bank.'

A trace now of dismay?

No.

Instead a smile. The cold smile, it seemed, of a trick contemptuously trumped.

'Yes, Miss Martens. I have, of course, recently had a considerable sum paid into my current account, as your inquiries, which I suspect must have been of borderline illegality, must have revealed.'

And no more.

'Yes, our inquiries, however much or little illegal, have breached the privacy of your bank account. As they have of others. I make no apology for that. I am investigating possibly very serious corruption in an élite squad of the police service, and I shall take whatever steps I see fit to prosecute my inquiries. Which include questioning you, Mr Quinton, about every aspect of your finances. So, tell me please, what was the origin of that *considerable sum*, a sum amounting in fact, allowing for some transfer charges, to precisely half a million American dollars.'

'Very well.'

Can this be it? The admission? An admission at least of something? Yet he is showing no sign at all of there being anything wrong.

'Since you feel it is your duty to ask, Miss Martens, let me tell you why that large sum was recently paid to me. It is simply that I came into a legacy.'

'Of exactly five hundred thousand dollars, American dollars?'

'Yes. Of American dollars, and of that nicely rounded-out amount. The legacy originated in America. Nothing so extraordinary, if you think about it. As you, or your assistants, apparently have failed to do.'

He shot a glance then at silent Adah Zaborski.

Who did not respond.

'Yes,' he went on chillingly. 'A legacy, as you might have realized had you thought about it, is apt to be for a stated sum. In this case the sum in question was half a million dollars.'

'But,' Harriet said, 'you almost immediately put in hand another transaction, with that precise sum?'

Maurice Quinton sat in silence, his leg still carelessly draped across the other knee.

Harriet raised her eyebrows interrogatively.

'Very well, since you seem to find it necessary to go into every detail of my personal affairs, I suppose I must satisfy your—'

He hesitated.

Was he going to say *Your damned intrusiveness?*

'Shall I say, your possibly necessary curiosity? All right. So let me tell you the history of that sum of half a million dollars. It was left to me by a distant cousin, who stated in his American will that I was his sole remaining heir. The bulk of his wealth, which was in fact very considerable, he left perversely, out of an intense dislike for the America where he had made his fortune, to a curious institution I had never before heard of, the American Society for the Restoration of the Queen's English.'

Once again he fell silent.

And now Adah Zaborski did intervene.

'I'm sorry, sir, but that fails to explain your transferring the sum to another account.'

'Quite right, Sergeant. You're very acute.'

'So?' Harriet jabbed in.

Another cold smile.

'So, Miss Martens, in view of the way this distant cousin of mine had disposed of his money, I decided that the sum was hardly mine to use for my own purposes. Indeed, there is a prior claimant. In quite the way of some depressing minor nineteenth-century novel, my cousin had a daughter, who in the course of time had a daughter herself, born *out of wedlock*, as they delight in saying. In consequence my cousin had absolutely cut this daughter of his and her descendants out of his will. Now, alas, the bastard child's mother has also died, and so I have conceived it my duty to set up a trust fund for her child's upkeep and education.'

A sharp look for Adah Zaborski.

'I will get my solicitor to give you the full details, Sergeant.'

Chapter Eight

On the whole Harriet disliked pubs. She felt that, though their rough conviviality could be enjoyable, it chimed a little ill with the notion she had always had in the depths of her mind of her true self. That notion she had perhaps looked at clearly only after C.A.G.D. Anstruther had put into her head the somewhat comical words *a female gentleman*. In her days as a junior detective in the Met she had spent hours in pubs, often drinking more than was strictly good for her, believing she would be a better police officer for having friendly relations with her colleagues. And she had enjoyed the gossip and the joshing.

But there had been as well an undercurrent of distaste. The gossip was sometimes, often even, idle and malicious. The jokes were generally merely crude and pointless. The opinions belted out were, in those days frequently either blatantly racist or mindlessly so and, on many occasions sexist. The alcohol that fuelled them fuelled in her, too, muzzy mornings and occasionally less alertness than she had thought it her duty to possess. Much inhaled tobacco smoke, at that now distant time when she had so often had a cigarette between her lips, had done her no good.

So it was with a frisson of antipathy that, bringing with her in her mind the inconclusive ending to her confrontation with Detective Superintendent Quinton, she entered the Earl of Lonsdale. However, she noted glancing at her watch, she was only a couple of minutes later than the target time she had set herself, to arrive a full quarter of an hour before the Boxer had said he would be there.

She saw with a glint of pleasure, looking round at the patrons arriving for the pub's flaunted Sunday lunches, that the Boxer had not come early, a trick she had fully expected in view of that threat not to wait *even a minute*.

She found a seat on one of the benches against the walls of the quieter, more tucked-away part the pub where she could keep an eye on the entrance doors. Taking off her rain-dampened coat and the hat that so nicely matched it, well sodden as it had become, she began to consider what she should get herself to drink. On her own, she would have probably chosen a glass of wine. But she saw the Boxer, no doubt about it, as a beer man, with very likely a favourite brew in every pub he regularly used. Setting white wine against his pint would at once mark out the opposition between them. Not a good idea. The chances might be slim, but if at all possible it would be very much of a plus to establish better relations than when she had heard those shouted words *What, she's arrived, has she? The Dozy Northern Tart*.

So she compromised. A bottle of Guinness. Not such a quantity of liquid to have to swallow as in a pint of beer, but not wimpish. Enough of the macho about it, too, to put on display the persona of a police officer's police officer. Irrespective of gender.

At precisely five minutes before the Boxer's rendez-vous time he arrived, hound's tooth black-and-white checked topcoat draped across his shoulders, no hat, no umbrella. Looking at him from her almost concealed place, Harriet suppressed a smile of triumph. One dozy northern tart not caught out.

Seeming not to notice her, though she had observed his quick sweep of the whole premises, the Boxer strode up to the small semi-circular bar that presided over this part of the house.

'The usual, Jim.'

His never-less-than-loud tones. Again, Harriet concealed a smile as a shining pewter tankard was lifted from its special hook and placed under one of the beer pulls.

Eventually, pint in hand, the Boxer turned and gave the room a steady survey, only allowing his gaze to rest on herself at its end.

He came over then.

'Didn't recognize you out of uniform, Miss Martens. Or I'd have brought you a drink, though I don't suppose I'd have guessed at a Guinness.'

Standing there, his boldly patterned topcoat wide open to show his waistcoat with that trademark gold watch chain swooping across it – today he was wearing a light-grey Prince of Wales cloth – he gave Harriet an up-and-down, frankly appraising look.

A touch angry with herself for allowing it, she acknowledged she welcomed the approval he was evidently giving to her well-cut lovat green suit, the crispness of her white blouse and the rightness of the simple amber brooch at its neck.

'Thanks, but I'm happy with what I've got.'

The Boxer thumped himself down on a chair opposite.

'Okay,' he said. 'A quiet drink in a pub where none

of my lot will see us. Can't do better than the Lonsdale
for that. When we set up in these parts, as soon as I'd
sussed out the lie of the land, I made it clear to the
lads they could frequent the Duke of Norfolk as much
as they liked, but they'd find themselves on an all-
night watch somewhere if I ever caught them poking
their nose in at the Earl of Lonsdale. Bloody aristocratic
all the pubs round here, you know, Earl of Lonsdale,
Duke of Norfolk, Duke of Wellington just along the
Portobello Road. But none of them, thank God, pooftah
places.'

Harriet gave the peacock display as appreciative a
smile as she could rise to. If she was to get anything
out of the quiet-drink session, this was her chance to
establish friendly terms.

'Yes, I'm glad to be here,' she said. 'I felt that as this
inquiry of mine's a pretty delicate business it would
be no bad thing if we could feel at ease with each other
when we discussed it.'

'Oh, yes?'

The two syllables could hardly have been delivered
more flatly.

'I mean, I know you by reputation. Who doesn't in
every force in the country?' Try another smile, even a
roguish one. 'But I know nothing of you as a person.
Are you married, for instance?'

He was. His P/R had told her that. But it might do
for a conversation starter.

'One wife. Two children, grown-up.'

Not exactly forthcoming. But an in of sorts.

'Ah, yes. I know all about children supposedly
grown-up. I've two sons myself. Old enough to be at
university, and young enough to behave pretty childishly from time to time.'

'St Andrews, isn't it, Mrs Piddock?'

Oh, so it's back to blatantly showing me you've been asking all about me, right down to my officially unused married name and where it is the twins are. All those useful contacts of yours.

But I'm not going to take that as a hands-off warning.

'Yes, the boys are up in Scotland. Bit far from Birchester, but it's one of the best universities in the whole British Isles, of course. And your children? How old are they now? College age? Or more? Both boys? Or what?'

'Boys, straight into the police.'

'In Dad's footsteps. Are they in the Met?'

'Liverpool and Newcastle.'

Minimal responses. All right, if I can't get you to play, move on.

'So tell me about these two in your squad who've been, shall we say, behaving childishly too?'

'Childishly? I don't think so.'

'No, you're right. Any police officer who extorts a bribe is behaving a good deal worse than childishly. They're betraying the whole service.'

She gave him a steady speculative look.

Was she perhaps, after all, talking to a man who was betraying the service on a scale enormously greater than DC Frecker's piece of extortion? Or DC Underwood's?

'I'd agree with that.'

Not the tiniest blink. But it would have been a lucky shot indeed.

'So what's to be done about Frecker and Underwood?'

'Get rid of the pair of them. Fast. Medical grounds discharges.'

Harriet thought rapidly. And then plunged.

'You seem, if I may say so, to have changed your mind about those two since we last spoke.'

The Boxer gave her a creaky smile.

'Not only a lady's privilege, Miss Martens. No, all right, my first reaction when I saw that *Sunday Herald* story was that no one was going to do the dirt on any of my lads. But I've listened now to those tapes recorded by that nasty piece of work Voles, and I can see those two idiots are past saving.'

Harriet took in that she had made an advance. And decided to push a little further.

'So you needn't have bothered,' she said, giving him a smile tinged with irony, 'with your neat little ploy of getting the pair of them to point the finger at yourself as the major bribe-taker that I'm here to look for.'

For a brief moment the Boxer seemed disconcerted.

'You got on to that then?' he said at last, grinning.

'They messed it up, your two bright lads. They were meant, I suppose, just to point lightly to your – may I say? – rather lavish lifestyle. To divert me into wondering about you. But they managed to produce the few words concocted for them each in precisely the same order. Your suits. Are they actually Savile Row? Your car, a Scorpio, I gather. And the fob-watch you've got in your waistcoat pocket at this moment, gold, of course.'

It had been a daring move. Too daring, she asked herself in sudden dismay? If I've simply shown him I'm no fool, well and good. But if he actually is the man in Pablo Grajales's pay, then not only have I warned him he's in my sights but I've quite possibly put myself in real danger.

'I can see I've underestimated you, Superintendent.'

The admission, though handsome, still gave no clue about the man sitting opposite in the Earl of Lonsdale's warm, beery, food-smelling Sunday atmosphere.

But the Boxer had more to say.

'All right, you told me when you came to Persimmon House on Thursday you were going to ask questions and expect answers. Okay, you've been tasked with this inquiry, and you're going to go on and on about it, like any damn nagging wife, till you think you've got what you want. Your privilege. But let me warn you. There are wives who go on nag, nag, nagging till maybe they find they've lost the husband who's been looking after them for all the years of their marriage. They kill the golden goose. And you, Detective Superintendent Martens, or Piddock, or whatever your name is, are in danger of killing my golden goose. The goose that before long, if I've anything to do with it, will lay one almighty golden egg, the crippling of the whole damn people-smuggling racket.'

A pause, if only for more breath.

Harriet jumped in.

'Yes, Commander, you said as much earlier. The work of the Maximum Crimes Squad is not to be interfered with. Oh, I see the virtue of that. But if the work's already in jeopardy, if there's someone, as that man Frank Parkins pretty well alleges, near the top of the Max who's been corrupted, then your work is being interfered with. On a wholly dangerous scale. And if by asking questions, if by asking and asking them, I get at whoever that is – and I grant you it's a big enough *if* – if my questioning exposes them in the end, I'll be wrecking the people-smuggling racket every bit as effectively as you hope you will.'

'No.'

A blank rejection, and a note of rising anger.

'No, Miss Sticky-nose, I tell you this. I chose each and every senior officer in the Max. I chose them. And I did not choose anyone who was going to be corrupted. All right, I was wrong about those two DCs. But I'm not wrong about any of my DIs, not about Browning, Phillips, Outhwaite nor Mary Smith. And not about DCI Griffin, nor even Detective Superintendent Quinton. Nobody at the top of the Max needs investigating. Nobody. Do you understand that?'

The lion defending its cubs all right, Harriet thought. No, more than that. The mother tiger not allowing even the smallest jungle beast so much as to sniff at her brood. But sniff I'm going to. If I find the least indication that all is not as it should be with any of those senior officers, I shall investigate it to the full. And I won't be stopped.

But I can see I'm not going to get any more out of the Boxer.

Abruptly the beery odour pervading the whole pub seemed overwhelming.

Right, at least I can get out now. Even the wind and the rain outside will be preferable to this.

She got to her feet, wondered for a moment if she should drain the still half full Guinness in front of her, decided she was damned if she would.

'Very well, I've heard you, Commander,' she said, snatching up her coat and her now all but dry hat. 'I've taken note. And sooner or later we'll see what's the outcome.'

In the street it seemed to be even colder than before. A sudden gust of icy wind took the hat off her head, swirled it for a moment high into the air, allowed it to fall.

Hastily stooping, she grabbed it and, keeping it clutched in one hand, marched away.

What is it, Harriet asked herself as at last she arrived at Pantsie Underwood's to put to him the questions she had planned to do first thing, what is it that gave him, trailing along behind sharply enterprising Freckles Frecker, the green light to extract cash from a criminal in his power? Will I learn from Pantsie now what Freckles refused to tell his bed-companion, even to the extent of forgoing his customary bout of sex? And can this be after all, despite what Adah has discovered about Quinton's finances, my way ahead?

She turned to scarlet-eared DS Watson, solidly striding along beside her, head down to the thin flurries of sleety snow racing across the street's front gardens.

'God, will this appalling weather ever come to an end? Who'd believe this is March?'

Watson gave her a grin.

'Won't get better till we get back to Birchester, ma'am.'

It was at least warm in the Underwoods' sitting-room, crowded with its shinily new-looking three-piece suite and big-screen television, though Harriet found she was regretting that Pantsie had once again brusquely sent his wife away when she had offered tea.

However, she got down to business without delay.

'Since I last spoke to you, Constable, certain information has come to me that makes me think you were
not as helpful as you might have been.'

Pantsie Underwood, upright on the edge of his
factory-fresh armchair, bristled.

'I answered every question you put to me, ma'am.
And, with respect, may I remind you that you were
perfectly satisfied at the time. You went so far as to
suggest, in fact, that I'd answered you so honestly I
earned some consideration in any disciplinary proceedings.'

'Yes, I did say that, or something like it. And you
may yet benefit from giving me your full co-operation.
But only if you now do more than provide the shortest
possible answer to every question I ask. Be a little
more forthcoming, Constable.'

'Ma'am.'

The response could hardly have been less co-operative, or more uncomprehending.

Right, let's see if he's capable of being jerked into
awareness.

'More co-operation, Constable. As much as you
gave Commander Boxall when he suggested what you
might say to me last time we met.'

From the look on Underwood's slab of a face it was
plain that her shot had gone straight home. He knew
what she had referred to was that list, *fancy suits,
Scorpio motor, gold watch.*

'For instance,' she went on, not letting go for one
moment, 'it seems to me that you could have told me
more, even a good deal more, about just what it was,
when you were using your safe-opening skills in Reynolds Liebling's flat, that made your friend Frecker
believe it was all right to go and talk to Arnie Voles.'

But the sergeant major opposite made one last feeble effort to thwart her.

'Ma'am, that was weeks and weeks ago. I can't recall anything more than what I told you on Friday.'

'Try, Constable.'

'I don't know what there is to tell, ma'am. I mean, all I did was to get to work on that safe in the wall in the bedroom there – behind a pretty juicy painting, it was – and open it up for Mr Outhwaite to go through the stuff inside.'

'No, you did something more. Did or saw. What was it?'

Then it was plain he knew he had not succeeded in keeping her at bay.

'Well, ma'am . . . Was it what made Freckles actually think it'd be all right to have our chat with Voles?'

'Got it in one.'

She sat still, drawing the answer out of him.

'Well . . . Well, ma'am, it was something a bit funny really. It was like this. Mr Outhwaite was going through the papers in the safe. I heard him sort of shuffling them. And— And . . . Well, it wasn't anything he exactly said.'

'So what was it, man? Speak up.'

She glowered at him.

'Ma'am, he sort of whistled.'

'Very good, Constable. Mr Outhwaite whistled. And what am I supposed to gather from that?'

'I don't know, ma'am.'

'Don't be stupid. You or Frecker took particular note of Mr Outhwaite whistling. Why was that? Was it something to do with the way he whistled? Was it that?'

'Well, yes. Yes, ma'am, I suppose it was. He kind of whistled in surprise.'

'Good. Now we're getting somewhere. Mr Outhwaite whistled in surprise. So what was it that surprised him?'

'It must have been something he found in the safe, ma'am.'

'Yes, it must, musn't it? You're obviously a brilliant detective, Underwood. So why don't you go on? Mr Outhwaite found something in Reynolds Liebling's safe that caused him a good deal of surprise. What do you deduce that it was? How about a piece of paper, a document of some sort? Yes?'

'Yes. Yes, ma'am. That's true, Mr Outhwaite was going through the papers in the safe. He'd told me to go and keep a watch on the mews from the sitting-room window in case Liebling might come back, though as we knew he'd just gone off to the States that wasn't hardly likely.'

'But Mr Outhwaite had sent you out of the way before he whistled in surprise?'

Thought apparent on the slab-face.

'Yes. Yes, I'm sure it was before, ma'am. Just a minute or so before. I bring it to mind now. I'd left the door of that bedroom open.'

'And Frecker, of course, heard this famous whistle of surprise as well?'

'Yes, yes, ma'am. He must've done because we talked about it afterwards. I'd sort of wondered what it was that made Mr Outhwaite whistle in just that way, and then— Well, that was when Freckles said he reckoned we could pay a bit of a visit to Arnie Voles.'

'So when Frecker was suggesting it was suddenly all right to extract money from Voles, did he say anything to you about what Mr Outhwaite might have seen inside that safe? Anything at all? Had he caught a glimpse of a paper or document Mr Outhwaite was looking at?'

'No. No, ma'am. You see, Mr Outhwaite had asked him to pop his head out of the flat's door to make sure it was all okay down the stairs. So he couldn't of seen nothing.'

'You're sure? He couldn't have seen anything?'

'No, ma'am. It was only when I happened to mention Mr Outhwaite's whistle of surprise that he said, yes, he'd heard it. And then, all of a sudden, he said we might have a go at Arnie Voles.'

Harriet could not restrain the faintest of sighs.

She glanced at DS Watson beside her on the new sofa. A swift shake of the head to say *Nothing more to be had.*

'Right then, Underwood. I'll see that your co-operative attitude, in so far as it went, is taken into account in the disciplinary process. Good-day to you.'

'All right,' Harriet said as they drove away, 'we've established that Mr Outhwaite saw something in that illegally opened safe of Reynolds Liebling's which caused him so much surprise he was unable to check a whistle of astonishment. So what do you think that could have been?'

'Well, it must have been a document of some sort, ma'am, I suppose. Might have been a pile of gold ingots or a big bag of cocaine, of course. But Underwood did say he'd heard papers being shuffled.'

'Yes. I think we can dismiss your ingots and your drugs. I doubt whether it would have greatly surprised DI Outhwaite finding those, even in an ordinary domestic safe if it was a criminal's.'

'You're right, ma'am. And it was a safe of that sort Underwood must have opened. I'm inclined to think anything more sophisticated and larger would have baffled him, however much he'd once learnt from his breaking-and-entering school pal.'

'No, I think you're wrong there, as a matter of fact. I see Underwood as being one of those people whose brains are, so to speak, all in their hands. If he wasn't a really top-notch safe-breaker, one of the élite, Commander Boxall would never have taken him on for the Max.'

Watson considered that.

'Yes,' he said after a moment. 'Yes, I see what you mean, ma'am. DC Underwood clever with his hands, but not so clever as a detective.'

'Oh yes. Not the sharpest of detectives, our Pantsie.'

'So what about Frecker, ma'am? When we saw him on Friday he sounded sharp enough to me, if more than a bit dicey. You going to have another go at him?'

'I don't think so, Sergeant. Or not this miserable Sunday afternoon anyhow. You're right, of course, about him being sharp. But from what Lambert and I got out of PC Witherspoon I know, too, he's totally obstinate. That may be because he does have a notion of what it is in that safe that's worth knowing about, and has ideas for exploiting that knowledge when he feels the time's right. But, no, I don't think we'll get anything out of him very easily. I see Mr Outhwaite as being the person to look into just now.'

'Yes, ma'am, I must admit I'd dearly like to know what it was that made a senior officer in the Max whistle in that way.'

'I think I can at least make a guess what sort of thing that must be. It has to be a letter of some sort.

Outhwaite was, we know, looking through papers. And I think it might well be a letter, surely to Liebling, which would compromise some person who cannot at any price allow it to get about that he, or she – or she, remember – has written to someone known, at least to the Met and the crime reporters of the nationals, as a top-ranking criminal.'

'Yes, I'd say you've hit on it, ma'am. A letter from . . . From some high-up. In the police? I hope to God not. Or in . . . Well, how about politics? Or the respectable business world? Someone at the top there? Any of those might be likely.'

'All right. But, to quote, Sergeant Watson, from Sherlock Holmes, as my husband frequently does, *it is a capital mistake to theorize before one has data.* So I think I'll spend the rest of this foul, sleety, snowy Sunday going through all the stuff we have on Mr Outhwaite. Then, first thing Monday morning, he and I will have a good long talk.'

Chapter Nine

On Monday morning before setting off to learn, if she could, why DI Jackson Outhwaite had whistled in surprise when he was going through the safe in Reynolds Liebling's flat, Harriet checked whether Sergeant Zaborski had been able to confirm Maurice Quinton's account of how he had acquired the exact sum of half a million US dollars. Not much to her surprise, Adah replied that, yes, inquiries into the information Quinton's solicitor had promptly supplied had confirmed in every detail the origins of the transaction.

'I've even checked on the Internet the American Society for the Restoration of the Queen's English. It exists all right.'

'Now I'll believe anything,' Harriet said, as she made her way out to find her noisy boneshaker of a car.

Her destination was the big and busy Cumberland Hotel at Marble Arch which, calling DI Outhwaite at his home in Buckinghamshire the evening before, she had suggested as a convenient point between Persimmon House in Westbourne Grove and the Business Park in Rotherhithe for a meeting where, as she had put it, he could talk about his colleagues without embarrassment.

Driving across London to the hotel, she kept a

careful eye out for whoever, moped rider or someone with a different vehicle, Pablo Grajales's London operator might have set to follow her. She did not spot anyone suspicious. Something that, with the press of traffic at that hour, was hardly surprising. Even when at last she found somewhere to park in the streets behind the big hotel she still saw nothing. But, she thought, failing to see a tail did not mean there was no one watching her every step.

DI Outhwaite, she saw when she spotted him waiting for her just inside the hotel entrance, was a gaunt-looking man seemingly in his late forties – actually only forty-two, she recalled from his P/R – greying hair cut close to a narrow pointed skull, grey eyes beneath sharply angular eyebrows set in watchfulness. She led him at once into the big foyer beyond, went directly over to the most secluded corner she saw and adroitly contrived to put him facing her in one of the foyer's deep black leather armchairs. A waiter came up and, without any consultation, she ordered coffee.

She waited then in silence. If the man opposite her had anything to hide about what he had seen in Reynolds Liebling's safe, a certain amount of nerves tautening might well pay off.

Once they had been served, still in silence she poured two cups from the squat steel pot between them, added milk from the little matching jug, and pushed forward the dimly shining steel pot of brown sugar crystals.

Then, when she had seen a hand reaching out towards the pot and abruptly being withdrawn, sitting well back in her chair she began on a deceptively friendly note.

'I hope you can appreciate the difficulties facing

me in my investigation, Mr Outhwaite. The *Sunday Herald* has made its allegations about serious corruption in the Maximum Crimes Squad and, whether what they've hinted at is right or wrong, they are allegations that have got to be looked into. Which leaves me in the unpleasant position of having to find out as much as I can about each of the squad's senior officers.'

She paused for a response.

And did not get much of one.

'I suppose so,' the grey man opposite muttered, indrawn as a crab.

Still Harriet kept to her relaxed tone.

'And that means,' she went on, 'I have to ask you to tell me what you think of colleagues to whom you are naturally loyal. But it must be done, DI.'

Another pause for a reaction.

'If you say so, ma'am.'

But, as one by one, she went though the list of the senior officers of the Max from Detective Superintendent Quinton down to Detective Inspector Phillips, she heard not even as much as she had gleaned long before from their personal records.

So at last she leant forward.

'I gather you yourself transferred to the Max from the Met Fraud Squad, Detective Inspector. Were you happy about that?'

Outhwaite gave her a small guarded smile.

'It wasn't exactly a question of whether I wanted to move or not,' he said. 'I was happy enough at the Yard most of the time quietly going through fraud suspects' figures. But when Commander Boxall says *Come* you go.'

She returned the smile, she hoped more warmly.

'Yes, I know what you mean.'

'Still, I'm pleased to be with the Max, of course. Who wouldn't be?'

'Yes, it must be very rewarding to be working on cases as important as the people-smuggling business.' And, pounce. 'Finding yourself going through the safe of a top-ranking international criminal like Reynolds Liebling.'

A redoubled look of uneasiness in the watchful grey eyes.

This it? Surely not as soon and easily as this?

And it was not.

'I hope you're not insinuating, ma'am, that breaking into Liebling's place was something the Max shouldn't have done?'

'No. No, Detective Inspector. We're not quite as innocent as that up in Birchester. There are times when the strict bounds of legality have to be stretched, even firmly broken. But I am interested in that afternoon you spent in Liebling's flat.'

And, yes, now surely a plain hint of unease in the grey eyes.

She cursed the hotel's discreet lighting, relaxing enough for its patrons, less than helpful for an interrogator.

'It wasn't an afternoon, ma'am,' Outhwaite said. 'We were in and out of the place in not much more than an hour.'

'But you found what you were looking for in the safe? Evidence? Even if it couldn't be used in court, considering how you got hold of it?'

'Well, we weren't looking for evidence, not as such,' he answered now more confidently. 'As you said, we couldn't have made much use of it, the way we'd have got it. But, no, what Mr Boxall hoped we'd find was some clue to Liebling's plans for the future.'

Right, let's ease off a bit now and come in all the harder later.

'I see,' she said, moving further back again in her slithery leather chair. 'A good move, of course. Much as I'd expect from Commander Boxall. But, tell me, why did a job of that sort land up on your plate? A figures man?'

'I'm not really sure, ma'am. Just I happened to be available, I think.'

'And did it turn out that your ability to read figures quickly was useful when you got into that safe?'

'No. No, not really.'

But a new hint of tension in that forcedly offhand answer? At the mention of the word *safe?* Getting near? Yes, time to dive in hard.

'But you did find something interesting? I gather you were heard to whistle in sheer surprise.'

'No. No, ma'am. No. Whistle? I don't think I whistled, surprise or not. Not when I was going through the papers in that safe. No, I didn't. Why should I have?'

'But you did, Mr Outhwaite. I know that.'

'Know it? I don't see how. You weren't there. Were you?'

'Let's just say I don't have to be somewhere to know what went on there. So what was it that caused you to whistle in surprise like that?'

A look of grimly silent determination in the poor light.

Harriet leant yet further forward.

'I asked you a question, Detective Inspector.'

'Well, I don't have to answer, do I? Not if your information's incorrect?'

'It isn't incorrect.'

She leant closer to him across the cups and steel jugs and basins thought necessary to serve two coffees.

DI Outhwaite sat still as a rock-carving, bolt-upright in his deep armchair.

'If you don't answer, Detective Inspector, or won't answer, you cannot do otherwise than make me suspect that something happened while you were investigating Reynolds Liebling's safe that would, at the very least, bring you into considerable discredit. At the worst it would lead me to think the *Sunday Herald* allegations were based on some knowledge, or at least strong suspicion, that you are the officer who has received a bribe from Reynolds Liebling.'

'That's not true. That's a damn lie.'

'Is it, Detective Inspector? If it is, you have only to account for your surprise when you saw something in Liebling's safe to make me see I have been misled.'

She sat peering at him in the dimness.

Opposite the gaunt shape seemed almost to wriggle from side to side on the deep seat of his chair. At last he spoke.

'Well, yes. Yes, I suppose I might have expressed surprise there in that flat. Even whistled. You— When you come across something totally unexpected, you may make some sort of involuntary sound which, I suppose, could be described—'

He came to an abrupt halt, shot out a question.

'Which of them was it? Underwood? Or Frecker?'

Plainly he hopes he'd bounce me into telling him. Yes, he very much wants to find out which of those two, despite his having tried to get them out of the bedroom where that safe is, might have got sight of whatever it was he saw. The one who, questioned later, could expose the lie he's about to tell.

No luck, DI Outhwaite. No luck at all.

'So just what was it that made you produce that *involuntary sound*, Detective Inspector? That whistle of sheer surprise?'

He had to answer.

A scratchy clearing of the throat.

'All right. Well, I didn't want to tell you, ma'am, because— Well, because I wasn't even exactly sure what it was I saw. For just a second. It was no more than a glimpse. One quick glimpse.'

'And why was it only a glimpse you got? You saw something when you were going through the papers in Liebling's safe that made you whistle in surprise. In surprise. At something, as you said, *unexpected*. But for some reason, you're saying now, you never looked properly at it, whatever it was. You just glimpsed it. Is that what I'm to believe?'

'Yes. Yes, ma'am. It is. It was just a glim— Well, to tell the truth when I realized what it was, what it might be, I pushed it back where it had been. Straight away. As if it was, well, you know, red-hot.'

'I see. So you saw something, a document, a letter, which was *red-hot*. Red-hot information. Information that – what? – you didn't want anybody else ever to see, other than Liebling, of course. Or was it information you had registered in your mind, taken in, which you wanted to be sure of keeping to yourself?'

'Ma'am, there were those two there somewhere in the flat. And— And, well, you know how trustworthy they are. Look at what it said about them in last week's *Sunday Herald*.'

'Yes, those two untrustworthy detectives were there in the flat with you, and you were anxious just a minute ago to know which of them had described your whistle of astonishment. Well, I'll tell you. It was both of them. They were both struck by it. So we come back to where we were, Detective Inspector. What exactly was it that you saw that made you express such aston-ishment?'

But she was not yet to get her answer.

'Well then, ma'am, if they both heard me whistle, which one of them was it that might have crept up on me at the safe there?'

'Why are you so anxious to know, Detective Inspector? Was what you were looking at, or, as you said, thrusting away after just one glimpse, was it so valuable, important, interesting, that you're worried that Underwood or Frecker, one or the other, might have got to share what you learnt?'

'No, no, ma'am. It was just . . .'

A silence.

'Just what, Detective Inspector?'

Even in the poor light he could be seen thinking.

'Just what, Detective Inspector?'

'Just— Just that, if what I glimpsed, and it was only a glimpse, might be . . . Well, pretty explosive. Then I wouldn't like to think either of those two, as I said, untrustworthy buggers had got hold of it too.'

'Very commendable, Detective Inspector. But that doesn't obscure the fact that, whatever this is, you yourself saw it. And I mean to hear from you precisely what it was.'

'Yes, ma'am.'

'*Yes, ma'am, yes, ma'am.* That's hardly good enough,

Detective Inspector. Now, out with it. What exactly did you see, see or glimpse?'

'Ma'am, it was a letter. Well, just the heading of a letter, as a matter of fact. Just the heading. A heading in what they call *embossed* type. In red.'

'Very well. What was that heading? And what was it about it that caused you, as you say, to thrust it back without looking at it more closely?'

'It— It was this. That piece of headed notepaper, and— Well, and I didn't really take any particular note of the address. But— Well, it was what I saw - glimpsed, glimpsed - printed under it that— Well, that made me whistle like that.'

'And that was?'

'It was just really four words, three and a half even. As soon as I'd just read those, that was when I thought the letter was red-hot.'

'All right. The four words? The three and a half?'

'They were *From the Hon.* - and then the half-word - *Maur.* That was when I stopped looking.'

'And why did you do that, Detective Inspector? Why?'

He shifted about again in the smooth black-leather armchair.

'Yes? Why?'

'It was— Well, it was because I didn't want to know, not for certain, what the whole of that letter was.'

'Very sensitive of you, Detective Inspector. But you must have had an inkling about such an explosive document. *Red-hot*, wasn't that the word you used? And in that case wasn't it your plain duty all those weeks ago to go to Commander Boxall and tell him what you had seen? Did you do that?'

'No. No, ma'am, I didn't. I— Well, as I said, I didn't

know what to think. And so . . . So, well, I just sort of pretended to myself I'd never seen the letter at all.'

'And that's your explanation, is it? Then, let me tell you, this won't be the last you hear about it.'

Back at the Business Park, Harriet – not followed there, as far as she could make out – set herself to consider what she had learnt. First, she realized, she had to double check on that half-word *Maur* which Outhwaite had said he had seen in red embossed lettering at the head of a letter in Reynolds Liebling's safe.

Maur is almost certainly the first half of *Maurice*, and Maurice is of course Detective Superintendent Quinton's first name, so that letter in the safe there looks as if it was from Quinton. But it could be from some other Maurice. So is Quinton actually an honourable? If he is, I'll have to take it that Outhwaite, whatever his motives for keeping Quinton's name back, was fundamentally telling me the truth about that letter. Nothing in Quinton's P/R to say he can lay claim to that *the Hon*, though it does give him a couple of other impressive forenames, *Gaskell* and *Fitzstephen*. If he is the Hon. Maurice, it would certainly be something to keep discreetly concealed in today's meritocratic police service. All too easily you could be marked out as a not-to-be-trusted élitist.

She called in reliable DC Higham and tasked him with looking into Quinton's antecedents. In less than ten minutes he came back. Yes, the Internet shows that Maurice Gaskell Fitzstephen Quinton is the third son of Sir Gaskell Quinton, thirteenth baronet, and thus entitled to call himself *the Honourable*.

So, if DI Outhwaite is right, the Hon. Maurice

Quinton, second in command of the Maximum Crimes Squad, is in secret contact with Reynolds Liebling.

But immediately she saw herself confronted by a dilemma.

All right, the information I extracted from Outhwaite points clearly to Maurice Quinton. But, on the other hand, I extracted that information only with the greatest difficulty. And it's hard to see why he was so unwilling to tell me what he knew. What is the strength, really, of the evidence for the existence of that telltale letter heading *From the Hon. Maur—*? No more than the word of a police officer who's been behaving extremely oddly, if not downright suspiciously? Why, after all, did Outhwaite suddenly push that letter back, as he told me he did? Fair enough, it should have been replaced in exactly the position it had been in when he found it. Liebling must never know his safe's been opened. But, if Outhwaite told me the literal truth, he didn't put it back with the utmost care, not by any means. Why?

Did he get rid of it in such haste only because he thought crafty Freckles Frecker might get to see it? And would then be able to make use of it? A letter to Liebling from Detective Superintendent Quinton would seem like a goldmine to someone capable of demanding money from Arnie Voles. But could Outhwaite be thinking of blackmail himself? Is that why he tried to avoid telling me anything about it? Is that why he didn't go to the Boxer long ago with his evidence of a letter in Liebling's safe apparently from the Max's second-in-command? Doesn't his failure to do that, putting aside that flimsy explanation of his, convict him straight away of being as corrupt as he slyly tried to make me believe Quinton is? Unless . . .

Yes another complication, a monstrous complication,

Unless Outhwaite did go to the Boxer, and was
sworn to secrecy. Because I can see the Boxer, presented with such evidence, deciding to keep the whole
business under wraps in the interests of preserving the
good standing of the Maximum Crimes Squad. He's
quite likely to have lain in wait for Quinton for all
these weeks till he got hold of some better evidence
than Outhwaite's assertion that the *Hon. Maur—* letter
existed, locked away in Liebling's safe. Then he'd hope
to deal with him in his own way, a man after all foisted
on to his pet squad.

Yes, that would be altogether in character for Commander Boxall, go-it-alone holder of the Queen's Medal
for Gallantry. And, yes, again, was that why the word
even slipped out when in the Earl of Lonsdale yesterday he was spewing out his list of his senior officers?
He had prefaced *Detective Superintendent Quinton* with
the word *even*. Definitely.

So there it is, my dilemma. Am I to believe that
the Hon. Maurice Quinton has really written a letter
to Reynolds Liebling agreeing to betray the secrets of
the Maximum Crimes Squad in exchange for some
large sum of money, a sum as large or larger than his
apparent inheritance from America? Or is DI Jackson
Outhwaite my man? Almost proven to be a decidedly
tricky liar? And, if he is that liar, doesn't that show
he's very likely the officer in the Max that Frank
Parkins has somehow got a line on?

So who to go for? Yes, Quinton. If he's my man,
he's in the best position by far to inflict terrible harm
on the Max's campaign against Pablo Grajales's mission
to swamp the country with illegal immigrants.

She called DS Zaborski in.

'Listen, Adah,' she said, 'are you certain that what Mr Quinton told us about that sum of half a million dollars was the exact truth? I know you've checked what his solicitor told you. But . . . Well, all right, that firm looks to be as respectable as any firm of solicitors in the land. Yet you and I have had experience enough of solicitors, some seemingly respectable, sitting there at interviews being purely obstructionist, let alone those specialists in wriggling criminals off the hook and even with the most respectable firms isn't it possible that, for a wealthy top-ranking client, a pop star, a footballer, a member of the aristocracy, they would on occasion stretch a point, produce a legalistic wriggle or two of their own? I'm sure just because a man's father is a lord he wouldn't be up to asking for a little delicate evasiveness if he'd got himself into some sort of serious jam. So, should you check again? Think at every point if there's some small thing that may not be quite what it seems?'

'Very well, ma'am, I will. But, with respect, let me say I do know my job. I have done the work.'

'Yes, yes. Of course. But if Mr Quinton is in fact playing for both sides, then we're up against someone very devious. I want to be one hundred per cent certain we're missing nothing.'

'Then I'll check and re-check. But I should warn you: that won't be something that can be done in half an hour. I wouldn't be fair to myself if I came to you any earlier than tomorrow morning, even if I stay up all night.'

'But it must be done, Sergeant. Because, look at it how you will, these are very suspicious circumstances. All right, that inheritance business looks as though it's all okay. But, think, it could be that Mr Quinton gets that big inheritance, and at first asks himself how he could make good use of the money for his own purposes, then he realizes that it's money that might have to be accounted for. So it occurs to him that there could be an equally large amount he could acquire that couldn't be checked. He could indicate to Reynolds Liebling he was ready to hand over information in return for a sufficient sum, one paid in a way that could be hidden, under the mattress, whatever.'

'Well, you know, ma'am, that if Mr Quinton has received a big sum in, say, fifty-pound notes, or in diamonds perhaps, it will be almost impossible to find it. He could have used deposit boxes here and there all over London. And elsewhere even.'

'All right, we'll leave it at that until you've re-checked that inheritance story. I mean, it is still possible that the half million dollars actually came from somewhere else, from Grajales eventually.'

'It didn't,' Sgt Zaborski said simply.

Chapter Ten

Feeling the frustrations of the day dragging uselessly at her mind after a long afternoon spent making repeated trawls through all she could remember of her meeting with DI Outhwaite had produced not a single tiny significant thing more, Harriet decided to call it a day. She had tried taking a break for an early supper at Billy's Diner and had forced down to the last mouthful the pale sausages, grease-laden chips and sad peas on offer. But, back at her desk again, no new recollection had surfaced.

She locked the desk drawers, put on coat and hat, ventured into the wind-whipped, rain-flicking outdoors, found the pool car and set noisily off on the tortuous drive to Ealing and Rekha Pathak's flat. Cursing all the way as the car's minimally efficient wipers barely swept away about half the rain streaming down the windscreen, she had just got over the river at Lambeth Bridge – a route, she had worked out, that would by-pass the West End traffic – when it came to her that she was not far from Chester Square.

Damn it, I'll go and see the Hon. Maurice Quinton. Who may, or may not, have written a letter to Reynolds Liebling. If he did, I might, coming to him out of the blue now, hit at least on some discrepancy, some tiny verbal slip, that shows he is my man.

Of course, he may not be in at this early evening hour. He may even be off somewhere, waiting on a bleak beach while people from Immigration hide ready to descend on some large party of wretched smuggled hopefuls. He may be dining out tonight and making his way, dinner-jacketed, at this moment to some yet smarter address than his own. But a call on the off chance might get me past that iron casing. Or show me at least a tiny crack in it.

Ten minutes later, the car parked not too far from the square itself, she was ringing at the bell of that well-furnished flat.

It was answered. There was Maurice Quinton already in casual evening clothes, a soft jacket in a shade of dark blue not far off black – a genuine smoking jacket, Harriet asked herself with a glint of malicious humour – no tie at his neck, feet in black leather slippers.

'I hope I'm not intruding, but I was nearby and I thought you might be able to spare me a few minutes.'

'Oh. Yes?'

A guarded answer, if ever there was one. So, a man with something to hold concealed at all costs? Or just a man who insists on keeping himself to himself, in his own private Elysium.

But, in any case, press onward.

'Yes, what I'd like from you, if you can spare me the time, is your perhaps more considered opinions of the senior members of the Max than you felt you could give me when I first came to see you with my Sergeant Zaborski. I realize—'

'The Max, Superintendent? You know, I've never much cared for that popular-papers expression. I am, for better or worse, second-in-command of the

Maximum Crimes Squad. And I like to hear it referred to as such.'

Harriet felt the sting of the rebuke. Despite priding herself on never letting clichés obscure the truth of things, she had over the past days come to take up unthinkingly the name Maurice Quinton had called, rightly if somewhat haughtily, the popular-papers expression.

'Yes,' she said now, 'I'm afraid I've got into the habit of using that abbreviation. But I agree. It devalues the work the squad does. I must try to cut it out.'

Her reward was a smile, just a little lifted up from bleakness.

'Then come in, Miss Martens. I can at least spare you a few minutes.'

Back again to his big room, now softly lamp-illuminated, its view on to the square hidden by the drawn silky-green curtains she was offered now, and accepted, a glass of sherry which, she realized at her first sip, was certainly not your everyday high-street wine merchant's offering. A classic bodega? The chair pulled out for her and placed opposite Quinton's own was the comfortably cushioned captain's one from in front of the elegant escritoire.

'Very well,' he said, looking across at her, as he settled himself in his tall, leather-covered armchair by the marble mantelpiece. 'I'm not entirely sure I like – what shall I say? – gossiping about my immediate colleagues. But if it's your judgment that my opinions of them will materially advance your investigation, I am at your disposal.'

'Yes, they would be helpful to me,' Harriet replied. 'I must admit I made much the same suggestion to Commander Boxall, but he was—'

She recalled that uncompromising *I chose them.*

'Not exactly forthcoming,' she concluded.

'I imagine not. He and I have a somewhat different approach to things.'

'I'm sure you do,' Harriet said, with a hint of a conspiratorial smile. 'But, tell me, has that produced any awkwardness? It wasn't Commander Boxall who chose you to join the squad when Detective Superintendent Mallard had his heart attack, was it?'

From the tall armchair opposite she thought she detected in the soft lamplight the smallest of acknowledging smiles.

'No. No, I wasn't Boxall's choice, I believe. However, I rather think going into the politics of that is best avoided. However, I am quite prepared to discuss, since you've asked me to, the officers immediately below me. Who would you like me to start with?'

'Well, shall we say DCI Griffin?'

'Hardly a suitable case for gossip, Mr Griffin. No, I worked under him once some time ago, and I think I know why Boxall picked him for what he likes to call his élite team. Griffin is a marvel of meticulousness. If ever I were to head another major murder investigation, I'd do my utmost to have someone like him to take charge of the admin. Nothing would go wrong. Not a thing.'

'I can appreciate how valuable that would be.'

She paused, thinking of what she had gathered from the DCI Griffin's personal file. 'And yet how limiting?' she suggested.

'Yes, you've hit on the right word. A fine detective, but a limited one. Limited in abilities and limited – and this is what you'll really be wanting to know, I suspect – in ambition.'

'I can see you're going to be extremely helpful to me.'

'Well, I have a certain advantage here, you know. For better or worse, I don't feel any particular sense of – what? – comradeship with any of my fellow Maximum Crimes Squad colleagues. So I am able to speak the truth about them. As I see it.'

One advantage of having got on to good terms with a man who sails away up there above the common ruck. As it seems I have, despite my expectations, succeeded in doing.

'Then DI Smith, Mary Smith?' she asked without further comment.

He gave her a smile that was near to being a grin.

'Will you leap up and slap my face,' he said, 'if I simply say to you: no woman would ever have the guts to take a bribe as big as Pablo Grajales would offer?'

'No, I won't slap your face,' Harriet answered, smile for smile, with the thought sharp in her mind that, if this man is actually taking a bribe from Grajales, then he's altogether capable of putting out a pretty ferocious bluff.

'Though I don't think you're right, as a matter of fact,' she went on. 'Or not about all women. On the other hand, I have read and re-read DI Smith's personal record and I have had her husband, who's a doctor as you may or may not know, thoroughly investigated. And I would agree that she's one woman who's safe from bribery attempts at whatever level. But I am glad to hear you confirm my belief, whatever the way you've chosen to do so.'

Quinton from the depths of his tall chair gave her a half-ironic bow in acknowledgment.

'DI Browning?' she asked sharply.

134

'Yes, Browning. Very well, he and Outhwaite are a pair, if you like. Boxall knew when the squad was formed that he would need people capable of working their way through minefields of figures, and both those two fit his bill. They're, if you like, his equivalent of that detective sergeant you brought with you the other day.'

'Not quite,' she said. 'DS Zaborski is something altogether out of the ordinary, while Browning and Outhwaite, from what I've seen of their records, are good honest figure sloggers.'

'Yes, I would agree. At least about my two colleagues, and I suppose I'll have to take your word for the exceptional stature of your DS Zaborski.'

'Right. But would you say there's nothing more to either Browning or Outhwaite?'

Through her mind went the hours she had spent earlier attempting to assess DI Outhwaite. A devious villain? Or a good plodding detective with a penchant for working with figures? Oddly sensitive, if his drawing back from finding out exactly what was in that letter was the truth? Or is he an out-and-out liar?

'No, I don't think there's much more to be said about either of them,' Quinton answered. 'Not really. Outhwaite's a bit of an awkward cuss, but no more than that I think.'

View from above. And perhaps the right one. Or perhaps not.

'Then DI Phillips?'

'There again a dedicated man. Dedicated in his case to rough-and-tumble. You must know as well as I do that there are people who join the police because they see the service as providing opportunities for physical aggressiveness. Boxall himself, not to put too fine a point on it, must certainly have started out with the enjoyment of that sort of thing in view. So, no, Phillips, too, is what we've called *limited*.'

'And limited morally, too?' Harriet asked, not wholly certain that being a bruiser, if that was what DI Phillips really was, made someone more susceptible or less to major bribery.

'No. I'm pretty sure, or as far sure as one can be about any ordinary human being, that Phillips, however much he relishes physical combat, is no more than a plain puritan when it comes to morals. I suspect he's a simple chapelgoer.'

'Not unlike yourself? Don't you make something of a point of Sung Mass every Sunday at Westminster Cathedral?'

Maurice Quinton smiled, if now with some reservation.

'Well, yes,' he answered. 'I do make a point of my religious observances. But I think one can draw a distinction between Westminster Cathedral at its most spiritual and, shall we say, some non-conformist chapel somewhere. Or, worse still, a messily ecumenical community church.'

'And you?' Harriet found herself asking. 'Are you like, DI Phillips, a good man? I mean, what did you join the police for?'

This was it. After all the helpful hints, and they had been helpful, this was the way to what she had come to learn, if she could.

Maurice Quinton sat back half an inch in his tall chair. But, after a very short pause, answered.

'I joined the police,' he said, 'to do what I was brought up to do, what I was born and bred to do.'

He gave her a slowly appraising look, as if

somehow seeking from her the fuller answer he was reluctant to produce himself.

But, sitting opposite him in the shaded light, she simply waited.

'Yes,' he said at last. 'I joined the police to do what my family has done for generations. Rule. To say what should be done, and to see that it is done. There's really hardly any opportunity to do that, in these days, you know, outside the police and perhaps the armed forces. There's certainly damn little opportunity in politics to see that what ought to be done is done.'

'An interesting answer,' Harriet said, her mind flicking back to the similar opinion Mrs Althea Raven had voiced. 'So you've no great respect for politicians? You've not had any ambitions in that direction? They're common enough among, shall we say, people like your family.'

Quinton darted her an uncompromisingly sharp look.

'Oh, I can see there's some attraction in politics. I'm not caught up by the everyday cant that tells us all politicians are there for what they can get out of it. One advantage of having been to a decent school is that one knows the people who have moved into positions of so-called power. And the ones I'm acquainted with at least – perhaps with an exception or two with the odd flaw in character – are, well, like the man who's actually commissioned your present inquiry, Ditzy Candover who was a couple of years ahead of me at Gordonstoun. He and others like him go into politics because they've been brought up to believe it's their duty to keep the country on an even keel, however much they suspect they'll really be tools of the mass hysteria of the media. And the same, in fact, *mutis mutandis*, goes for a good proportion of the top people on the Labour side. But, as for my having ideas in that direction, no, none whatsoever.'

He smiled.

'So, if it has entered your head that I might want to rise to high office in Parliament, and might stoop to accepting a bribe to aid me on my way, you can forget it.'

Harriet decided that the declaration needed no reply.

'Well now,' Quinton went on, 'are there more of my colleagues you'd like me to put under my microscope?'

'No. No, I don't think there are. I don't suppose you've any comments as pertinent about anyone under the rank of detective inspector. So I'll say goodnight.'

Quinton took up the book on the table. Harriet saw, without surprise, that it was calf-bound, gold-trimmed. The Odes of Horace.

Back eventually at Rekha's flat, unexpected news awaited.

'Do you know something?' Rekha greeted her, almost before she was fully into the room. 'I rather suspect my phone's being tapped. And I can guess why.'

'Not because someone wants to pry into the secrets of social work, that's for sure. No, I'm sorry. It must be me. Or, rather the Boxer. Christ, how does he dare?'

And then, suddenly, a whole train of events fell into place in her mind.

Yes, a man on a moped has been following me. And not only when Watson's sharp driving proved it. No, I've been tailed almost from the time I got down here. When I was standing in the rain outside the Business Park hoping for a taxi to go to the *Sunday Herald* there was that man crouching over his moped speaking into a mobile. And then, when I arrived at Frecker's flat, what did I see flung on to the chair where the Witherspoon girl's bra was, a hooded jacket. And, yes, none of the fug you'd expect if Frecker had been, as he claimed, cooped up there all day. His wretched electric fire must have been switched on only minutes before Watson and I arrived. Damn it, while we were making our way from where we had parked the car at the end of the street Frecker, following us from Rotherhithe, must have nipped in, told la Witherspoon to scram and been ready to greet us. No wonder there was something impudent about his expression.

Yes. Oh, yes. The Boxer's surveillance expert – and, right enough, he is expert – has been trailing me ever since I began looking into the affairs of his pet Maximum Crimes Squad. And, damn it, damn it, damn it, there I was thinking distant, powerful Pablo Grajales had fixed his deadly eye on—

'Listen,' she said then, 'I believe I know what that bastard, the Boxer, has been doing. He's been doing more than bug your phone. He's had me tailed, damn him, by one of those DCs of his on suspension. You know, when I first went to see him, to introduce myself formally, quite abruptly at one stage he dropped his hostile manner and asked me, very nicely, if I was being properly looked after down in London, whether I had a reasonable hotel. And, like a fool, as I see now, I told him I was staying with a friend – oh, and, yes, a former Met detective, I said – in Ealing. Nothing more than that. But it'd be quite enough for someone with the Boxer's record of cases detected to get on to you and have his phone tap installed. I'm really sorry.'

'Oh, it doesn't matter. Not a bit. And it's nicely ironic that the Boxer will have scarcely learnt a thing. Almost all your calls were on your mobile.'

'Yes, piece of luck for me that I didn't want to make you sit there every evening while I indulged in wifely chat with John, though as a matter of fact I never told him any more about the inquiry than I've told you.'

'And that, frankly, has been sadly disappointing.'

'Sorry, again. But I'm not going to risk even the slightest criticism from now on of the way I'm conducting the inquiry. The Boxer would jump at any chance to get it driven into the sand.'

'You're right. He would. Not, to do him justice, that he'd actually protect anyone causing— What was it the *Sunday Herald* said last week?'

'A wider scandal.'

'Yes. If the Boxer finds someone senior in his élite team is corrupt before you do – and such things have happened – then he'll deal with whoever it is his own way. And I wouldn't like to be in that person's shoes.'

'But, listen,' Harriet said suddenly, 'if he's having your phone tapped, do you think he's gone a step further? I mean, should we even be having this conversation? Or, not unless we go into the kitchen and run the taps as hard as they'll go?'

Rekha grinned.

'I've checked. No hidden mikes. Not as yet anyhow.'

'All right then. So let me remove at least some of your disappointment at not being fed your titbits.'

'Go on, go on. Speak, speak.'

Harriet laughed.

'I'm not going to tell you very much. My sense of

duty's still there. But there is something, something I heard this evening as a matter of fact, that I'd like another opinion on. In your Met days did you ever come across the man who's now Detective Superintendent Quinton, the Hon. Maurice Quinton?'

'No. No, I didn't, though I know a bit about him. From girly gossip with other old friends. He's Number Two in the Max now, isn't he?'

'Yes. And let me tell you he wouldn't like hearing you refer to that élite organization as *the Max*. I incautiously did so when I was talking to him an hour or so ago, and did I receive a sharp rebuke? *I am, for better or for worse, second-in-command of the Maximum Crimes Squad, and I like to hear it referred to as such.*'

'Yes, that sounds like the man my ex-colleagues giggled about.'

'Right. And it's something he said along those lines that I want your take on.'

'Shoot. I'm always good for saying what's what.'

'Okay. I'd called at his flat, in Chester Square no less, on the off chance of squeezing something out of him about— Well, about something we've learnt. Won't say more. But, by way of getting to the nitty-gritty without raising any hackles I began by asking his opinion of his fellow senior officers, and soon we seemed to be getting along pretty well, so I asked him then, point-blank, why he had joined the police. And this is what he said. Almost a one-word answer. I went into the police, he answered, to do what I was born and bred to do. *Rule.*'

'You do seem to have been getting on well. I don't suppose he'd have been anything like as frank with any other fellow police officer. Certainly not one from the Met. But perhaps seeing you as a provincial, a mere

Birchester detective, made you seem like someone it didn't matter what he said to, what he admitted.'

'No, actually I don't think it was that. I think I'd somehow implied, if not in so many words, that I came from his own world, if not quite so high up the scale. My accent? I don't know. Perhaps just my general attitude.'

'Well, let's assume you're right. And what you want to know, I suppose, is what that *what I was born and bred to do* tells you about him as a possible recipient of some mighty bribe? Whether he'd scorn any attempt to buy him, or whether he'd feel he was above such common or garden prohibitions?'

'On the ball, as usual.'

'Okay. You've come to the right top-of-the-tree Brahmin family to get the authentic inside view.'

'And that is?'

'Six of one and half a dozen of the other, actually. Yes, someone, believing they're born to lay down the law would, I like to think, be above consorting with criminals, however high up, and taking their money. But, on the other hand, even in my family we had one terrible black sheep. And, yes, he ended up in gaol after, as a minister, taking a colossal bribe. So, I'm afraid it's: you pays your money and takes your choice.'

'Thank you for nothing.'

'No, no. Not nothing. Just an unbiased view.'

'Right. Yes, I see that.'

She sat in silence for a moment or two.

'Actually, there's something else about Maurice Quinton I'd like to sort myself out over.'

'All complications neatly tidied by professional lady. Charges reasonable.'

'It's this. I was thinking about it in the car coming

from Chester Square. Is Quinton actually someone who ought to be a police officer?'

Rekha laughed.

'Why, for heaven's sake? If someone's gone shooting up to be a detective superintendent in almost no time, then he's surely in the right profession. As you, of all people, ought to know.'

'Oh, yes, I'm not questioning Maurice Quinton's abilities as a police officer, as a detective. No, what I found myself asking in the car was: should a man make a career in the police in these days who believes he's there to rule, to see that people do what he thinks is right for them?'

'*In these days*? You mean, in this so-called democratic country?'

'Yes. Yes, I do mean that. Damn it I was born in democratic Britain. I was taught in school, upper-class though my school was, that one of the great things this country has achieved was the establishment of democracy. And, yes, I suppose, I've always gone along with that. So you can see why what Quinton said to me this evening gave me something to think about.'

'Okay,' Rekha said, 'you've come to the right person with your terrible doubts. Don't forget, if I, like you, was born in a democratic country, my parents certainly weren't. They were born in a country ruled by an aristocracy, or strictly an oligarchy, of British civil servants and soldiers. And those people certainly thought they knew what was best for us.'

She gave Harriet a cheeky grin.

'And this is the point,' she said. 'We liked it. Not all of us, of course. There were plenty of hotheads, brought up on British notions of the all-conquering idea of democracy, who with a bomb or two and plenty of massive demonstrations put the opposite point of view. But it's my belief, and it was my parents' too, that India was a happier, better place under that pretty benevolent British rule than without it.'

'Oh God, one moment you're promising to tidy up all my complications, and the next you're doubling them. You're telling me now that democracy isn't the unambiguous Good Thing I was taught it was.'

'Well, is it? Ask yourself. Ask the person who so easily got on the best of terms with the Hon. Maurice Quinton.'

'Jesus, I don't know. I mean, I really do believe I like living in a society where – all right, one or two exceptions – every one is as good as their neighbour.'

'Well, time you learnt, Detective Superintendent Martens, that life ain't exactly all sweet simplicity. If you'd been brought up in India, you might have it in your head, just as firmly, that people have different places in society. There are people who are born, like your Mr Quinton, to rule, and there are people who are born to be – what? – carpenters, say. All right, both are equally meritorious, provided they do their duty as it should be done. But between the ruler and the carpenter there is a gulf fixed.'

'Point taken. Or I suppose it is. But, more than that. I'm beginning to think now that an undemocratic friend may be like your bad-apple cousin, someone prepared to take large sums of money because he thinks he's somehow got a right to them. You know, it could be that I was chatting happily away this evening to the subject of Frank Parkins's *wider scandal.*'

Chapter Eleven

It was with more than a little eagerness that, as soon as she arrived at the Business Park next morning, Harriet called in DS Zaborski to hear the outcome of the rechecking of Maurice Quinton's finances. But she got none of the new evidence she had hoped for.

'Ma'am, I have gone over again every possible doubtful transaction, every name Mr Quinton's solicitor gave me, and I've found nothing other than as it ought to be. I'm sorry.'

'Yes. Well, I suppose I should have expected nothing else. I'm sorry that I gave you so much extra work.'

'Glad to do it, ma'am.'

'Right. And you know what we'll have to do now, in view of that letter DI Outhwaite says he saw in Reynolds Liebling's safe.'

'I imagine you'll be seeing Mr Quinton.'

'I saw him last night, as a matter of fact. I'd hoped really perhaps I might catch him out in some tiny slip or other. But it turned out to be just an informal chat, asking his opinion of his fellow senior officers. However, now it's going to be very much an official interview, across his desk at Persimmon House. And once again I want you to be there.'

'But— But, ma'am, surely there aren't any more questions of a financial nature to ask him.'

'No, I know there aren't.'

She gave Adah a grin.

'So I want you to invent some for me,' she said. 'And I want you to put them to Mr Quinton yourself. If I simply question him about that letter in Liebling's safe – if that's what's really there – incriminating evidence on the face of it, then what can he do but blankly deny any such document exists? He'll know it must be still locked up in that safe. It has to be, or Liebling when he comes back from the States will guess the Max has been in his flat. So Mr Quinton will know I can prove nothing. But now look at it this way. If I go to him, with you, and seem to be asking a few extra questions about a transaction that's perfectly aboveboard, then he'll be off his guard and, possibly – just possibly – I'll see my way in.'

'Well, if that's an order, ma'am, I'll come of course. But give me half an hour, if you can, to cook up some likely sounding questions.'

'Certainly. More if you need it.'

It was not, however, at Persimmon House that Harriet eventually confronted Detective Superintendent Quinton. Exercising over the phone the sort of bland obstructionism every officer in the Max seemed to put in front of her, he had produced objections one by one to every time she had suggested for a formal interview.

No longer in any way the slippered conversationalist of the evening before. Instead a man who had at once realized why he was to be interviewed, however little he might know what he would be asked. Who had realized that, and, because he had something very much to conceal or perhaps merely because he felt whatever he had to do was more important than this intrusive inquiry, was putting obstacles between himself and the officer who was to question him.

'No, Miss Martens, I have a meeting then.'

'Very well, can we say an hour later?'

'I'm sorry, but I have to be over at the Yard after that. Some administrative nonsense.'

'All right, when do you expect to be finished there?'

'Oh, not till almost one o'clock, and I shall be going home to lunch then, as I usually do, unless pressure of events means I have a sandwich at my desk here.'

Pounce.

'Then I will come to Chester Square at one. I probably won't need to keep you long.'

She felt she could almost hear him at the other end rapidly turning over in his mind whether he could say he was having lunch at his flat with someone who couldn't be put off. And deciding at last that enough was enough.

'Very well. At Chester Square. At one.'

Quinton was there before Harriet, with Sgt Zaborski beside her, rang at the flat's bell on the dot of one o'clock.

So how long, she wondered had that appointment at the Yard really lasted? Or had it even existed?

'I had hardly expected to see you so soon again, Superintendent,' he said coldly. 'And – is it? – Sergeant Zabrinski?'

'It's Zaborski,' Harriet snapped out. 'Zaborski.'

Battle lines drawn already, she thought. All last

night's easy friendliness gone up in smoke. I wonder why.

'Yes, of course, Sergeant Zaborski,' Quinton said, leading them into his elegant, if austerely male, room. 'Nevertheless I fail to see why she is here now.'

He went over to the tall leather armchair near the mantelpiece, sat himself in it and stretched out his long legs.

He made no offer of a seat either to Harriet or Adah.

'There are some points I would like to have thoroughly cleared up arising from your statement to us on Sunday,' Harriet said, with an equal coldness.

'My statement? I wasn't aware that I had made any statement. Do Sergeant Zaborski's skills extend to verbatim recording?'

'Mr Quinton, I detect, frankly, a hostile tone in your replies to me. May I ask why? Why should you feel hostility towards the inquiry I am undertaking into these serious allegations about the Maximum Crimes Squad?'

Quinton's chilly smile appeared once more on his lean face, giving Harriet a sudden glimpse down the long tunnel of the ages of a feudal baron casually ordering a serf to be flogged.

'Hostility, Superintendent? I don't think so. Certainly I'm not aware of feeling any hostility towards you. Or even towards your able assistant.'

'Then,' Harriet said, 'you will have no objection to answering the questions arising from her investigation of the details of your finances you gave us on Sunday and the subsequent information your solicitor, on your instructions, passed on to her.'

'None. None whatsoever.'

And Adah Zaborski, feeling, Harriet guessed, no little hostility of her own, launched herself.

'Very good, sir. Then, first of all, may I ask how it came about that, when you received the legacy from your cousin in America, the whole sum was transferred to your current account here in England?'

'It just was, Sergeant.'

'Despite the losses that accrue in converting US dollars into pounds sterling? A not inconsiderable amount in this case. Why wasn't the whole capital kept in America? You could have had access to it there, once you had decided where to invest it.'

'Really, Sergeant, I hardly think my investments are any business of yours. I'm not one of your Birchester petty fraudsters, you know.'

Good, good, Harriet said to herself. She's getting under the skin of this man seemingly so different from the one I was talking to last night. He'll make a mistake before long. With any luck, he will.

And Adah, knowing her role, went on needling.

'It's hardly a question of petty fraud, sir. What Detective Superintendent Martens is investigating, at the request of the Inspectorate of Constabulary, is the possibility that a senior officer, or senior officers, in the Maximum Crimes Squad, have been corrupted. Corrupted by criminals with massive funds at their disposal. Her investigations revealed that you, sir, recently received a very substantial payment from America. Very well, you accounted for it to us on Sunday. But if queries have arisen from our subsequent investigations, there can be no question of it being *none of our business.*'

For a long moment Maurice Quinton – the Hon.

Maurice Quinton, third son of the thirteenth baronet – looked across at her down his long nose.

'Very well. Ask what questions you conceive to be necessary.'

'I asked why the sum which came to you as a legacy, a legacy my inquiries have established as valid, had to be transferred to this country. If you intended, as you told us you did, to establish a trust fund for your cousin's granddaughter, then would it not have been the obvious procedure to set up that trust in the United States where disbursements would take place? Why wasn't the simpler method used?'

A glint of anger in the blue eyes.

And again Harriet said to herself *Good, good.*

But there was no sign of anger when Quinton eventually brought himself to reply to what, no doubt, he saw as an impertinent question addressed to him by someone from the lower orders.

'Simpler? Yes, I suppose it might have been simpler to leave the money in the States. But I happened not to think of it. Not all of us spend all our time agitating about money, you know. I live here in England, and as far as I'm aware I shall continue to live and work here for the foreseeable future. So it seemed to me the obvious thing, for all that it wasn't obvious to you, to have direct control of my somewhat informal trust here.'

'Mr Quinton,' Harriet broke in, seeing her chance to move the questioning in the direction she intended it to take, 'when you say you have no intention of not living and working here, do I take it that you mean to pursue your career in the police?'

The sudden question, answered to an extent in the friendly atmosphere of the evening before, produced a guarded look, and a quick glance towards Adah Zaborski, as much as to say *Pas devant les domestiques*.

But Harriet was having none of that.

'Is that your intention, Mr Quinton?' she repeated.

'Yes,' Quinton answered, after a moment. 'Yes, it is. Why should I have any other intention? For better or worse I have made my career in the police until now, and I see no reason to give it up. None at all.'

'Right, in fact you're talking with someone every bit as determined as you seem to be to have a career in the police. Yet, it has occurred to me, that a man of – shall we say? – your abilities might nevertheless be beginning to look elsewhere. Tell me, did you hope when the Maximum Crimes Squad was formed that you might be chosen to head it?'

But she got an oblique answer.

'You see us as two of a kind, do you, Miss Martens?'

And a sudden edge of steel.

'Then let me ask you something. Do you regard the inquiry so unexpectedly thrust into your lap, when one might have thought it would go to a successful chief constable, do you see it as a means to move yourself more swiftly to the highest ranks? And are you, I wonder, exceeding your proper limits in order to achieve what might look like a striking success?'

'Certainly not. All right, you and I both know that we could rise higher, if the right opportunities presented themselves. But that doesn't mean, in my case, that I would make opportunities for myself that didn't properly exist.'

A sharp smile directed at her, with something of the crocodile in it.

'But you think I would create such dubious opportunities?'

Harriet was up to that.

'I don't know you at all well, Mr Quinton. So I must at least examine the possibility. It is relevant, highly relevant perhaps, to my inquiries.'

'Very well, but all I can do is to repeat what I have said already. I have no ambitions outside the police service.' A slight hesitation then. 'But, yes, I will admit – why not? – that I do have ambitions within the service. I'm not ashamed of them. Why should I be? If one is born with certain abilities, superior abilities I don't hesitate to say, then one should exercise them to the full. It is one's duty even to do so, however much in these days it may produce stupid envy from those unlikely to rise further than the lower ranks.'

For an instant his cold gaze flicked across to Adah Zaborski, silent and self-effacing.

Harriet found herself at once giving him an answer.

'But what you fail to take into account, Mr Quinton, is that there are other élites than the one you lay claim to. There is, for instance, an élite of intelligence. Intelligence that can come, yes, like a wind-blown seed, to anyone, anywhere. As it has come, for instance, in the form of exceptional mathematical ability, to Sergeant Zaborski here.'

Maurice Quinton sat for a moment silent at this rebuke.

'Very well,' he said then, 'I take your point. But, let me say, it doesn't by any means negate my own. If, yes, there are, as you called them, other élites, there still remains the élite created by the process of breeding through the ages. We're quick to apply that to racehorses, to prize boars even. But, in these days when democracy is a cant word on everybody's lips, from plebs to politicians, we shy away from that.'

Then his outstretched legs came hard down on to the Persian carpet, and in a single swift movement he was on his feet.

'But now you must excuse me,' he said. 'Unless I switch on my microwave I shall never get my lunch.'

He left them standing.

And what he has just said, Harriet thought, is something I would very much like to pursue. A man who believes he has something you could call almost a divine right to tell lesser mortals what they should or should not do – as all that about racehorses and prize boars means he does – may well feel his career in the police, rapid rise though it's been, ought to be going even higher and faster. And to achieve that he may believe a large sum of money could in one way or another speed him onwards and upwards.

But, damn it, he must have seen, more quickly than I did, that he had said a little too much. Hence the urgent need to switch on his microwave.

So how can I confirm now that DI Underwood was telling the truth about that letter? Because it's a long leap from hearing the Hon. Maurice Quinton saying he believes he has a right to rule to getting some sort of evidence that, in order to speed the day when he can exercise that right, he has taken money from Pablo Grajales.

But, wait. If you believe yourself to be one of the true élite, as Maurice Quinton really seems to do, then won't your ambitions in the police go as high as seeing yourself as the youngest, and most forceful, commissioner ever? And to achieve that what would you need? Answer: media backing. Yes, it's possible that a wide media campaign could position an officer of obvious talent to be in line as next commissioner. And if ever such a campaign were to get under way, then money would have to be spent. On plain old-fashioned sums paid to journalists like Frank Parkins, and, no doubt, on heavily entertaining others higher in the scale.

Yes, a good few Groucho lunches to Mrs Althea Raven and the other ravens of the media world. A man like Quinton could, surely, then have gambled on just one illegal act, one piece of corruption, being justified if it enabled him to advance his destined career to the highest heights.

Yet can I be right in all this? Has the dozy northern tart flown up to high, icy outer-space regions? Unreal regions?

She found she had, almost unconsciously, been pacing up and down the length of the big room, careless of the dim gold-framed landscapes looking down at her, of the view of the wind-brushed trees of the square outside, of the pervasive delicate scent wafting from the big camellia in its wide porcelain bowl between the tall windows. And leaving Adah Zaborski standing composedly beside one of the little gilt chairs.

Space-high or not, she argued, I have at least got one tangible clue in my sights, the letter in Liebling's safe. However little chance there is of me ever actually touching it, of confirming as hard evidence that red embossed heading, *From the Honourable Maur—*

And then she realized, with something of the feeling of awaking from a dream or nightmare, that she was actually looking at something uncannily almost the same as the letter she had had in her imagination.

But this was a letter there in real fact, lying squarely in the centre of the leather-bound blotter on the escritoire where her marching steps had brought her. It was a letter, evidently just begun and perhaps abandoned when the doorbell had sounded.

> *Dear Father,*
>   *I am sorry not to have written on Sunday, but – what shall I say? – pressure of business is, I suppose, the phrase I must use, seeing my work is still very much secret.*

She blinked and bent to look more closely. And, yes, there could be no doubt about it. She was looking at a letter on Maurice Quinton's own personal creamy white writing paper. And the address at the top, *Flat 3, 10 Chester Square, London SW1* had above it the words *From the Hon. Maurice Quinton.*

In flat unembossed dark-blue print.

At once, regardless of any consideration of good manners, she pulled open the escritoire's narrow drawer and peered inside, a tiny thought at the back of her mind trusting she was not going to be caught a second time rifling the drawers of a desk.

And, yes, as expected, there in a neat pile was, not some big, rubber-banded bundle of currency notes, but a stack of writing paper exactly similar to that of the unfinished letter she had just seen.

So the letter DI Outhwaite so precisely described to me just never existed. Yes, bugger it, DI bloody Outhwaite had me completely deceived. Given those teasing three-and-a-half words just pointing to Maurice Quinton, especially when I'd learnt about that seemingly mysterious half-million dollar sum, I jumped at the idea that it was Quinton who was the man in the Max that Grajales has bribed.

Clearly now he was not.

My whole fantastically piled-up tower of suspicions and daring, space-reaching hypotheses – the commissionership, for God's sake – has crumbled in one instant to dust. A scatter of dust on the rich carpet under my feet.

Right, Mr bloody Outhwaite, I'm coming to see you.

Chapter Twelve

Harriet allowed herself, standing at the escritoire in Maurice Quinton's elegant room, one small jet of revenge for the way he had kept her on her feet, together with Adah Zaborski, while he stretched out in his tall armchair.

She opened the door he had left by in order, so he had claimed, to switch on his microwave. Then she called out loudly.

'We're off now, Mr Quinton.'

And, with Adah quietly grinning behind her, she walked straight out.

But in the car she began to think.

All right, what Outhwaite saw in the safe of a known criminal was not a letter from Maurice Quinton. That had been Outhwaite's hastily conceived invention. But he must have seen a letter of some sort, or perhaps a document. And, whatever it was, it had been something that had caused him to whistle in considerable surprise. Would he really then at once have thrust it back out of sight without reading it? However much he might have feared Freckles Frecker's sharp eyes would see what it was? No, there would be a dozen ways to prevent Frecker getting sight of it, at least for long enough to give it a quick scrutiny.

So what is it Outhwaite learnt? Surely something

that, when I interviewed him at the Cumberland, he knew he had at all costs to prevent me finding out about. Which was why he concocted his ingenious suggestion about that letter heading, the three-and-a-half words, the red embossed print. And another factor. What Outhwaite saw cannot have been anything innocent. If it had been, he would have had no reason to produce that elaborate invention.

But wait. This needs a little more thought. Precisely how much of what Outhwaite said to me was invention? I was pressing him hard about his surprise at what he had seen, and he was anxious at all costs to keep from me what it really was. So isn't it likely that, under pressure, he had been able to do no more than alter just one vital circumstance. To substitute Maurice Quinton's name for— For whose?

Yes, I very much want a word with you, Detective Inspector Jackson Outhwaite.

But this time I am not going to talk to him on my own, no, I want a witness with me. This will be no soft informal chat. Sooner or later I'll be going for the kill, hard as it may be. So, back to the Business Park, leave Adah there, with her head in her lofty world of computer-screen figures, and take with me to Persimmon House ever-alert, ears-flapping human recording-machine, DS Watson.

'There's nothing I can be sure about, of course,' she said, after she had briefed Watson as they drove through the still rain-whipped streets. 'But I hope, by jumping on the least discrepancy I'll get to discover now what Mr Outhwaite really saw in Liebling's safe. And then . . . Well, then the end of the inquiry may be in sight.'

'Can't be too soon for me, ma'am,' Watson said. 'I

spoke to the missus on the phone last night. She said it'd been a gorgeous spring day in Birchester. A gorgeous day, would you believe?'

Harriet, looking at the rain-splotched windscreen in front of her, could only feel that the very elements were against her.

But at Persimmon House she met yet another obstacle. It was a simple enough one. She was repeatedly told no interview room was available. With a bite of rage she thought how easy it would have been at Greater Birchester Police headquarters to book an interview room, and to spend as long as necessary there in getting the truth out of any difficult suspect.

Damn it, she thought at last, the northern tart, however dozy, is not going to be put off like this.

She marched into the Boxer's outer office.

'Listen,' she said to little Miss House, 'would you ring down and say that Commander Boxall wants the use of an interview room. As of now.'

A deep blush appeared on Mary Mouse's twitchy-nosed face.

'I— Mr Boxall never— But if he—'

Harriet looked down at her as mercilessly as if she were the Boxer himself berating *my girl*.

'Find somewhere for me quickly.' she said. 'I have an interview to conduct.'

Ten minutes later she was sitting at a table in a ground-floor interview room, DS Watson beside her. Summoned by internal phone, Detective Inspector Outhwaite entered.

'Good afternoon, Mr Outhwaite,' she greeted him. 'I have come, with Detective Sergeant Watson here, to ask you some further questions concerning what you told me at the Cumberland Hotel about the raid on Reynolds Liebling's flat.'

Had the smallest dart of apprehension instantly appeared on Outhwaite's gauntly grey face? Hard to tell.

She gave him no hint that she had noted the give-away flicker.

'Take a seat, Inspector,' she said. 'It's just a few things to check back on. But I thought it best not to talk to you in the squad room.'

DI Outhwaite subsided into the chair opposite, his face now showing no more than a readiness to comply with whatever he was going to be asked.

Hit now straight away? Why not? If that flick of dismay was there, this is the time to go after him.

'Detective Inspector, when you told me what you saw in Liebling's safe, why did you invent a letter to him supposedly written by Mr Quinton?'

'Invent?'

For a second, no longer, the accusation appeared, yes, to have stunned him. But recovery was swift.

'I don't know what you mean by *invent*, ma'am,' he banged back in apparent anger. 'What I told you I'd seen there was exactly what I did see.'

'No, Inspector.'

'No? No? How can you say that? Who was there, seeing it? Me or you? I told you what I saw. What's the idea, pretending I saw something else?'

'I'm not pretending, Detective Inspector.'

'If you're not, then how— How can you know what it was I saw?'

'For one simple reason, Detective Inspector. You went into a little too much detail when you were

160

describing that totally imaginary letter. A detective inspector of the Metropolitan Police ought really to have enough experience of liars to know it's those extra details they think are so convincing that in the end give them away. All that stuff about the embossed printing of the letter-head, and in red. Red. You never thought, did you, that a man of Mr Quinton's sort would hardly have red lettering on his private writing paper?'

She was rewarded by the dark flush that spread over the lean grey face in front of her.

Yes, no wonder he feels ashamed. Caught out by a dozy northern tart.

But give him no time to recover now.

'So why did you do it? What was it you really saw?'

Hammer at him. Hammer at him.

'Come on, I want to know.'

But, however short the time she had waited for her answer, it had been too long.

'I don't understand what you're talking about, ma'am.'

All right, a check. But keep on at him. Keep hard on at him.

'You don't understand? Then let me put it to you in plain terms. You described Mr Quinton's personal writing paper, as having the address in red embossed lettering. However, I have seen Mr Quinton's paper. And the address on it with, as you correctly guessed, his name above *From the Hon. Maurice Quinton*, is in unembossed lettering in a discreet shade of dark blue. So, come now, what was it you saw in Liebling's safe that caused you, in order to conceal its existence from me, to invent that wholly spurious letter-heading?'

For a little Outhwaite still sat in silence. Then at last he grunted out a sullen, plucked-from-the-air reply.

'I suppose someone like Mr Quinton could change his notepaper any time he took it into his head. He— He may have written what I saw on some paper he stopped using before he ordered a new lot with – what did you say? – dark blue printing.'

'Someone like Mr Quinton, Detective Inspector? So what do you think Mr Quinton is like?'

'Why d'you want to know what I happen to think? I can't see that that's got anything to do with anything.'

'Tell me, Detective Inspector. What do you think Mr Quinton is like?'

A glowering moment.

'All right then, if you're so keen to hear. Then I think the Hon. Maurice Quinton is nothing but a poncy upper-class shit.'

'Yes, I rather expected you to say something like that. I imagine Mr Quinton's manner has earned him quite a lot of resentment. But I'm a little surprised that you referred to him as *the Hon*. He goes out of his way, I've gathered, not to draw attention to his – shall I say? – position in society. So how did you come to know he's an honourable?'

'I just happened to see the envelope of a personal letter addressed to him here at Persimmon House, and I noticed it had that silly *Hon* stuck in front of his name.'

'And so, when I was pressing you a bit too hard, you took advantage of this piece of chance knowledge to invent a letter that might have been the one in Reynolds Liebling's safe? Is that it?'

'No, it isn't. I've told you the letter I saw in the safe was from the Hon. Maurice, and so it was.'

'And I have said I don't believe you. But this interests me. Why did you pick on Mr Quinton when I was questioning you? You could have chosen any other officer in the Max to send me off on a wild-goose chase. So why Mr Quinton?'

'You know why.'

Harriet let pass this tacit admission, if it was such, that the letter had been pure invention. The words were there, she knew, securely lodged in silent Sgt Watson's retentive head.

'No, tell me, Detective Inspector,' she said. 'Why Mr Quinton?'

'I've told you already. He's a poncy shit. I've no time for that sort of so-called gentleman. My grandfather was a servant in the house of— Never mind who. He was a garden boy. *Boy*, when he was old enough, when World War One broke out to go straight into the army. And he had some tales to tell about the gentry. Queer folk, he used to say. *Queer folk the gentry, think they're a different breed altogether*. A different breed, he said, as if they were cut off from the rest of us by some dividing line. What they thought of as proper men and women on one side, and something different on the other. Cattle. Cattle, that's what they thought of my grandfather and his like.'

And, yes, Harriet said to herself. Yes, that's true of my own family, or partly true at least. Grandmama, who lived to be almost a hundred, used to think like that. Unwittingly speak like that. I don't know about Grandpapa. I think he grew to be more circumspect, but I rather guess that was the way in his innermost thoughts he saw the world. Gentry and others. Gentlemen and Players, as they used to say in the old cricket reports.

'And you had no other reason for putting Mr Quinton's name to that letter you told me you'd seen? There wasn't something you knew about him, or just suspected at the back of your mind, that made you think that, if any senior officer in the Max had any contact with Reynolds Liebling, it would be him?'

It was possible still, she thought. Possible, despite all Adah Zaborski had found out apparently clearing him, that Maurice Quinton was the officer in the Max of whom Frank Parkins had heard something, something with a whiff of suspicion about it.

But she got no helpful answer from DI Outhwaite.

'I said, ma'am, that I saw a letter from him in Reynolds Liebling's safe. And, red embossing or dark-blue, whatever you like, you can't prove that what I saw was any different.'

She looked at him long and hard.

'I'm disappointed in you, Detective Inspector,' she said at last. 'Deeply disappointed.'

Sitting beside Sgt Watson, silent as usual, as he drove them back to the Business Park, Harriet set herself to work out the implications of the little she had learnt before dully obstinate DI Outhwaite had confronted her with the inescapable fact that, with Reynolds Liebling's safe intact, there was absolutely no knowing what the letter in it contained.

It's possible, of course, she argued, that his suggestion that Maurice Quinton is simply using a new sort of personalized writing paper, is absolutely correct, however hastily the notion was produced, however much it was a sullen response to my unexpected question. So can I have been too subtle in thinking Quinton would never have used writing paper with red embossed lettering? And in going on to argue from my one single deduction that Outhwaite invented the letter?

Right, I have to admit I may have been too quick in drawing the conclusion I did when I saw that pile of writing paper in Quinton's escritoire. It's all very well being top of the class at school, getting my first at Cambridge, using my brains as much as my will to rise up through the police ranks. But there's a danger in being too clever. You can delight in your superiority to the point where you come to rely on it unthinkingly.

So did I go beyond the mark in working out that a man who was a son of the thirteenth baronet would never use such vulgarly brash type on his personal writing paper?

No, damn it, I don't actually believe I did go too far. I made a valid deduction based actually on evidence. The evidence I have accumulated all my life about what the manners and customs of a certain class are.

All right then, now I have to ask again: who did write that letter?

By way of answer a thought came to her. A sudden thud of realization.

Yes, only one thing for it now. I have got to get into Reynolds Liebling's flat myself. I've got to have to get his safe opened, find that letter and read it myself.

For some moments Harriet sat there in the appallingly noisy car contemplating what it was she was faced with. Then, as much to put off the moment of final decision as anything, she turned to consult Sgt Watson, silent at the wheel while the great detective had communed with her inner self.

'Sergeant, I'm sorry. I've been sitting here like the Sphinx, not even asking you what you thought of our friend Outhwaite.'

'Dodgy,' Watson said. 'That's what I think of him.'

'Right. But tell me, what exactly was it he said when he seemed to concede that he did in fact invent that letter apparently from Mr Quinton?'

'What he actually said was only this: *You know why.*'

'Yes, I remember now. I'd asked him why he had chosen Mr Quinton as the writer of whatever letter or document he'd seen in the safe. And, instead of denying once again that he had invented the letter, he replied – you've got it exactly, I can hear him now – *You know why.* Which I took at the time to be an admission that the letter was an invention. But now I'm not so sure. He could have been replying to what I had actually asked, about why Mr Quinton was the person he picked on if he had invented the letter. Without thinking, he answered that I would know why. He just didn't take into account the implication that he'd been lying about the letter.'

'I see what you mean, ma'am. Or at least I think I do. And I believe you're very likely right. DI Outhwaite was not really admitting that letter was something he'd cooked up just to get out of the jam you'd put him in.'

'Yes, that's it,' Harriet said.

And found she had sunk into her own thoughts once again.

One thing. There can be no doubt now that it was a letter which caused Outhwaite to whistle in involuntary surprise. Needing to produce an instant response, he said he had seen a letter. Not some other sort of document. Not a sheet of paper with figures on it and a name. Just that he'd seen a letter.

All right, he embroidered a little too much, with that stuff about the heading. But, under pressure as he was, he can't have gone too far away from the truth. So, he saw a letter from someone, and it made him realize he'd somehow struck gold. Yes, gold. Surely the possibility of blackmail of some sort. For money most likely, or possibly for power.

And the letter he saw could still have been written to Liebling by some other member of the Max. Or – I doubt if it'd be worth Liebling's while to get his claws into any of the lower ranks – by one of the Boxer's specially chosen senior officers.

Yes, there's really no getting away from it. I've got to find out who that letter was written by. I've got to get into that flat, come what may.

But how? I haven't got an expert safe-breaker like Pantsie Underwood on my team. I'm by no means sure we have anybody in Birchester who'd fill that bill. And, though I suppose I might manage on my own actually to get into the flat – have to find out if Liebling's still in the States – I could no more open his safe than fly to the moon.

So . . .

So I'll have to make use of expert safe-breaker, suspended Detective Constable Underwood. And that means I'll have to get the Boxer to co-operate with me. It's the only way. I can't possibly cajole or bully a man like Underwood into breaking into that safe simply because I want it done. For one thing, he'd very likely refuse straight away. Even if he doesn't, he'll expect me in return to get him completely off the hook on the corruption charge. Which I cannot do unless afterwards I tell C.A.G.D Anstruther what I made Underwood do, what I did alongside him. And Mr Anstruther's not going to approve of that. Not in any way. I'd be on my way back to Birchester in ten minutes if he got to hear I'd been illegally breaking into Liebling's flat.

So, no way out of it. It's see the Boxer once again. Go begging.

If there's something you don't want to do, do it at once. That had usually been Harriet's way ever since she was a schoolgirl. But she did not, back in her poky, bare-walled office, at once pick up the phone, call Persimmon House and ask for an appointment to see the Boxer. She chickened out. For the duration of a fleeting thought she had tried to persuade herself that she would be acting sensibly if she spent the evening thinking about what tactics she should use to secure the Boxer's co-operation. But she had known this was no more than prevaricating.

So by the time she left the Business Park, much earlier than she usually did, she had brought herself to phone little Mary House and had secured an appointment with the Boxer for next day. Half past eleven. Yet before she had reached Rekha's she had fully admitted to herself there was nothing to do by way of working out how the Boxer could be persuaded to tell Pantsie Underwood to break into Liebling's safe. When she faced him it would be, she thought, a matter of playing it by ear.

But she had failed to take into account Rekha's interest in her affairs.

'Harriet,' she exclaimed when she came in, 'what

are you doing here so early? Don't tell me you've got to the heart of that man Frank Parkins's tremendous secret? You've gone to the great C.A.G.D. and presented him with a report to shake the nation?'

Harriet shook her head.

'No, I've scarcely got that far.'

'But you have got some far?'

'I don't know. I rather think the truth is I've got right to the heart of a considerable mare's nest.'

'And you're going to stay stumm about it? To me? What you need, my girl, is a stiff drink.'

Drinks, of considerable stiffness, on the table between them, Rekha went on where she had left off.

'All right, we know that Detective Superintendent Harriet Martens, sometimes known as the Hard Detective, never, never, never tells anybody anything she ought to keep confidential. But, come on, open up.'

Harriet produced a worn-down grin.

'All right. The complication I've got myself into is this. One of the Boxer's DIs whom he sent to break into the flat of a criminal called Reynolds Liebling—'

'Know about Liebling. He's in the gossip pages. A numero uno party-goer, they say, and sometimes slip in something like a *close friend of Colombian gang boss Pablo Grajales*.'

'Right. Well, in Liebling's safe this DI saw a letter, a letter he successfully refused to tell me about—'

'Blackmail stuff then. Bet it is.'

'If you keep interrupting, you'll never hear what my trouble is. And I find I'd rather like you to know.'

'Silent as the grave. Or, in my case, the funeral pyre.'

'Okay. Well, the long and the short of it is that I have to find out what that letter contains, and the only way I can do that is to break into that flat myself, assisted by an expert safe-cracker. That's to say by suspended DC Underwood, who's broken into the same safe once before. On the Boxer's orders. And, of course, to obtain Underwood's services, as they say, I've got to go and beg them from the Boxer.'

'Succinct. And, yes, I see how tangled your mare's nest is.'

She took a hefty swallow of her whisky.

'Okay, let Rekha Auntie help you out.'

'If she can.'

'I can always try. After all, it's my profession to find ways round intractable situations.'

'Right, let's hear the top social worker's answer.'

Rekha sat thinking, fingers drumming on the soft material of the sari draped across her knee.

'The way I see it,' she said at last, 'is that you'll have to take advantage of the Boxer's worst qualities.'

'I'm not going to let him rape me, if that's what you mean.'

'Well, no. Not exactly. But I think you'll have to let him patronize you. Which is almost as bad.'

'Okay. But how?'

More thought. But not for long.

'Yes, this is what you'll have to do. You'll have to go to him and say you're about to sign off the inquiry. You know that's what he's wanted all along, yes?'

'Oh, yes. You should have encountered all the obstructive tactics I've had to battle with.'

'Good. So you tell him you're calling it a day, giving the Max a clean sheet and all. Then you go on to say *Oh, Boxer, dear, do just let me after all try just one little thing more.* And he'll pat you on your pretty head and promise to help. You'll see.'

Chapter Thirteen

On the stroke of half past eleven next day Harriet was there at Persimmon House asking the Boxer's ever-subdued, sleek-haired Miss Mouse whether he was disengaged.

'Oh, yes, he is, but he said you were bound to be—No. He said, even if you were late, I was to send you straight in.'

Harriet allowed herself a grim internal smile. So the Boxer was as determined as ever to put down the dozy northern tart. And, little did he know, but she was about to allow him to put her down as definitively as he could have hoped. The enemy was about to admit defeat, however craftily.

Behind his desk, still littered with the set-aside reports and unanswered correspondence which a man who despises paperwork inevitably accumulates, the Boxer sprawled in his big chair. The usual well-tailored suit, in pale grey today, with the familiar gold chain of his pocket watch stretched across its waistcoat. And, Harriet noted, as at the Boxer's nod she took the chair opposite, the remembered sharp tang of his expensive aftershave mingling with the smell of cigarillo butts in his ashtray.

'Okay, miss, you wanted to see me?'

Harriet was prepared for the contemptuous *miss*

and let it sail by. No sign of resentment must interfere with bringing into play Rekha's tongue-in-cheek ploy of the evening before, if in a decently modified version.

'Yes, Commander, I thought you should be the first to know that I have come to the conclusion that my inquiry has gone as far as it can.'

She was rewarded by the smallest sign of surprise on the Boxer's weather-beaten face. But he was quick to recover.

'You can't say I didn't tell you. There was never anything to inquire about.'

Then Harriet saw how she could bring in, earlier than she had ever thought she might, the tricky matter she was there to raise.

'There was something to inquire into,' she said, giving the answer a touch of sharpness which she hoped would produce a response leading the Boxer further in. 'There was the behaviour of your DCs Frecker and Underwood.'

'Not much wrong there either,' the Boxer snapped. 'DCs have made the scrotes wriggle ever since there were DCs, at least in the Met they did. Don't know what happens in the countryside. No, the only trouble with those two was they let that sod of a journalist, Parkins or Piggins or whatever, get that evidence.'

'Well, that's a point of view, Commander. And it's lucky, of course, that Frank Parkins never found out it was what they'd done in the way of breaking and entering that allowed them to think they could get money out of Arnie Voles.'

'What those two were doing in Reynolds Liebling's flat was my business, and nothing else. That's why I've let them off as lightly as I did. Discharge on medical grounds, keep their pension rights.'

'Yes. But, let me say at once, I'm a hundred per cent certain you were doing the right thing in having Liebling's safe opened.'

So much for the flattery stuff and the abasement. But now . . .?

'However, as a matter of fact, there is one small point arising from DI Outhwaite's examination of Liebling's safe I'd still like to get cleared up. If only for my own satisfaction. I doubt if anything about it will appear in my report to Mr Anstruther.'

'It had better not, miss.'

Silence across the desk now.

So my ploy's gone for nothing?

But, no.

The Boxer heaved himself forward in his big chair.

'Well, what is this *small point*? Mustn't let the lady from the North go home unsatisfied.'

Another little bitter pill to swallow.

'That's good of you, Commander. Well, it's just this really. In the course of my inquiries I learnt that while DI Outhwaite was going through the contents of the safe he let out a distinct whistle of surprise. That rather intrigued me. I wondered, for instance, if he'd come across some strong evidence which the Max could use. Had he? Did he report anything to you?'

The Boxer directed a thoughtful look at the ashtray in front of him with its little pyre of cigarillo butts.

'No,' he said at last. 'No, I don't believe he did. So did you ask him what had surprised him like that? Or did you just let it drop?'

'No, I didn't let it drop, as a matter of fact. I questioned Mr Outhwaite at some length.'

'And?'

'And I have to say he didn't give me any sort of

satisfactory reply. He attempted, in fact, to persuade me that what he had seen was a letter, written to Reynolds Liebling, by Mr Quinton.'

'He attempted to persuade you? Are you saying he did or he didn't see a letter from Mr Quinton in that safe? Am I to understand that my second-in-command is linked up somehow with that shit Liebling?'

'No, Commander, I'm not saying that. No such letter from Mr Quinton existed. DI Outhwaite is not, if I may say so, a very skilled liar. I was able to prove what he said was pure invention. He piled on too many details.'

She was letting nothing escape her as she looked at the big man opposite. And, though she could not have sworn to it, she thought he had for an instant worn a look of regret.

So, she registered, as I've suspected no love lost between the Boxer and the second-in-command foisted on him when Superintendent Mallard had his heart attack. The Hon. Maurice Quinton never exactly a soul mate for the Boxer.

'I see that Mr Anstruther may have known what he was about when he chose you for this business, Miss Martens,' the Boxer said now, a certain thoughtfulness showing itself on his face. 'But if Mr Quinton wrote no such letter, what was it that Outhwaite saw and whistled in surprise about? Did you get that out of him?'

'No, Commander, I didn't. DI Outhwaite persisted in sticking to his claim that he saw, if only for an instant, the heading on a letter that had come to Liebling from Mr Quinton. And, though I'm quite sure he's lying about the sender, I don't doubt there is a letter in that safe which Outhwaite saw and which considerably surprised him. In all probability it was written by some senior officer, not necessarily from the Max. Or possibly even by someone outside the police who should not in any circumstances have been in correspondence with a man like Liebling.'

'Not necessarily an officer in the Max, you say.'

'No, not necessarily.'

'But it might be. I suppose it might be, if it caused Outhwaite such surprise.'

'Yes, of course, it might be.'

And now the crunch.

She took in a breath.

'And as far as I can see,' she said, 'there's only one way to find out. And that's for you to send DC Underwood with me into Liebling's flat – I suppose Liebling's still in America – and open that safe again.'

The Boxer looked at her. Impossible to tell, she thought, what's going on behind those flushed red cheeks, that aggressive nose.

'Well, miss,' he said at last. 'You're not afraid of asking one hell of a lot.'

'No, I'm not. It's got to be done. You know that. There's that letter in the safe there with a signature on it that may well be that of one of your senior officers.'

'Or it may not.'

'All right, it's not a certainty, of course. But if that letter wasn't from someone in the Max, then it'll be from someone somewhere who shouldn't ever have been writing to Liebling. Why did he lock it up like that if it isn't something important to him? Why did DI Outhwaite whistle in surprise when he caught sight of it?'

Again the Boxer fell silent, regarding her with all

the suspicion of one of the boxer-dogs that had given him, together with his earlier prowess in the ring, his nickname.

And then he spoke.

'No, you're wrong when you say there's only one way to find out what Outhwaite saw. There's another. And it's the way I'm going to take. This time it'll be me who asks Jackson Outhwaite the questions, and I'm willing to bet I'll get my answer.'

Then, without the least show of politeness, he banged out something more.

'There's someone I've got to meet now. So good-day to you.'

All Harriet felt she could do at that moment, as she watched the Boxer flip open the lid of his silver cigarillos box, was to dart him a single glance of defiance. However little she could see how she could in fact defy the man who had, with abrupt contempt, whisked Detective Inspector Outhwaite from under her very nose.

Deflated. That's what I feel, Harriet said to herself as she left the Boxer reaching into his big silver box. Damn it, I thought it was going so well. I thought the Boxer was bound to want to know what it was Outh-waite saw. And he did. Of course, he did. But – my sense of my own worth – it never occurred to me that, if I'd got nothing out of Outhwaite, anyone else would think they could. Which comes of not reckoning with the Boxer's sense of his worth, fifty times more inflated than mine. And perhaps with some reason. Think of his record of successes, let alone his Queen's Gallantry Medal.

None of which makes my situation look any better. If I'm to bring the inquiry to a successful end, I have to know what it is Liebling's got in his safe, whether or not it is, as I think it almost must be, something implicating a senior officer of the Max. Finding out if a top officer in the Max is corrupt is what my inquiry was set up to do. Why I was selected by Mr Anstruther as the most suitable officer to conduct it.

And now it's all in the Boxer's court. All right, use what strong-arm bullying tactics he will, he may still not get Outhwaite's secret out of him. But I can't deny that it's very likely he will. And if he does, then that secret will stay in the Boxer's head, no matter what happens to Outhwaite. And my inquiry really will have got nowhere.

'Oh, Miss— Miss— That is, Superintendent.'

It was Miss Mouse. Or, rather, it's little Mary House.

'Yes? Is there something I can do?'

'No. No, Superintendent It was only— Only I just wondered if Commander Boxall really is about to go out. Because— Because I know the commissioner wants to speak with him. On the phone. That is, I've said he'll be in all morning. I thought he would be if he had that appointment with you, and I . . .'

And, poor kid, she hasn't dared ask the Boxer whether he'll wait in, as she's made the mistake of telling the commissioner's secretary he will. Permanently reduced to jelly. Really, bloody macho Boxer ought to have a bit more consideration.

'No,' she replied, realizing that despite the way the Boxer had dismissed her he did not in fact have any intention of going out. 'No, I don't actually think Mr Boxall will be going out. He's just lit another of those awful things he smokes.'

She gave Miss Mouse a grin, as cheerful as she felt she could make it.

'And that's despite the fact that, if I'm not mistaken, there's a big *This Is A Non-Smoking Area* notice inside your front door here.'

Wearily then she set off in search of the car she had eventually managed to park in one of the smartly decorated little streets north of Westbourne Grove, as far away from Persimmon House as the Boxer had once predicted she would have to go if she ever tried coming to the area by car. Finding the wretched vehicle at last, she got in but made no attempt to move off. The long drive back to the Business Park seemed more than usually unattractive. All the way down to the river, then across whichever bridge seemed less likely to have a traffic hold-up. Not nowadays a regular driver in London she had not once guessed right yet, nor had Birchester-born Sgt Watson when he was driving. Then when she had arrived in south London there was the task of wriggling through still hardly familiar streets to reach at last her not exactly welcoming office. Where on her desk, bitterly reproachful, there would be grottily familiar stacks of the personal records of every member of the Max.

So she sat, increasingly conscious of the invading chill – the rain for once holding off – and tried to find, in the remorseless pattern of unsuccess her investigation seemed now to present her with, some way forward. But, go over the ground as she might, she came every time to the same blank wall. She had to find out who had written the letter in Reynolds Liebling's safe and the Boxer had refused to give her Pantsie Underwood, safe-cracker.

At last, heaving a sigh, she straightened her shoulders, slipped the ignition key into place.

No point in sitting all afternoon in pretty-pretty Notting Hill. To hell with the Boxer and his kidnapping of DI Outhwaite. There must be something to be done in dreary, dull, depressing Rotherhithe.

But, before she had driven for much more than a minute, the Boxer, the bloody Boxer, made his presence felt once more. Out of the corner of her eye, as she waited for the traffic in her path to give her time to cross Westbourne Grove, she glimpsed his unmistakable burly figure in that dazzlingly-checked topcoat marching into an ultra-smart fish restaurant a little further along the street.

But then, as her thoughts about the man and his machinations began to churn once more, she realized the person following him into the restaurant also seemed familiar.

An instant later and she had got him. Frank Parkins. The Boxer had after all had an appointment outside Persimmon House, if not an absolutely immediate one. He was going to lunch with the man she had clashed with after he had caught her burrowing into his desk drawers.

Now, why the hell is the Boxer eating with Frank Parkins in a place like that? Parkins, the man whose allegations about the Boxer's squad were the whole reason why it was being investigated? And hadn't the Boxer boasted *I don't have time for long lunches . . . I've got a major investigation on my hands*? And, come to that, what was it he had called Parkins? Yes, *that sod of a journalist . . . Parkins or Piggins or whatever*. So why is he lunching with him now?

But at that moment the traffic flowing nose-to-tail

along Westbourne Grove mysteriously left a gap. Harriet shot into gear, put her foot down, crossed into the street she had been eyeing.

But as she drove slowly south, questions came bubbling up in Harriet's head. Why was Frank Parkins taking the Boxer to lunch no doubt at the expense of the *Sunday Herald*? Has he decided the time has come to settle that *You owe me one* debt, made at Herald House? Is he hoping to sideline my investigation in favour of his own by telling the Boxer what he caught me doing in his office? Does he reckon that the Boxer, armed with the information, could pass it on to Mr Anstruther and so get me right off his back? Or can it be this? That Parkins has found out something new about one of the senior officers in the Max and is hoping to use it as a lever to learn yet more? Even the ultimate answer? Or, again, is Parkins just Mrs Althea Raven's emissary? Has she decided I am in her way? And that by fair means or foul I'm to be neutralized?

What wouldn't I give to be the waiter in that smart-as-paint restaurant, my ears flapping. What wouldn't I give to know what's going on there.

Chapter Fourteen

As, back at last in her office, Harriet leadenly contemplated her stacks of exhausted personal records, something came to her. Perhaps the sight of Outhwaite's name on the topmost file, sending bubbling up once more her fury at the way the Boxer had hi-jacked him, somehow triggered a quite different thought.

Yes. Surely there was something in Outhwaite's P/R, the very first time I read it, that, ever so slightly, smelt wrong. To do with an internal investigation . . .? Years ago. That had resulted, yes, in the dismissal, and sending to prison, of a detective constable. On the face of it, it was a plus mark on Outhwaite's record. And it had been annotated as such. But there had been something – didn't I feel then? – not quite right about it.

Events, she realized now, had made her put that faint feeling aside, almost forget it. But not altogether. It had certainly scratched at her mind, just momentarily, more than once since she had first felt it.

Pricked by curiosity now, she went back to the file.

All right, the Boxer by battering and bullying at Outhwaite may get to the bottom of whatever lie he's telling about what he saw in Liebling's safe. But that may not be the only way to bring to light whatever may be behind his devious behaviour.

Almost as soon as she began to read the file she hit on what it was that had caused her that faint uneasiness. It was a note commending Detective Constable Outhwaite, as he had been then, on having found evidence that resulted in a fellow detective, DN 746 Richard Reader, being found guilty of corruption. But, as she re-read it now, it was seeing Reader's police number that brought back to her, jangling like an alarm bell, what earlier had obscurely bugged her.

Could it be that Reader had retained the number, though not the prefacing two letters, allocated to him when he had first joined the Met? Because, if so . . .

She flipped back to the start of Outhwaite's file.

Yes, that was it. When Jackson Outhwaite had become a police probationer his number had been 745. So Outhwaite and Reader had probably joined the Met in the very same intake. Blood brothers, as it were. But there had been no comment in the file on the close connection between the detective who had found evidence of corruption and the detective who had been corrupted and paid the heavy penalty suffered by any police officer sent to prison among criminals.

In the file she read now with sharp concentration every entry, however routine. And, yes, there were two more references to Reader, first to PC Reader and then to DC Reader, that made it clear the careers of the two officers had run for much of the time side by side. It was always possible that the two had been at loggerheads from the day they met, that honest PC Outhwaite had taken against shifty PC Reader. But, thinking of the man who had evaded and dodged her every question both in the dim light of the Cumberland Hotel and in the harsh glare of the Persimmon House interview room, she reasoned that the situation could well have been the other way about.

All right, much to the credit of DC Outhwaite if he had denounced a corrupt officer, even though the man had been a friend. But that hardly fitted the pattern of the DI Outhwaite she knew, the man who had lied and lied about whatever it had been in Reynolds Liebling's safe. No, devious DC Outhwaite, in those distant days, had decided for some reason to shop his mate.

And at once she saw what that reason could well have been. Within a month of Reader's trial and conviction Detective Constable Outhwaite had become Detective Sergeant Outhwaite, and – flip, flip through the file – before much longer he had gained promotion to detective inspector.

A man on the make, Jackson Outhwaite.

For a moment Harriet hoped that the Boxer would get to the bottom of what Outhwaite had seen in Liebling's safe, and would make him pay the penalty for concealing it.

But it was for a moment only. No, it was not going to be Commander Boxall who discovered what it was that lurked behind Frank Parkins's hints of *a wider scandal*. It was going to be the dozy northern tart.

And to do that, she said to herself, I'm going to have to track down ex-Detective Constable Reader – he'll have finished his sentence some time ago – and find out from him all about his former friend. And I won't be at all surprised if I get hold of something that will crack that man on the make wide open – perhaps even before the Boxer has his crushing interview with him, or series of interviews. Because DI Outhwaite isn't a man who'll break easily.

The weather in the Midlands, not very far from Birchester, was much less cold than it had been earlier in the day in inhospitable London. From time to time, even, the sun had briefly shone. Harriet had arrived at Gralethorpe because it was at an address in that small industrial town that, in the course of a long, long evening on the Internet – she was no expert in using it though she could cope well enough with a computer – she had located Gralethorpe-born former Detective Constable Reader. She had taken an early train to the town, and now, shortly before eleven o'clock, she was hoping to find unemployed Richard Reader in the narrow little house she had just located after tramping through its soot-grimed but somehow warmly familiar streets.

She put a gloved finger on to the cracked button of the doorbell. It rang, though it had looked as if it might have long been disconnected. And, more, the twanging sound from inside almost immediately produced the clump of heavy footsteps.

The door opened.

The man standing at it, hunched, untidily grey-haired, cheeks blotchily red, looked a good deal older than DI Outhwaite, and for a moment Harriet thought she would have yet another layer to penetrate before she came face-to-face with Outhwaite's fellow novice PC. But then she remembered what Detective Constable Reader must have gone through, convicted as a result of the evidence his former friend had produced. A long stretch, with his fellow prisoners knowing he was from the other side of the fence. It would have taken a toll.

'Mr Reader?' she asked without hesitation then. 'Mr Richard Reader?'

'What d'you want?'

The jabbed-out words could hardly have been less hostile.

'Mr Reader, you're not going to welcome me, but it's important that I speak with you. I am Detective Superintendent Martens, of the Greater Birchester Police, at present tasked with an inquiry into certain circumstances affecting the Maximum Crimes Squad in London.'

'I don't care a—'

'Affecting in particular Detective Inspector Jackson Outhwaite.'

The beaten-down look of sullen indifference on the red-blotched face changed in an instant to an undirected glare of fierce hatred.

'Jackson? So bloody Jackson's got himself into that – what d'you call it? – élite squad? Yes, sodding élite. I might have known.'

'May I come in, Mr Reader?'

'Come in. And welcome, if there's anything Dick Reader can tell you about tread-in-your-face Jackson Outhwaite, you're welcome to it.'

Facing Dick Reader in the tiny, starchy front-room – there was even an aspidistra wearily flying its dusty flag beside the window – Harriet launched into the account of why she was visiting him which she had carefully constructed as her train had made its way northwards.

'For reasons I won't bother you with, Mr Reader, I have recently had to question DI Outhwaite about a certain document he, and he alone, has had access to. It is a document that I believe will be vital to my inquiry. However, DI Outhwaite has consistently refused to say what it was he saw in it, and I want to know why that is. On the face of it, he has a first-class reputation as a detective—'

'If you believe that, you'll believe anything. Jackson Outhwaite's fine reputation is so much crap. Always was, always will be.'

'Go on, Mr Reader. Tell me why you say that.'

'Oh, I'll tell you all right. I've known Jackson since the day we both joined the Met together.'

A bark of a laugh.

'Oh, yes, on that day, when as raw recruits we were given our numbers and the two came one after the other and I heard his Yorkshire accent, I thought, well, here's someone who's not a stuck-up Londoner. So, here's a pal. And I went on thinking he'd be a friend. For a week or two anyhow. And then little things Jackson Outhwaite did began to make sense to me. Nothing you could really put a finger on, but they added up. Getting himself just in front of me queuing in the canteen and taking his pick from the dishes. Putting himself behind me when we'd been making a bit of a row and the duty sergeant was looking for someone to put on parade in full uniform at nine o'clock at night. Things like that.'

'But you went on being friendly?'

'No. No, I didn't. But I didn't quarrel with him, I'm not the quarrelsome sort. Even in prison – you'll know I did a three-stretch – when time after time I smelt piss in my tea mug I didn't pick a fight with anybody. It's not my way. So I never picked a fight with Jackson Outhwaite, little though I liked him. But that didn't stop him in the end doing worse than pick a fight with me.'

'Yes, I've read his record. It was his evidence that got you convicted, wasn't it?'

'Yes, Jackson Outhwaite got me sent down. To that hellhole Polecroft Gaol, with the screws treating you all day and every day as something sub-human, and the cons not much better. Mind you, I'm not saying Jackson's wasn't good evidence, though he made the most of it standing up there in the box. Yes, I took all right. I took, when it was just a sensible thing to do, never very much, never when it really mattered. And, yeah, when Jackson shopped me I'd perhaps for once taken more than was sensible. And, yes, Jackson didn't take. He had his eyes on other ways of feathering his nest. Wanted to go on and up, did Jackson. And he did that, didn't he? The bloody élite Max, you said. You'd think that makes him an élite detective. But he bloody isn't. Not however well he might have done in the Max.'

'And why do you think that, Mr Reader?'

Dick Reader gave a twisted grin.

'Because fucking Outhwaite isn't in the police to do what police officers are supposed to do. Keep the Queen's Peace an' all that, put as many scrotes behind bars as possible.'

A silence then. Eyes in the red-blotched face sunk in thought.

'Right,' Harriet said eventually, 'I'd agree with that, Mr Reader. A police officer should be there to put the criminals where they belong. But, from his record at least, it would seem DI Outhwaite has been doing just that. It's what brought him into the Max. To the top.'

'But that's not how Jackson Outhwaite used to see it. No, Jackson thought he was in the police for what it'd bring him in the end. He kept that pretty close to his chest. But I know better.'

'How? How do you know, Mr Reader?'

A grin.

'Obbo. That's how. I've been on obbo with Jackson on many a night, the two of us DCs. Many a night, and all night. Sitting there in some beat-up old car, watching some house where something was being planned. And nothing happening. No little party of crims coming hurrying out, getting into a motor, racing off to ambush some security van when the crew are half-asleep. But obbo's when people start talking. On obbo. That's when they say things they'd never breathe a word about in the pub or the canteen or wherever.'

'So what did DC Outhwaite say to you on nights like those?'

'Oh, he didn't let it spill out all at once. Jackson's too fly for that. But on one night or another, even in the day sometimes when we'd been sitting on our arses for maybe twelve hours or more, little bits would come out.'

'All right. So what did you learn, there on obbo with him?'

'Greed. That's what I learnt. Jackson Outhwaite was eaten up by greed. And he still will be. Leopards don't change their spots, that's what they say, isn't it? Well, Jackson was eaten up with greed then, and he'll be eaten up with it now. You know what he used to say?'

'Tell me.'

'He used to say it was his dream to quit the police, just like that, and go off somewhere with some bint to sunny Spain, West Indies, I don't know. *But I ain't got the cash, Dicky boy*, that's how he'd always end up. *I ain't got the cash. Not yet. But one day I'll have it. Enough and to spare. You'll see.*'

Harriet thought then that she, too, saw. Saw what

had motivated DI Outhwaite on his way up, up and up till he'd got himself into the Max. Till he'd got to where, if he kept his eyes open and had a stroke of luck, the really big money would be within his grasp. He must have joined the Met with ambitions oddly comparable to those, she had learnt, that had fired as different a police officer as the Hon. Maurice Quinton. Quinton had wanted in a dyed-in-the-wool democratic age to exercise the power he believed was his by right of inheritance. And Jackson Outhwaite had wanted, in an increasingly money-directed age, to get his hands eventually on a fat capital sum. The two of them were in a way a pair, if a curiously linked one.

But I have to be a little more sure about what the bitter man in front of me has asserted, she told herself. A little more sure.

'Yes, you paint a vivid picture, Mr Reader. But, tell me, you said earlier that your fellow probationer, 745 Outhwaite, was never a taker, whether it was sensible at the time or not. So doesn't that rather contradict that picture of him as a man eaten up with greed?'

'No. No, it don't. I tell you, I know Jackson Outhwaite. I was close to him, or at least I was till the time he married. Some Yorkshire lass. From where he came from. After that I saw less of him. But, before, we were often stationed at the same nicks all over the Met area. Oh, there's not much I don't know about Jackson. Not much? There's nothing I don't know about that shit. I had time enough to think about him in stir, didn't I? And, I tell you, hide it though he did, Jackson Outhwaite went into the police with one aim only, and he stayed with it every inch of the way. Money. The big pile. That's what Jackson's always wanted, and a big haul somehow was what he thought he could best get hold of by joining the Met, heavy blackmail, going over to one of the big gangs. Anything.'

'Thank you, Mr Reader. And I rather think before long you'll be hearing something about your fellow recruit that'll more than please you.'

Harriet did not get back to the Business Park till the early darkness of a dismal London day was beginning to fall. She felt confident now that, if Frank Parkins did have any information that would give grounds for his claim of *a scandal that goes much wider*, she knew who it was he had had in his sights, even if it was not yet clear how she could use what she had learnt. But as soon as she entered her office she saw, pinned to the top of her pile of messages and reports, a note heavily underlined in red.

A Miss House has rung four times now. Says ring her back BUT BE CAREFUL.

Miss House, Miss Mouse. What can she have been calling about? And so urgently? One thing, plainly she had not been relaying any message from the Boxer. There would have hardly been that *ring back but he careful* if she had.

Right, let's find out.

'Miss House?'

'Speaking. Is— Is that— I think it's all right. I mean he won't be— Is— Is that—'

Flap-flap-flapping could be allowed to go on only so long.

'It's Harriet Martens. Now why have you been ringing me all afternoon?'

'It— It's because— Oh, Miss Martens, I don't know now whether I should.'

'My dear girl, it's too late for second thoughts. You've let me know you have got something you want to tell me. The only thing to do now is come out with it.'

'Yes. Yes, Miss Martens. You're right.'

'Well then?'

'Miss Martens, it's this. Commander Boxall— He— Well, he's— Miss Martens, Detective Inspector Outhwaite has reported sick. He's gone home, Miss Martens. Been sent home. I— I think it was the— It was Commander Boxall, Miss Martens, he made him go. There was a— Well, a sort of terrific row when DI Outhwaite went in to see him. I heard. I heard voices. Well, I couldn't quite make out . . . But I heard your name. And— And Commander Boxall was in one of his rages. You know. Well, you don't, I suppose. But—'

'All right. I don't think you need tell me any more. You're right that I needed to know about Mr Outhwaite, and, yes, no one was going to tell me if you didn't. But now I understand what's happened, and I'm grateful, very grateful, to you for putting me in the picture.'

To murmurs and gulps at the far end Harriet put down the phone.

So the Boxer has done what he said he would do, she thought. He's found out what it was Outhwaite saw in Liebling's safe.

Well, thanks to scared little Miss Mouse managing somehow to pluck up her courage, at least I know what he's done. And perhaps that's something.

And, whether the Boxer takes further action or not, he's put Outhwaite firmly out of account. Retirement on medical grounds. That's what it's going to be once again. A cover-up. Something went badly wrong in the Boxer's élite Max, and he's managed neatly to bury it.

Can I unbury it? Go and see Outhwaite at home,

on his supposed sick-bed, and get him to tell me what it was that, under the Boxer's battering, he confessed to at last?

Plain answer: No.

No, if I know anything Outhwaite will have been so scarified by the Boxer that he won't dare ever say anything about what it was he saw in Liebling's safe. He'll know, if he talks to anyone about what he found out, he won't go on enjoying a quiet retirement on medical grounds. If he breathes a word to anyone, it will mean prison for him. Even if it's on a trumped-up charge.

I know the Boxer. And that's what he'd do. No question.

Chapter Fifteen

No, the fact of the matter, Harriet said to herself sitting there at her desk, is that I was too late getting on to ex-Detective Constable Reader. The Boxer's been too quick for me. If I'd known what I now know about Outhwaite I might have broken him myself. If Outhwaite had been able to hold out longer under the Boxer's battering-ram questioning, I might still have been able to get at him before he told the Boxer who really wrote the letter in Liebling's safe, who it is in the Max that Grajales has bribed.

But I didn't. Too late. Too late. There's nowhere else for my inquiry to go. I'd got almost to the end. Narrowed it all down to that letter in the safe. All I needed to do was to take Pantsie Underwood and his clever fingers back into that flat, get that safe open again, see who did write that explosive letter. But the Boxer trumped my ace. He's defeated me. That's it. Defeated me.

Her internal phone rang. For some moments she let it go on ringing, too weary to deal with whatever the caller wanted. Then at last she stirred herself.

'Superintendent Martens.'

'Ah, you are still here, ma'am.' It was the constable on duty at Reception. 'Ma'am, there's a— A gentleman here who says he wants to see you. A Mr Parkins. Mr Frank Parkins.'

The note of curiosity was so plain it almost oozed out of the phone.

Oh, he knows who Frank Parkins is all right. And he's busy wondering what the chief crime reporter of the *Sunday Herald* wants with me. Perhaps all along down there he's been another of the Boxer's eyes, watching my every move. But Frank Parkins, the man I saw just yesterday trailing behind the Boxer as they went into that fancy fish restaurant in Westbourne Grove. Waiting at Reception now. The man who said *You owe me one.*

So what can he want now?

Only one thing to do. See him.

'Yes. Thank you. Tell Mr Parkins to come up.'

Frank Parkins came slouching in. The twisted-teeth smile on his dully complexioned face brought into Harriet's head at once the single ominous word *predatory*.

She had no time to wonder why the impression had been so strong.

'So this is the secret headquarters of the ace investigators from— Where was it? Ah, yes, Birchester.'

'A headquarters, Mr Parkins, where, for better or worse, we don't welcome visitors.'

'But then I'm the Press. Makes a difference.'

And, in a small sunburst of illumination, Harriet guessed what had brought her this visitor, and who was behind him.

Yes. Yes, of course, the reason Frank Parkins gave the Boxer lunch is because Mrs Althea Raven must have ordered him to cripple the detective who had refused to leave the discovery of the rotten apple in the famous Maximum Crimes Squad to be given to the world in the pages of the *Sunday Herald*. And, knowing the Boxer, as he must do, Parkins has gone to him to ask him to dish whatever dirt on me he might have acquired while defending himself from an awkward inquiry.

She took the battle to the enemy.

'Tell me,' she said, 'what did you talk about when you were lunching Commander Boxall yesterday?'

She had the pleasure then of seeing she had disconcerted him.

But it was only for the shortest of moments.

'Yes, I was doing that. The Boxer and I get on rather well, and he was good enough in the course of conversation to tell me one or two things about you, Miss Martens. Things about Birchester's famous Hard Detective that I didn't know before.'

'I think I said to you the other day that I'm not particularly enamoured of that label your media colleagues have chosen to stick on me.'

'No? No, I suppose you're not. But it gives us a good headline, you know.'

'A headline? What headline?'

'Well, it wouldn't be one on a story about your little inquiry into the Max's naughty boys. No, it'd be about something quite different.'

Before she could stop herself Harriet spoke.

'What on earth—'

Frank Parkins smiled then. Twisted, tobacco-stained teeth well to the fore.

'You know,' he said, 'it rather depends on you, Miss Martens, whether that headline appears or not.'

He stood looking at her expectantly. But now she had herself under control. Parkins was not going to get a panicky demand out of her twice.

'Not interested, Miss Martens? You know, I think you should be. After all, you wouldn't much like to see *Hard Detective in Love Tangle* all across one of our pages, would you?'

And then Harriet knew what it had been that the Boxer had told Frank Parkins.

The Boxer's inquiries about the dozy northern tart who was poking her nose into his squad's activities must have gone even deeper than tapping Rekha's phone and having Freckles Frecker tail me. The Boxer will, of course, have known someone in the Greater Birchester force. He knows officers everywhere, and knows how to call in favours. So I can imagine how pleased he must have been when he learnt that interfering Detective Superintendent Martens, Mrs Piddock, had not all that long ago had an intense affair with a detective inspector from the neighbouring Leven Vale force.

But Parkins, still looking at her in much the way a surgeon might look at a mass of guts under his poised scalpel, was going smoothly on.

'Yes, you know, that's what you'll see bright and early next Sunday. *Hard Detective in Love Tangle*, though I expect our headline writer will manage something even juicier, once he puts his nasty mind to it. You'll see what it is then. That is, unless there's something you're prepared to do for me, and after all you do owe me one. As I seem to remember pointing out to you after a certain event that took place in office.'

So, Harriet thought, he doesn't believe he settled that debt when he was talking to the Boxer. And I'm damned if I'm going to let him settle it any other way now, however many columns he devotes to my *love tangle*.

'You know,' she said, 'I don't think I'm very interested in settling that little debt.'

A glint of fury in Parkins's somewhat bloodshot eyes.

'Oh, well, if you won't play for me, perhaps you'll play for someone else. For my boss, Mrs Althea Raven, in fact. And, let me tell you, she's a lady who makes sure that when she asks she gets the answer she wants.'

'Yes, I've met Mrs Raven. She gave me lunch last Saturday. At the Groucho. But I didn't then give her the answer she wanted.'

'Yes, she told me you had been unco-operative. But now I think the time's come to change your mind. You know what Mrs Raven wants. She wants you to sit here for a week or two more and do damn-all. So are you going to do that? Or are you going to see your private life spread out all over our pages?'

All right, Harriet thought at once, nicely ironic that it so happens the Boxer has done Mrs Raven's work for her. As far as I'm concerned there's no more to be done in the inquiry. So shall I tell Parkins that? Send the messenger back with good news? Or bad news, if Mrs Raven wants her precious public-influencing paper to be the one that breaks the Max? If I tell her that her messenger came here on a fool's errand because the Boxer has succeeded in hushing up altogether what went wrong in his squad, what will she do? Shrug her elegant shoulders, I imagine, and register that one stratagem hasn't come off.

So why not tell this journalistic truffle-hound what he's not at all expecting to hear? Right, here goes.

'As it happens, Mr Parkins, I have some news for you. My inquiry has come to an end. There's been no corruption in the Max, beyond what those two small-fry managed to do. You can go back and tell your esteemed employer just that.'

Frank Parkins looked astonished. Almost comically so.

'I— I don't believe you,' he got out at last.

'Oh, it's true. Perfectly true. You were right in your insinuations in your original story about there being something more astray in the Max, however you got a sniff of it. There was something astray. But it was nothing like as serious as I dare say you hoped. There wasn't, I came to realize, any corruption at a high level. It was just a simple disciplinary matter. If you still don't believe me, you can call your friend, Commander Boxall, and he'll confirm it all.'

The *Sunday Herald* star reporter stood there looking like a schoolkid whose bottle of Coke had fallen to the ground, smashed.

But then, just as Harriet was about to get rid of him, he perked up. Some kindly adult had, it seemed, bought him another Coke.

'All right,' he said. 'No skin off my nose if I tell Mrs Raven our big story's fallen to the ground. It won't be the first, nor the last. But, you know, you still owe me something, and my little threat just now is still poking out of my sleeve.'

Harriet was momentarily puzzled.

Okay, he still does have that nasty story about me he learnt about from the Boxer. And I suppose he could still plaster it across a page in the *Sunday Herald* next week. But what point would there be? Sheer malice, of course. Yet I don't quite see Frank Parkins, unpleasant fellow though he is, wasting his time, and his paper's columns, out of mere malice. No, he must have . . . He must have, damn it, something he still wants from me.

At once she found out what it was.

'All right,' Parkins went on, 'I've lost my big Page One lead. But there's still juice to any story about the great almighty Max, especially if it's not altogether to their credit. So I'd be obliged, Detective Superintendent Martens, if you would give me full details of that *simple disciplinary matter* you tried to slip past me. It'd probably make a better story than *Hard Detective in Love Nest* but I'll use that if you'd rather.'

Harriet considered.

I can't, of course, give him his *details*. Even if they really existed, it would be a blank betrayal of my duty to do it. But they don't exist. They're only the Boxer's smokescreen. So how much will that headline, those revelations, affect me? Oh, they'll hurt. That's certain. No one likes their private affairs to be broadcast to the world. Okay, film and TV stars, and footballers, people who've plunged themselves into the public eye, have to put up with that sort of intrusion. But I haven't set myself up in front of an admiring public, all ready to be knocked from my pedestal. Yes, I'm called the Hard Detective. But I never did anything to award myself that absurd title. So, I've the right, if I want, to have my private life left private.

But, make no bones about it, Frank Parkins, slouching there against the filing-cabinet, won't hesitate to ride roughshod over that vague right of mine if I don't tell him what he thinks I could. But I can't. There's nothing to tell. And, what's more, I can't even tell him that there is nothing to tell.

So, am I ready to bite my lip and endure seven

199

days of licensed prying? And worse. Poor John, and all our friends, will know the whole bloody public is reading that stuff, that true stuff, the details of my love-life sprawled all across a page of the *Sunday Herald*.

But worse again. It will mean the image of Hard Detective is for ever discredited. All right, that in itself hardly matters. But something else matters a great deal more. Because any story about the Hard Detective's not altogether salubrious private life is going to affect her standing – my standing – as an effective police officer. More, it will affect my standing as the officer chosen to conduct an inquiry that has to be carried out with the utmost efficiency while being kept well under wraps.

It will affect my standing with C.A.G.D. Anstruther. It will fill him with doubts about me when I tell him, as in any case I will have to, that my inquiry has revealed nothing

No, that's the final sticking point.

She braced herself to bring all that the *Sunday Herald* could do down on to her head.

But then into her mind there came a little gem-like thought. One last wild, daring, illegitimate hope.

'Right, Mr Parkins,' she said, 'you reminded me just now that I owed you one. But what you don't know is that you owe me. You've owed me one just as long as you say that I've owed you. Because I didn't only go through your desk drawers, you know. I worked my way into your computer, too.'

'What a talented detective.'

'Yes, it so happens that I am,' she lied. 'I'm rather a dab hand at using computers. At getting, quick as you like, on to things stuffed away in them which their owners think are safely secret.'

'Secret?'

A look of plain fear flashed for an instant on to Parkins's face, a widening of the eyes, a tiny drop of the lower jaw.

He recovered almost as quickly. But Harriet guessed then that her hasty shot had landed somewhere near the bull's-eye. Frank Parkins had got stored in his computer something, some fact he had found out in a way no reporter was entitled to, or even something to do with his own private life – a cache of kiddie porn? – that could land him in criminal trouble.

Right, I've got him. By the balls.

'So, Mr Parkins, I'll bid you good evening. I expect you can find your own way out.'

It was still, however, with a deep layer of depression welling up in her mind that Harriet left to make her way – that interminable drive – back to Rekha's flat. All right, I've stalled bloody Frank Parkins, and I suppose bloody Mrs Althea Raven is off my back too. But the fact remains that I was summoned down to London to find out who in the élite Maximum Crime Squad was corrupt, if anybody. And what have I found out? That one of the squad's senior officers, DI Outhwaite, is beyond doubt corrupt, but that in no way now can I touch him. The Boxer, damn and blast him, has taken it all into his own hands. Yes, Outhwaite is going to suffer. But he will suffer, in whatever way the Boxer finds to make him suffer, in secret and in silence. I can hand Mr Anstruther no report saying that, yes, there was corruption in the higher reaches of the Max, and naming the officer responsible. Even if I were to name Outhwaite as being unfit to serve in the Max, I have no evidence I can produce to substantiate my accusation. Much less can I name the officer who wrote the letter Outhwaite found in Liebling's safe. No, all I can do is to state my inquiries and have found nothing to justify the *Sunday Herald* allegations of a wider scandal.

What I want to do, and can't, and can't, is go tomorrow to see the Boxer and tell him that, no, whatever I indicated earlier – how stupid to try that schoolgirl wheeze of Rekha's – my inquiry is still very much active. That I intend, however many difficulties are put in my way, to find out what DI Outhwaite confessed to him earlier today and to put the full details into my report. But those details will necessarily have to include, if I'm to have any hard evidence, what is in that letter Outhwaite saw. And to do that I will have to get that safe opened, put my hand into it, pull out that letter.

And I can't. I can't. In any possible way.

All very well to squash a cheap example of humanity like Frank Parkins with a well put over piece of—

No. No, but wait. I didn't succeed in bluffing Parkins because he was *a cheap piece of humanity*. He isn't. Not altogether. No, I bluffed him because he knew he had something he wanted to keep hidden.

And, when all's said and done, won't a man like the Boxer, a monster like the Boxer, have plenty of things in his past that he wouldn't like to think might be exposed in a report made to a senior member of Her Majesty's Inspectorate of Constabulary. To the man, the gentleman, who, I really believe, would never agree to let them be quietly forgotten. So can I play the same trick once more? On the Boxer, that altogether tougher proposition than flaky Frank Parkins?

But, damn it, I'll try. I'll try.

He prides himself on always being at his desk by at least nine. Right, he'll find me there waiting for him.

Chapter Sixteen

Mary House was, as Harriet might have expected, already well established at her desk outside the Boxer's office even before she herself arrived at Persimmon House some ten minutes before nine next morning. She did her best to put the mousy little girl at ease as she fluttered and fluffed, torn between offering coffee and dreading seeing her boss come booming in with some complaint about her guardianship of his telephone.

At two minutes to nine the Boxer appeared, flaunting like a flag-of-war the dark, well-tailored suit in a fine flecked tweed that Harriet had seen before.

But, Harriet thought with a tiny jolt of pleasure, just for one instant his stride checked when he saw me standing here.

'Thought you'd be on your way to Birchester this morning, Superintendent,' he said however, breezily enough.

'No, I'd like to see you for a few minutes, Commander,' she said, doing her best to make the request a simple matter of business.

The Boxer looked at her, his big broken nose poking forward aggressively. But then he turned, swept open his office door and, with a body gesture that was somehow not a bow, ushered her in. He shut the door behind him, marched round to his big chair, crashed down into it, reached across the desk to his cigarillos box, pulled one out.

'No use offering them to you,' he said cheerfully. 'You'll be one of the people who take notice of that damn thing in the entrance hall. *This Is A Non-living Area.*'

Harriet ignored all of that and took the chair in front of the desk.

'Commander,' she said without more preliminary, 'will you kindly tell me why you put an officer from your élite squad, and one who's actually been suspended, on to following me all the time I have been conducting my inquiry.'

And the Boxer blinked.

There could be no doubting it.

'Furthermore,' Harriet leapt onwards, 'I have reason to believe the phone in the flat in Ealing where I'm staying has been tapped. Do I take it that this too was on your instructions?'

'Yes. You can.'

No point in hoping the Boxer would stay on the run. But no point either in taking this lying down.

'You're aware that such an unauthorized intercept is illegal?'

'Oh, come on, sweetheart. It's done every day.'

'Commander, may I remind you I am the officer tasked with investigating circumstances in the squad under your command that have given rise to considerable disquiet in the Home Office and elsewhere. As such, I think you would do better, whatever the difference in our ranks, not to address me as *sweetheart.*'

'All right, if you're so touchy. But let me point something out to you. I'm not the only one who takes steps to find out what people are doing that might interfere with their business. You've been on at my Mary Mouse to keep you informed about what I'm doing, haven't you? I keep my ears open, you know, even when I'm not in my office but happen to be coming towards it. And, let me tell you, that young lady's going to pay for her indiscretion. I don't know whether just to put her across my knee or to give her whatever piece of paper you hand out when you sack someone. But one of those it'll be. You can be sure of that.'

Harriet decided to take no notice of the macho jibe in so far as it was directed at herself. But protecting little sleek-haired Mary House was another matter.

'I think we'll hear no more of that, Commander,' she said. 'If I have been inquiring more deeply than is strictly above board into your squad's affairs, and your own, let me tell you I haven't inquired without some success. Whatever in the end I put in my report to Mr Anstruther I can, should I wish, include some facts about corners that have been cut by the Maximum Crimes Squad which would do you considerable harm. So, to put it plainly: hands off Miss House.'

All right, she thought, I think I've said enough to make him realize his famous squad is not above reproach. But have I given him too much warning of the bigger bluff I'm on the point of trying? He's no Frank Parkins to cave in at a single word.

'You think you can shop me to your big boss, do you?' the Boxer replied. 'Well, we'll see about that. But, since you're here, there's something I can tell you that, as they say, may be of assistance to you. Since it seems this inquiry of yours, which you led me to believe yesterday had come to an end, appears to be still active.'

It was Harriet's turn now to be disconcerted. This was a sudden change of attitude surely? What could it mean?

She bristled with suspicion.

'Yes,' the Boxer went on, spending longer than necessary now lighting up the cigarillo he had taken from his silver box. 'It's about that nasty piece of shit, DI Outhwaite. Or ex-DI Outhwaite, as he soon will be.'

He enveloped Harriet now in a cloud of evil-smelling smoke. She knew better than to show she was aware of it.

'Outhwaite,' she said. 'So what was it, after all, that made him whistle in surprise when he saw it in Reynolds Liebling's safe?'

'I wish I knew.'

Harriet almost jerked back in surprise. Could it be that the Boxer had failed to get out of Outhwaite what he saw in the safe? She could hardly believe it.

The Boxer produced a grin, if hardly a cheerful one.

'So my Mary Mouse didn't have all that much to tell you,' he said. 'I thought she'd have heard more of what Outhwaite said while she had her little ear pinned to my door. Voices were raised. Or mine was certainly.'

'Miss House did phone me, yes,' Harriet said now. 'But all she had to tell me was that you had sent DI Outhwaite home sick. I thought you must have got out of him what he'd seen in Liebling's safe and had decided to deal with him in the way you were proposing to deal with DCs Frecker and Underwood. Sweeping any wrongdoing under the carpet. But I wasn't right, it seems.'

'You weren't. I don't like having to admit this, but that bugger Outhwaite was too good for me. I had him in here for two solid hours, and he clammed up, as if his life depended on it. Oh, yes, he saw something in that safe all right. His looks alone told me that. But I'm damned if I could get out of him what it was. I suppose he thinks it's something that's going to let him put the bite on somebody in a big way. But I think he's hardly got round to it yet. And before he does I'm going to find out what it is he's on to, whether he tells me or not.'

'So, how do you think you'll manage that?'

'Quite simple, Miss Martens. You're going to tell me. You're going to pay a call on Mr Reynolds Liebling, in his absence in the United States of America, of course. And, with the able assistance of one DC Underwood, you're going to open that safe in his bedroom – you'll find it behind a pornographic painting, so they tell me – and you're going to go through the contents until you see just what it was that made Outhwaite whistle. Should be pretty obvious when you set eyes on it.'

'You're suggesting I illegally enter Reynolds Liebling's flat? That I order DC Underwood to open the safe there?'

'I'm sure you'll be just as ready to do that as I was, dear lady.'

And Harriet knew that she was.

In the middle of the afternoon on the following Monday Harriet found herself looking at a well-developed woman, all rosy-tinted flesh, and an even better developed dark-skinned man, very hairy about the buttocks, painted at the climax of gratification. Competently painted, if not rather more than competently. Must have cost Reynolds Liebling a penny or two, she thought.

Pantsie Underwood, as ever the stiffly look-alike sergeant major, lifted down between his surgically gloved hands the heavily-framed canvas to reveal the wall-safe behind it. The safe, which, so the Boxer had said, his use-for-anything tail, Freckles Frecker, had once, from a convenient window a little way down the mews, contrived to see Liebling going to.

Pantsie put the grotesque painting, face-down, next to his open leather bag on the big king-sized bed.

'I'll need a few minutes, ma'am,' he murmured, ineradicably the police officer despite the dubiousness of his present activity. 'More even. Took me the best part of an hour to get her open without a trace the last time.'

'All right, I'll just go into the sitting-room, keep an eye out through the window.'

She left him.

But should I stay there watching him? Just in case he gets that safe open more quickly than he's said, gets to the letter before I do. But Pantsie, the thick. I don't see him trying anything like that, even if he's got the remotest idea of the importance of the letter. And if I hover over him he'll be conscious of me. He'll fumble. Make mistakes. No, better leave him. And in any case I might find something in the sitting-room that'll be some help to the Boxer. The safe's not necessarily the only hiding-place here.

In the standardly luxurious room next door she took out her own pair of dead-white surgical gloves, pulled them on and then wandered about, free to poke

209

and pry. For a little she had no better result than satisfying her mild curiosity about the life-style of Pablo Grajales's London lieutenant, and, whatever the degree of her interest, it soon failed to keep at bay her inner tension.

Christ, if by some fluke someone reports that there are intruders in here . . . If I suddenly hear the sound of that creaky one-person lift outside . . .

She went over to the nearer of the two windows, peered out along the narrow rain-dreary Mayfair mews, deserted at the afternoon hour which the Boxer had with careful precision chosen for the expedition.

All right, I'm a police officer and I'd like to see Liebling and all the other London villains Grajales uses safely locked away. But the man to see to that is the Boxer. And, looking at the co-operation he's now giving me, I'm pretty sure that he's actually devoting his full energies to that task A good police officer. Or at least a good thief-taker, a very good thief-taker.

So I ought to be giving him in return what help I can. And, damn it, that's what I'm doing at this moment. I'm waiting to get my eyes on the contents of that safe in the bedroom there, so as to find what it was that so surprised and, yes, delighted Jackson Outhwaite, the man who joined the police on the chance of one day being able to lay hands on a fortune in illegal cash. And, when I've seen what's in the safe, I'll happily share my discovery with the Boxer, provided it looks as if, in any way at all, it would help in his task.

She stood there looking out at the shining cobbles of the tucked-away mews, watching the rain, which had hardly ceased over the whole weekend while she

had been impatiently waiting for the moment the
Boxer had chosen for the break-in.

Is it going to go on coldly sloshing down, day after
day, while I struggle against all the obstacles in the
way of my investigation that have been put there by
the people who resent any inquiries into themselves,
however properly undertaken? Jesus, it's ridiculous.
The bloody weather could have been especially
arranged as one final maddening hindrance. But
perhaps – yes, fix on it – what friend Pantsie is doing
at this moment will bring all this to a conclusion. And
in days, if not hours.

Go in and see how he's getting on? No. He's not
had anything like time enough yet. Leave an expert to
get on with an expert's work.

She turned away from the rain-streaked window
and wandered over to the three shelves of a small
alcove bookcase opposite, her curiosity aroused once
more. What sort of books would Reynolds Liebling have
there, the man who has hanging opposite his big bed
next-door that blatant piece of painted porn?

The answer, she thought wryly when she looked
more closely, is just what I ought to have expected. So
many dummy spines.

But, wait. A hiding-place? What will I . . .

Pulling at the topmost row of dummies, she
brought the whole façade forward on the hinges at its
foot. And, behind, found no more than two long mirror-
backed shelves crowded with an assortment of bottles
and glasses.

She skimmed along the row, almost idly listing the
drinks a man like Liebling would think necessary for
his own use and to offer the party pick-ups Freckles
Frecker had watched him bring home. A wide variety

of liqueurs of the stickier sort. And whisky, of course. Three kinds of impressive Highland malts, plus a three-quarters empty bottle of bourbon, presumably for himself.

Abruptly she halted her survey. Hadn't there been . . .?

Yes, between the first two of the liqueurs, a wide-shouldered bottle of coffee-laced, rum-based Tia Maria and a slimmer bottle of Bailey's coffee and Irish whiskey, there was a chink of space, and – she must have noticed it subliminally – behind there was no mirror-backing to the shelf.

She pulled out the bottle of Tia Maria, the stickiness round its thin neck clinging to the fingers of her white gloves.

And, yes, a small wood panel, an inch wide and three long, was revealed. She pressed it experimentally with the forefinger of her other hand. A section of the mirrored strip behind gave way.

A gun.

What I might have expected, she thought. Of course, Liebling won't have been able to board an aircraft with a weapon. So here it is, waiting for him when he returns. Whenever that will be.

For a moment she wondered whether to relieve him of it. But, no. No sign must be left of there having been anyone in the flat.

Replacing the door of the hidey-hole, she glanced at her watch. Time now to go and keep an eye on Pantsie?

But, no. He had still been less than a quarter of an hour working at the safe. Let him be for a bit. But I'll make sure I'm there before that safe door swings back.

No one's going to get hold of that letter before I see it, not even thick-brain, clever-hands DC Underwood.

But, damn it, I wish he'd get a move on. All right, from what the Boxer's team found, when they were in here before, we're perfectly safe from interruption at this time of the afternoon. And, yes, the Boxer told me specifically that Liebling was still in America. But . . .

But somehow I'm uneasy.

Okay, so I ought to be. I'm in here, in someone else's flat, a senior police officer playing the breaking-and-entering merchant. If by any wild chance I'm caught here with Pantsie, say by a curious neighbour unexpectedly at home, or Liebling himself yet more unexpectedly coming back from the States, it'll be the end for me. The end of my career. Arrest. A trial . . . Sent down. I would be. And, make no mistake, a woman police officer in a women's prison would have just as hard a time as broken and bowed-down Dick Reader.

God, I'm going to go and have a look at Pantsie.

She took three rapid paces towards the bedroom. And stopped.

No, it's panic. I'm panicking. And I'm not someone who does that. I am not.

She allowed herself then an almost inaudible chuckle.

I'm the Hard Detective.

Yes, the Hard Detective, even though I've been weak enough, if it was a weakness, to agree to the Boxer's illegal scheme. Yet shouldn't I have done? I think I should. I still think I should. It was the only way to find who it is Jackson Outhwaite intends one day to blackmail. Who is the one betraying the Max.

But something else. Something I've stopped myself

thinking about. Or, whenever the thought surfaced I've pushed it down. Why, after all am I the one who's here? Why really has the Boxer left it to me to do this? Why did he insist it should be me? All right, he had his arguments. *I can't, for God's sake, use one of my own senior officers. It bloody could be the man – or even the woman – who wrote that letter to bloody Reynolds Liebling.*

All right, something in that. Except that if anything goes wrong, I'm the one who'll be caught in the act.

She pushed back the rows of dummy volumes.

I could just check on Pantsie now. He may be quicker getting that safe door open this time.

But, hearing what she thought might be a shower of hail battering at the window, she went over to it. Not hail. Just yet heavier rain. Would it ever stop?

Down at the far end of the mews she noticed, through the blur of the rain, that a man had come in at the narrow archway. A burly man, dressed somehow a little differently from the average passer-by. In a light-coloured trench coat, broad across the shoulders, with a light-coloured, broad-brimmed hat. Head down against the chill rain, he was striding purposefully along like a person knowing exactly where they're going and in a hurry to get there.

And, yes, hadn't there been the sound of a taxi reversing just beyond the archway?

Liebling, she thought. Yes? No? Yes, it must be. It's Reynolds Liebling. He looks every inch like an American. He's not safely away in the States. Not at all.

Reynolds Liebling is here, and heading for home.

Chapter Seventeen

As Harriet went barging at top speed into the flat's bedroom, she saw that Pantsie was just stepping back from the safe.

'Open, ma'am,' he said triumphantly. 'Twenty minutes, less.'

'Shut it. Shut it up, and put that painting back. Liebling's coming up the mews.'

Pantsie was slow to react. He gave the little solid door of the safe a long lingering look, as if totally loath to leave his handiwork. On the shelf inside Harriet saw four or five neat piles of papers.

On top of one of them – God, almost certainly – whatever it was that had made Jackson Outhwaite whistle in surprise.

Can I? Can I? Dart in. Snatch the lot, bundle them up?

No. No, no, no. If Liebling finds us, it'll be too late to learn who wrote that letter. It'll be all up.

She hurled herself across, slammed the safe's heavy little door closed.

'The painting,' she hissed. 'Get it back up.'

Now, at last, Pantsie seemed to realize the need for speed. He picked up the picture, lifted it, hung it.

Not daring to stop and see if he had got it exactly

in position, Harriet turned to the door, thinking like a search-engine.

Yes.

The lift. Ought to be down at ground level. Was there when Pantsie had dealt with the front door and came in. I'd have heard it if anyone . . . I was straining to listen. So Liebling, will he use it, even though it's only one floor up? Yes. Yes, he will. He would.

Any luck, we've got a chance.

She turned back to Pantsie, coming out of the bedroom.

'Listen. We're going to wait just outside the flat door. Then, if we hear the lift beginning to come up, we're going to go, fast as we can, down the stairs. But quietly. Quietly. With luck, we'll be able to get past without him having any idea there was ever anyone here.'

'But what if he doesn't use the lift? I wouldn't.'

'You're an economy-conscious Brit. Liebling's a free-spending American. He'll take the lift. So, come on. You've got your kit? Get going.'

Pantsie lifted up his heavy tool-bag, shook it in her face with a touch of insolence.

'But, Christ, shut that bedroom door. It was closed when we came in. Shut it.'

Pantsie's tiny spurt of truculence vanished. He swung back round, sergeant major stiffness momentarily gone, and carefully pulled the bedroom door shut.

'Right, out we go.'

On the cramped landing outside they waited, alert for the least sound from below.

Then it came. The just audible click as Liebling's key turned in the lock of the outer door.

Harriet felt the tension suddenly pulling hard at all the muscles of her abdomen. She tried to quieten, even more than she had already, the sound of her breathing, and was conscious that Pantsie, beside her, was puffing like an exhausted athlete.

Footsteps down below, plain to hear on the tiled floor.

The lift? Am I going to hear its grille-door being used?

Then, yes. An uprush of sweat flooded out all down her front as, at Liebling's press on the button, the criss-cross door below clashed heavily open.

She began, involuntarily, to count.

One, two, three, fo—

The reversed clunking as the lift door closed.

'Now.'

Swiftly she led the way down the dark staircase. Up on tip-toe. Hardly daring, despite the loud covering noise of the lift-motor, even to breathe.

Behind her Pantsie was not as silent. Heavy-footed.

She turned, gave him a glare, finger to lips.

How much time do we have? If the lift's fast it could be outside the flat at any second. And then, with the lift-motor silent, if some movement we make catches Liebling's eye, or if he hears some sound, will he suspect there's something wrong? Turn and peer down the stairwell? He's a criminal, damn it. Always alert.

Ground level.

She hurried over to the house door, careless all of a sudden about how much noise she might be making. The tap-tap of her heels.

In the gloom of the unlit hallway it was difficult to see where the lock of the door was.

And up above . . .?

Then the tiny gleam of the Yale's brass knob entered her vision. With fingers in an instant sweat-slippery inside her thin surgical gloves she twisted at it. It moved round. She tugged the tall door open. The blissful feel of cold, rain-washed air.

From behind her Pantsie came blundering out, head down, ready to pelt off along the inviting stretch of cobbles in front. She caught his elbow in a grip that should have made him wince with pain.

'Come back, you fool. If he hears footsteps running away like that, he'll be after us before we get to the top of the mews. He's got a gun in there.'

Sharply she pulled him flat against the wall of the house, hopefully not visible from above unless a window was fully opened. And there, tugging off their clinging surgical gloves and with the icy rain now heavily battering at their faces, they waited.

How long, Harriet asked herself. Count to a hundred? No, more. Two hundred. Three.

But at last, with her good, new green coat heavy once again with rainwater and Pantsie's stiff mackintosh looking equally wettened from collar to dripping hem, she decided it was safe to go.

'But keep a steady pace,' she said to Pantsie. 'Think of yourself as just off out to get cigarettes or something.'

'In this rain?'

'Yes, damn you, in this rain. Just don't draw attention, right?'

But, at the top of the mews, she was unable herself to resist giving one last backward glance. The distant windows of the flat looked gleamingly black. No pale face up against one of the panes, staring out half-suspicious of people in the mews at this dead hour of the day.

Or had there been something? Not a face, but a glint of movement? Someone moving purposefully, behind the panes' shiny blackness?

No telling.

'Right,' she said to Pantsie. 'Make your own way back home now, and forget any of this ever took place. I'll be in touch with Mr Boxer, tell him what happened.'

'Ma'am.'

In the wonderfully warm comfort of Rekha's flat – no point after the out-of-nowhere fiasco in going to the Business Park – Harriet, in Rekha's absence, draped her sodden coat across the sitting-room radiator, went into the bathroom, wrung out her hair, set her heated comb to warm up and changed tights and shoes. At last, beginning to feel a little more human, she sat down and began to take stock.

All right, there in that awful dully luxurious flat waiting for Pantsie to get the safe open, I told myself, a mad burst of optimism, the whole business could be brought to an end, successfully, successfully, in a few days.

No, damn it, I said *in days, if not hours.* I bloody allowed myself to think it could all be over in a few hours.

But now? Now, how long will it be till I can go to C.A.G.D. Anstruther and hand him a report naming the officer of the Maximum Crimes Squad in the pay of Pablo Grajales? It could be weeks. It could be months. In all probability now, it's a report I'll never be able to write.

Bugger it, what appalling luck to have Liebling come back just at that time. I should have gone in at the flat earlier. I should have challenged the Boxer's decision to wait till today. It never does do to put things off out of some mimsy sense of super-abundant caution.

And, damn it, I was all in favour of getting hold of Pantsie straight away, the moment the Boxer said he wanted me to see inside Liebling's safe. I'd have gone in there on Saturday night. I can't see there'd have been any real obstacle to burgling the place under cover of darkness. Okay, this afternoon the mews was deserted. Most of the young executive types with flats there busy, I suppose, earning their fat salaries and fatter bonuses. But late in the evening on a Saturday most of them would have been out on the razzle somewhere or down weekending in the country.

So why did the Boxer of all people—

Then she saw it.

No, damn it, I know why he insisted on exactly four o'clock this afternoon. I know why he told me his pet Freckles Frecker, often keeping obbo there, had said this was a guaranteed quiet time. No, the Boxer was adamant that his chosen moment was the only really safe time to go in for one reason only. Because he'd been told by his FBI contacts that Liebling had booked a London flight. A flight arriving, in fact, when, if all went according to plan, a taxi from Heathrow would bring him to the mews at some point during the time Pantsie would be working slowly away on the safe door. Didn't he tell me it'd taken him a full hour the first time he'd done it?

Pantsie there at the safe. And myself, that bugger must have thought, standing there urging him on.

Christ, this is it. I should never have abandoned believing the Boxer would stop at nothing to make sure my inquiry got nowhere. He wants me gone. No, he wants me disgraced, if not shot by that American criminal. And wretched Pantsie being shot alongside me is a sacrifice he'd cheerfully have made.

He's a swine. A lunatic even. A man prepared to do that, just to make sure no one interferes with his wonderful élite Max. It's not really that he's determined to carry out the task the squad's been given, come what may. No, it's that he's determined the squad's success will be a triumph for him. The best detective at the head of the best squad the police has ever known. That's what the Boxer wants to be hailed as.

And he's not going to be.

If there's a senior officer in his precious squad who's in the pay of Pablo Grajales, that man, or that woman, is going to be named by me in a report to the Inspectorate of Constabulary. They're not going to be offered a quiet retirement *on medical grounds*. All right, I may have to allow the Boxer to wangle that much for bloody Outhwaite, since that seems more or less to have been done already. But for the officer Outhwaite was intending to blackmail, no, no escape. Trial at the Central Criminal Court. The full blast of publicity for the less than perfect Maximum Crimes Squad, and, damn it, the resignation of its overbearing boss.

She heard then Rekha's key in the door. For an instant she experienced a chill reprise of the moment when, with Pantsie snortingly breathing beside her, she had waited to hear the key being turned in the house door in the Mayfair mews.

But by the time Rekha came in she had recovered

enough to snatch her coat from where it was draped it over the radiator and be standing with it, still steamily damp, across her arm.

'Sorry,' she said, 'I've been trying to dry this on your radiator. But I think it's had enough rain steamed off now that it'll be okay just hanging up.'

'Not to worry,' Rekha said. 'Worse has happened in here than getting a coat dry. But what have you been doing letting it get so wet? And, come to that, why are you back so early and . . .? Well, actually you're looking pretty awful.'

'Awful? Yes, I suppose I must be. To tell you the truth, I'm a bit shaken up.'

'What's happened, for God's sake?'

'Well . . . Well, it's this. I've just realized the lengths some people are prepared to go to stop me doing my job.'

'Some people? No, don't tell me. The Boxer?'

'Him.'

'What's he done now? Wasn't tapping the phone here enough?'

'It wasn't. Not by any means. No, the devious sod's just tried to have me caught red-handed by a top-ranking American criminal, with a gun hidden in his flat, while I was breaking in there.'

'My God, you were doing that? And— And the Boxer did what you said? Even if you weren't shot, it would've meant the absolute end for you. Disgrace. I don't know, prison, anything.'

'Oh, I've thought of all that, believe me I have.'

'So what are you going to do? Have a blazing row with him? Or . . . Or can you report it all to lofty C.A.G.D. Anstruther? It'd at least put paid to the Boxer's career, if you could.'

'But I can't. I can't really. For one thing, I haven't got any hard evidence. Only a series of coincidences. Like that I suspect the Boxer knew about the time this fellow Reynolds Liebling was due to fly in from the States, and that the time he suggested, or even insisted, I go into that flat being pretty well exactly when Liebling would have got back there. Not enough, not when—'

She came to a halt.

'Yes? What?'

'I don't know, but swine though the Boxer may have been to me, what I might put in my report would mean the end of a career in the police that's been an example to everyone. I mean, whatever he's done, he's actually a dedicated police officer, a Number One detective, and . . .'

'And, sweet little Miss Martens doesn't want him out on his ear, élite copper that he is?'

'Well, yes. Yes, put it however you like. Much as at this moment – or at least until a moment ago – I was furious with the Boxer, I know he'll do more good, much more good, at the head of the Max than anyone else who's likely to replace him.'

'You're the one who's seen him at work,' Rekha said, 'and I haven't. Or only from a distance, and years ago. But— Well, are you really sure he's the élite figure you've painted him as? Okay, he's a leader. He's full of get-up-and-go. And, yes, if you're going to say someone's an élite figure that's something they'd have to have.'

She paused for a moment, took in a breath.

'But wouldn't an élite figure have to have something else? Something more? I wouldn't say this to just anyone, not in democratic Britain, but I know from my Brahmin ancestors all down the years that there are other qualities the true élite possess. Oh, not always. There are always the ones who go wrong, even a good many of them. But the others, the majority, possess – what? – a selflessness, the habit, engrained and engrained through centuries, of putting the greater good before their own wishes.'

'So, what you're saying is I should after all take my case against the Boxer to C.A.G.D. Anstruther?'

Rekha gave a sharp little laugh.

'But you can't, can you?' she said. 'You made it plain to me just now. The evidence you've got is practically non-existent. And, besides, as you also said, the Boxer, élite figure or not, does a damn good job.'

'So what am I going to do? I just don't know. I can't— No. No, I do know what I'll do. What time is it?'

'What time? What are you— It's almost five to six. I was thinking *Drinky-drinks.*'

But Harriet was reaching for the phone.

And then turning away.

'No, better be the mobile. The Boxer's tap may still be on, and I don't want him to know he's not beaten me yet.'

Chapter Eighteen

Harriet, zapping at her mobile, found, as she had been pretty certain she would, even at two or three minutes before six, Adah Zaborski still at her computer at the Business Park.

'Listen,' she said to her, 'there's something I want you to do. It's been at the back of my mind for some while, but I think the moment has come to look into it. Hard. See if it stands up, or if it's just a go-nowhere idea.'

'Ma'am?'

'It's this. I've reason to believe that DI Outhwaite when he had access to Reynolds Liebling's safe got hold of something about a fellow senior officer which he could use to blackmail him.'

'Ma'am.'

'Okay, your work on Outhwaite's bank account revealed no large sum paid in. But can he have been hiding such a sum anywhere else?'

'Yes, of course he could, ma'am. Easily. He could have an account, even half a dozen accounts here and there, under another name or under half a dozen other names. The only difficulty there would be that, when the Proceeds of Crime Bill becomes law, as it will do before too long, bank managers will be under an obligation to report suspicious payments to the

National Criminal Intelligence Service. Mr Outhwaite
will know this. Anyone working in a fraud squad will.
It's what we've been waiting for.'

'So you think he'll have had to find some other way
of hiding his big payment?'

'The only really safe way to conceal receiving a
really large sum is by getting paid only in untraceable
cash or, say, in diamonds. But those present certain
difficulties when it comes to converting them. Buyers
ask questions.'

'So it's get cash and stick it under the mattress,
bury it in the garden?'

'Well, there are better places. Especially if you don't
want whoever shares your bed or digs in your garden,
such as your wife, to know what you've acquired.'

'See what you mean. But, here's the thing. This is
what's occurred to me. Anyone who's demanded such
a large sum must still want to be able to use the money.
So can they take it in relatively small amounts and use
those to pay off their bigger recurrent bills? Wouldn't
they then show up on a bank account, only in a nega-
tive way?'

'Oh, yes, that could be done.'

'Well now, look at it this way. If it's a fellow senior
officer that Outhwaite was hoping, perhaps still is
hoping, to get a really big payment out of, enough to
let him march out of the police, go to Spain or somewhere, live the life of Reilly, then in fact that officer is
unlikely in any case to be able to find a big, big sum
in one fat lump.'

'Yes, ma'am, you're right. Whoever it is, on the
level of pay they're getting, they couldn't disburse, say,
fifty or sixty thousand pounds just like that. No, if
someone's paying Outhwaite, then it's perfectly likely

they're doing it by instalments. They'll have had to. So Outhwaite may not have been waiting to demand money all this while. No, he'll have had a payment, some payments perhaps, already. And they'll have been of amounts, say, not much more than a thousand at any one time, sums that would look more or less reasonable when paid in, a betting win, a lottery win, anything like that. Sums I could possibly have passed over. Ma'am, I'll get on to it.'

'Now?' Harriet asked.

There was a silence at the far end. But not a long one.

'Well, ma'am, I was thinking of calling it a day in a few minutes. It's actually just after six now. But—well, but, yes, if you think it's worth pursuing straight away, then, yes, I could work on, through the night if necessary.'

'And give me a call the moment you've found any-thing? At one o'clock, two, three, four, whenever?'

'Of course, ma'am.'

Harriet's bedside clock showed 2.37 when her mobile woke her with its discreet burble.

'DS Zaborski, ma'am.'

'Yes? Yes? You've found something?'

'Well, ma'am, this may turn out to mean nothing, but it is odd. Definitely odd.'

'Go on.'

'Well, it didn't actually take me all that long to go through Mr Outhwaite's account figures again, and, as I really knew I would, I didn't find any sums paid in, however small, that couldn't be simply explained.'

'No betting wins, a thousand quid, a bit more?'

'No, nothing that, looking into it, wasn't a wholly likely credit.'

'You're telling me nothing, Sergeant.'

'Yes, ma'am. But what I remembered then was that Mr Outhwaite's finances run closely with those of his wife. Well, I had realized that the first time I checked and I got Sergeant Downey to hack into her account too. I took it that you'd approve, ma'am.'

'Oh, yes, I approve. If this is the only way we can get at the truth of what's happening in the Max, I approve all right.'

'Yes, ma'am.'

Said with a trace of *rather you than me*.

'And you found something when you checked again now? In her account, in Mrs Outhwaite's account?'

'Well, it's actually Lady Annabella Outhwaite's account. Or – and this is why I didn't get on to it sooner – an account she had in her maiden name, Lady Annabella Foxbury, though made a joint one with him at some stage. But, yes, I found what we were looking for in Mr Outhwaite's own account. There were credit payments that on the face of it looked innocent enough, but when I examined them in more detail it became pretty clear they weren't what they had been made to look like. I can show you exactly why in the morning, but it'd take some time.'

'No, no. I'll accept your word for it,' Harriet said, thinking with a dart of amusement that it had turned out the *Yorkshire lass* Dick Reader had told her Outhwaite had married was the bearer of a title.

'But how much is involved in it all?' she asked.

'Well, this is what pretty well proves it, to my mind, ma'am. You see, none of those payments were for round sums. And that's always been a way of disguising certain payments, ones that should have been for an exact thousand, or ten thousand or whatever, by having a little extra added on to them so as they look natural. But these were for— Well, here's an example. One thousand and twenty-three pounds.'

'Yes, I see. I suppose if I was paying illegally acquired sums into my own account, I might add a few pounds to make the sum look less like a round-figures bribe.'

'Yes, ma'am, I dare say you would. But that would be where you made your mistake.'

'Mistake? How?'

'By rather carelessly making the odd sum one in pounds. You might get away with that once. But if anyone who knew what they were about examined your account, a series of payments in odd figures in pounds alone, no pence, would stand out a mile. And actually those ones were all for one thousand plus a figure in the twenties. A real give-away, to anyone who knows how to look'

'Oh, yes. So what you're saying, am I right, is that the Outhwaites' joint account has had sums paid in that, if my suspicious are at all right, came from an officer in the Max?'

'Yes, ma'am, I'd say so, or certainly paid by some-body for highly dubious reasons. Over the past couple of months they've been paid, or, to be accurate, Lady Annabella Foxbury has been paid a total of £12,237 exactly, in effect ten payments each of one thousand and each plus something in the twenties. And none of the sums were dividends or anything like that. She doesn't appear, in fact, to have had any income at all other than those payments. But there's no way at present of showing where those sums in amounts of

a thousand-plus came from originally. Of course, if
Outhwaite is blackmailing a fellow officer, then they
are most likely from that officer, by however roundabout a route. I might be able, say, by the day after
tomorrow to get hold of some other figures from
Sergeant Downey that would lead me some way
towards the original source. But even that would
require an unusually lucky break, and it's probable
that the payments will have been in cash originally.
Untraceable.'

'All right. If there's nothing more you can do till
you get those figures, there isn't. I shall be going down
as early as I can make it to that cottage the Outhwaites
have in Buckinghamshire. But I'll take DS Watson with
me. So, have tomorrow, or rather today, off. And thank
you.'

DI Outhwaite's home, Oaktree Cottage, lay a mile or
so outside the neighbouring Buckinghamshire village.
Harriet stood beside the car some fifty yards away,
looking at it, with beside her DS Watson, flap-ears
doubly reddened by the never-ending icily rain-flecked
east wind. Despite the hours she had lain awake plan-
ning the moves ahead after Adah Zaborski's call, she
had got to the Business Park before eight, in time to
give her team her customary swift daily briefing,
however little she was able to tell them. Originally she
had wanted to make a start even earlier, but then
she had calculated there would be nothing to be gained
by arriving before the Outhwaites were up and about.
This was no occasion for the dawn knock at the door.

'Cottage?' she said now to Watson. 'That's hardly
my idea of a cottage.'

The house in front of them, behind a quickset hedge out of which there stood the oak, now lightning-blasted, that must long ago have given it its name, looked as if it would have been once a farm labourer's dwelling. Now, however, a long wing, evidently recent, had been added to one side and on the other an extension held a two-car garage as well as a pair of stable-doors.

Harriet's conjecture about the latter was confirmed in a moment by the sound of a loud whinnying.

'A riding-horse,' Watson commented. 'It'll have cost a pretty penny all this. I can't see how it could have been done on a DI's pay.'

'No. But remember the wife is one Lady Annabella, Lady Annabella Foxbury originally. DS Zaborski tells me that she's got no income of her own at present, but she may have had some capital once.'

'Funny, I wouldn't have said Outhwaite's the sort to catch himself an heiress. Not by the look of him. Not exactly outgoing, and not any sort of a hunk.'

'Well, you never can tell when it comes to sexual attraction. But I'm inclined to agree with you, they're not quite the couple I'd have expected. When I was interviewing Outhwaite informally at the Cumberland Hotel last week, he came out with something his grandfather, who was a gardener at some big house somewhere, used to say about his employers, that they were – I can't quote as accurately as you, Sergeant – a different breed altogether. Queer folk, I think he said, who treated those below them as cattle, something of that sort.'

Watson looked distinctly shocked.

'Oh, yes, there were people like that, not all that

long ago. Though I doubt if we'll find Lady Annabella's quite from such a world as that, not outwardly at least.'

'I look forward to finding out,' Watson said, with a touch of tartness.

'Then into battle.'

It was Lady Annabella herself who opened the new-looking oak front door to Harriet's brisk knock. It could be no one else, Harriet thought. Probably late thirties, if groomed to look younger. Tall, with blonde hair down to her shoulders framing a pale face looking coldly out from blue eyes on either side of a long perfectly shaped nose. For a fleeting moment Harriet found herself reminded of Detective Superintendent the Hon. Maurice Quinton's just this side of effete good looks.

'Yes?'

The word delivered as if to someone selling something, or to a pair of identically dressed Jehovah's Witnesses.

Harriet had her warrant card ready and flipped it open.

'Detective Superintendent Martens and Detective Sergeant Watson. We'd like a word with Mr Outhwaite.'

'Would you indeed? But perhaps he won't want a word with you.'

'Then I'm afraid he'll have to change his mind. I am here conducting an inquiry on behalf of the Inspectorate of Constabulary.'

'Yes, we know all about that. It's done my husband enough harm as it is.'

She actually made as if to close the heavy door.

Harriet, rather than putting her foot there to prevent her, simply leant an inch or two further forward.

'If my inquiry has done any harm to Mr Outhwaite,'

she said, 'that can only be because he has behaved in a manner not in accordance with his duty as a police officer.'

'And if he has, his superior, Commander Boxall, has dealt with the matter.'

She looked now as if she was contemplating barging Harriet back before slamming the door shut. Harriet took a half-pace further forward. And stayed there, immobile.

'Look,' she said. 'You know very well that, even if Mr Outhwaite is on sick-leave, he has not yet been signed off as medically unfit. He is still a serving police officer, and I have the right to order him to see me. So shall we come in?'

And now Lady Annabella did step back.

Harriet was quick to make her way inside, contriving to leave the door wide for DS Watson. She found then, not greatly to her surprise, Jackson Outhwaite standing just inside the first room she came to.

'Mr Outhwaite,' she said sharply. 'I'd like a word. In private.'

Outhwaite glowered at her, but made way for her to enter with Watson, ears already at the high port, close on her heels.

'This may take a little time. May we sit down?' Harriet asked, giving the room a quick survey.

It said, in its every aspect, *real country cottage*. No kitsch horse brasses hung either side of the big open fireplace. Nothing cheap. But solid oak furniture, softly gleaming, a high-backed settle, a corner cupboard, two or three little low tables and with them two deep, squashed-looking armchairs covered in a dulled flowery-patterned chintz. On the far wall a long-case clock was heavily ticking.

'All right, sit all you like,' Outhwaite said. 'But I can't see what you want that'll take more than a minute to answer.'

Harriet was tempted to jump on the mutinous reply to get at once to what she must find out from the man who, it seemed almost certain, was blackmailing a fellow senior officer over the letter in Reynolds Liebling's safe. But she thought a more roundabout approach was likeliest to undermine that truculence.

'Well,' she replied, almost the soft detective, 'I'm afraid that what I have to inquire into is somewhat delicate. So one question and one answer will hardly suffice.'

Outhwaite looked puzzled.

Harriet made herself keep hidden the trickle of pleasure she felt at this sign that she had succeeded in putting the man opposite at a disadvantage, however tenuous.

'So what do you want to know then?' he asked, lowering himself into one of the chintz-covered armchairs at an angle to the uncomfortable wooden settle where Harriet had seated herself, Watson beside her.

'There's no way to put this nicely,' Harriet said, almost praying that the ice she had felt in the grey-faced detective at the Cumberland Hotel and yet more in the interview room at Persimmon House was glistening with the first watery traces of melting. 'What it's my duty in essence to learn from you is how can you, on a detective inspector's pay, keep up a house like this? A two-car garage? Even a stable?'

'My wife's a rich woman.'

A take-it or leave-it statement.

'I don't think so,' Harriet replied without harshness,

Adah Zaborski's investigation of Lady Annabella's bank account firm in her mind.

'What do you know about her?' Outhwaite shot back, however. 'She's the daughter of a lord, a big landowner, isn't she? Why shouldn't she be rich, bloody rich?'

'She isn't, not at this time,' Harriet replied, still with unemphatic gravity. 'We know about her finances.'

'How? How can you? All that's someone's private business.'

Was there now a hint of panic? Harriet gave it no weight.

'Not when that person is married to someone under suspicion of illegal activities,' she said, laying out the words like the cards of a winning hand in some trivial game.

'But I . . .'

He faded into silence.

'No, you're not someone above suspicion, are you?' she said, reasonably. 'Rather the other way about, in fact. After all, why are you down here on what's supposed to be sick-leave, if Commander Boxall wasn't convinced, however much you wouldn't answer when he questioned you, that you're guilty of something. So we come to the difficult point once again. The money for this place, the horse in the stable there, all that, where does it come from?'

'It doesn't come.'

A light flicked into life in Harriet's head at this abruptly delivered answer. Had she now hit the right spot? Was the truth beginning to appear?

How to tease it at last to the fore?

'Yes,' she said, tones dulcet. 'I guessed the trouble might be that.'

Outhwaite, in the depths of the chintzy armchair, gave her a single querying look. Was it with a touch of something like hope?

And then in an instant he seemed to crumble into wracked despair.

'God knows, I should never have got together with her.'

The words had come tumbling out, as if he had had no control over the thoughts churning in his mind.

For a moment or two he sat in silence. But the marks of despair were plain to see on his drained face.

'It was bloody odd that I did,' he said eventually, with a laugh that was as much a groan. 'It was the first time in years that I'd gone back up to Yorkshire. For my old man's funeral. And that was touch-and-go. We'd grown far apart, the two of us. I'd never wanted to live the sort of life he did. Did I tell you, there in that hotel, that my grandfather was a gardener at a big house? Well, if I did, I didn't tell you, too, that my dad just took over when the old fellow died. Gardener to Lord Foxbury. But I wasn't going to follow in his footsteps, as everybody just expected me to do. So I did the first thing that came into my head so as to get away. I went to London. I joined the Met.'

Harriet thought of what Dick Reader, Outhwaite's old friend and enemy, had said about what he had learnt during long, dull hours of night surveillance from his fellow officer. His skewed reason for joining the police, that hope of his that one day somehow a career there would lead to money. Money enough to escape for ever from the looming shadow of thraldom among a lower species.

But she kept silent. And, as she had hoped, more

words came out of the mouth of the suddenly sad man in the squashy armchair.

'Yes, the most damn stupid thing I ever did, going back for the funeral. The most stupid and yet, in a way, the best thing. Or so I thought.'

He sat forward.

'God knows how it happened,' he said. 'But Anna-bella, Lady Annabella, was there at the burial, like all the family who were at home. Noblesse oblige, as they say. And, I suppose it was because I wanted to show I was now as good as them, I went over afterwards and— And I bloody well chatted her up. She was not much more than a teenager then, you know. God knows what she saw in me . . . No, I do I know. I know now all right. She saw— She saw a servant. A servant for free, a servant for life. She's never quite said that, but that's why she married me, married me almost before I knew what was happening. Because she knew even then that she was not ever going to have the money to live the life she'd been brought up to. Never the need to do a hand's turn. And a servant I've been ever since. Doing all the work of the house, all that gets done, grooming that fucking horse, polishing the bloody woodwork, everything. She's got a way with her, runs in the family. She says *Do it*, and I do it.'

Outhwaite shook his head from side to side like a spaniel shaking off water.

'That's how it's been,' he said. 'You asked how we could run this place on a DI's pay. Well, that's the answer. All right, Annabella had a bit of capital. It's what bought the cottage in the first place. She just said she had to live in the country, never mind me working in the Met. It paid for the new building, all that. But after it was just run up the bills without another thought and leave the work to the servant, the unpaid servant.'

What an extraordinary story, Harriet thought. What a crushing reversal it must have been for him when, thinking he had achieved the freedom he had always wanted by marrying the daughter of a monied landowner, he found she hadn't any income of her own, only a small sum in capital. Then finding himself a wage slave twice over, first to the Met and then yet more to the woman who, as he said, had married him for what she had seen she could make him become.

So . . . So, now when he's found after all, when he must have despaired of ever doing so, what would seem to be a golden key to the life of freedom that's always been his goal, now what has he done? I think I can make a pretty good guess. He's been putting the monthly payments he's been getting from— From who? Who? He's been putting them into the Lady Annabella account without telling her anything about them. I can see her, well enough, as the sort of young woman, brought-up in wealthy circumstances, who never checks her bank statements. And he's been intending, when he's gathered in enough, just to disappear. No longer the unpaid servant, a free man.

Poor devil. Still fighting to believe, no doubt, it's not all going to come unstuck.

But it is going to. I'm going to unstick it.

If just now he shook his head like a spaniel emerging from a dirty pond, I'm not going to give him a reassuring pat.

'All right,' she said, 'you were married and you found you'd become the unpaid servant you were telling me about. A miserable life. But then in a stroke of luck you came across that letter in Reynolds Liebling's safe and realized someone else, a fellow officer in the Max, was going to have to pay and pay to let you break your bondage. Yes?'

A grunt perhaps of admission. Or perhaps not.

'So, tell me,' she said, almost holding her breath, 'tell me now while you can still get yourself out of the worst of your trouble, who was it who wrote the letter in Liebling's safe?'

But now the spaniel failed to wag its tail. It bared its teeth.

'I said before, I saw nothing there. And there's nothing I'm going to add to that.'

When I've got so far. So far into his head. He can't just go back, like a spring released, to that brute state of dumbness.

And I'm not going to let him. I'm not.

'That's not good enough. When Commander Boxall interviewed you and you refused to give a plain answer to his questions, you were glad enough to get out of it by taking sick leave with a view to a medical discharge. But, let me tell you, if I have anything at all to do with it, you won't be seeing one of those tame medical officers who've been giving out *Unfit for further duties* certificates for years. Those days are gone. You had better reconcile yourself to appearing in court.'

'Why would I find myself there? I've done nothing wrong.'

'Then why are you here, pretending to be at death's door?'

'I'm not. I wasn't feeling well when Commander Boxall saw me, and he suggested I take some time off. That's all.'

'But it's not what Commander Boxall told me.'

'What else but that could he tell you? He'd got nothing to tell.'

'No, of course he hadn't. You refused to answer his questions. But now you're going to answer mine.'

Outhwaite sat there in silence for a few seconds. Then he replied.

'All right, ask me what you like. I've told you everything I can, but if you want to go on asking, ask.'

Harriet thought hard. Plainly he believes he can't be touched. He thinks he's only to sit here saying nothing each time he's asked about that letter that nobody – damn it – has seen or can get to see now, and in the end he'll be able to scrape up everything in the Lady Annabella account and get out of the country. And he might yet pull it off. If he's tough enough. We've nothing on him, not a jot of real evidence.

Then, perhaps because in her mind she had pronounced the words *the Lady Annabella account*, she glimpsed a tiny possible penetrative way ahead.

'Very well, let me ask you this: why in your so-called joint bank account with your wife are there concealed a number of sums amounting to exactly £12,237?'

And the shot went home. She had guessed right: Lady Annabella must know nothing of what was in her account. Outhwaite's sullenly grey face had looked abruptly as if it was a target in a shooting gallery and the bullet had gone right through the nose.

'I don't—' Then recovery began to set in. 'What the hell are you lot doing prying into Annabella's private bank account. I'll have you out of whatever bloody police force you belong to for that. You see if I won't.'

'It's the Greater Birchester Police,' Harriet

answered. 'Birchester is a city in the Midlands, in case you don't know.'

It wasn't much likely that it had been DI Outhwaite who had shouted out *dozy northern tart* in the office next to the Boxer's in Persimmon House. But make it clear to him, as crudely as may be, that he isn't being questioned by anyone he can bluster into silence.

'I know where Birchester is, and I don't care. You had no right to go poking into Annabella's account.'

'Not if it's where you've been hiding away from your wife the money you're being paid to keep silent about that letter in Liebling's safe?'

Yes. Yes. I've got him rattled now. He knows I've only to tell Lady Annabella what's there in that account and she'll guess what he's intending to do. Skedaddle. And she'll stop him.

'I've told you I didn't see any letter.'

'Come on, we're past all that now. You saw a letter in that safe, not of course the one you so carefully described to me with the Hon. Maurice Quinton's name at its head? In red embossed print? But you did see a letter and the officer who wrote it certainly wasn't Mr Quin—'

'And what makes you think it was an off—?'

Harriet could see him regretting the wild challenge even as it was still spilling out of his mouth. *What makes you think it was an off—* What made me think it was a police officer? Just my cast of mind. Because I've been looking for a renegade police officer ever since Mr Anstruther entrusted me with the inquiry that Sunday morning. But it never needed to be a member of the Maximum Crimes Squad. It could be someone else, anyone else, anyone who would be ruined if it was known they communicated with Reynolds Liebling.

'Mr Outhwaite,' she said, the thrill of the chase running hot once again. 'I have Detective Sergeant Watson sitting here beside me. He has heard every word that's come from your lips, as I have. Together the two of us can offer evidence that will very likely see you spending a number of years in prison. However, if you now tell me who is the person you have just referred to, the one who isn't after all a police officer, I think I can say your honesty will serve you when it comes to presenting a case against you. Or even that it may be considered that there's no case to present.'

Now, is it going to come? The name? The answer? The name, so unexpectedly, not of an officer of the Max, but of someone else? Of who? Who?

Yes, have I beaten the Boxer? Have I overcome every obstacle there's been in my way? Is this my answer at last?

Chapter Nineteen

'Bloody Lord Candover. That's who, if you've got to know.'

Outhwaite shot upright from his squabby chintz-covered chair, face flooded with red-raging anger.

'Yes. Bloody high-and-mighty, idle party-going Lord Candover, that idiot who's my boss, your bloody boss, the – what's it? – minister of fucking state at the Home Office. And the Boxer's boss, too, come to that. I suppose it's Lord sodding Candover who set you up to poke your nose into what that bloody *Sunday Herald* story hinted at. Yes, sodding penniless Lord Candover, weeping into his wine that he's only got his ministerial pay to keep him from the gutter. The gutter where he fucking belongs.'

As the released torrent of abuse poured out, Harriet sat there on the hard wooden settle feeling facts and events whirling round and re-patterning themselves in her head.

Lord Candover penniless. Yes, true enough, to the extent at least that he was supposed to be in dire financial straits. I've seen the odd snide gossip-column reference to that, generally coupled with some tale of his never-ending party-going. But Candover, after all, the man who wrote the letter in Liebling's safe? Yes, easy enough now to see how Liebling, crook and society darling, must have been sent to London with the sole purpose of getting at that influential, vulnerably *penniless* and, yes, *ditzy* figure. Wasn't that what Maurice Quinton, his old schoolfellow, called him, *Ditzy* Candover? *Ditzy*, meaning, yes, this is the word: *unsound.*

And why did Grajales plan all this, send Liebling to London? Suddenly obvious now. The famous, much debated Euro Fence. Once set up, it'll deal a tremendous blow to Grajales's people-smuggling empire. But now, with Candover in his grip, Grajales must be within an ace of sinking the scheme. It's already strongly opposed in all the votes-rich little Englander circles. One strong anti-voice from within, and British backing for the idea will be so tepid nothing will ever be finalized.

Then other thoughts rushed in.

Frank Parkins's *Sunday Herald* so-called scoop. Yes, he had had one, or the tiny signs of one. But not what he'd guessed at. No, who was it who had insisted that the way to deal with Parkins's hints, was not under Section 49 of the 1964 Police Act with an inquiry by a chief constable, but to have some lower-ranking provincial police officer conduct it? Lord Candover. His idea to give the inquiry to an officer too far down the pecking order, too lacking in the ability to go up against entrenched high-powered obstruction, to get anywhere.

The pattern complete.

She rose to her feet, sweeping up with her stony-faced DS Watson, whose big red ears had just heard more astonishing words than they ever yet had.

'Jackson Outhwaite,' she said, 'I am arresting you on suspicion of making false statements to the police.

I warn you: you are not obliged to say anything, but it may harm your defence if you do not mention when questioned something which you later rely on in court. Anything you do say may be given in evidence.'

Jackson Outhwaite, detective inspector and feudal serf, stood there mutely, the high red flush on his cheeks gradually fading.

'Right, let's go,' Harriet said.

She went across and opened the door, leaving Watson to escort Outhwaite after her.

'What the hell do you think you're doing?'

Lady Annabella was there, not three feet away, standing where she must have heard everything, confronting Harriet like a chatelaine of old defying a party of drunken outlaws robbing her of her absent lord's goshawks and gerfalcons.

But Harriet was not going to enter any feudal past.

'I regret to say,' she answered matter-of-factly, 'that I have just arrested your husband. We are taking him to New Scotland Yard. Perhaps you should inform your solicitor.'

'Fuck you, fuck you, fuck you.'

Lady Annabella, transformed in an instant from brave figure of ancient romance to everyday virago, shifted half a step back allowing the three of them to pass. Harriet lifted the latch of the new oak front door and led the way out. DS Watson, hand at Outhwaite's elbow, took care, she noted, to close the door quietly and politely behind them.

Then, outside, she saw with astonishment that the rain, which had seemed ceaselessly to be blowing into her face from the moment she had arrived in London, had simply come to an end. Looking up, she saw a last black cloud scudding away, and, yes, beyond the

245

shadow of the long wings of the house there was sunlight.

In the far corner of the rank lawn between house and hedge, she realized, a large old forsythia bush had apparently just that minute come into bloom. Can it have all come out while we were inside, she asked herself. Hardly. But, for all that she must have seen it before going up and knocking at that raw oak door, it looked as if it really might have come to life in just that short time in one great joyous starburst of spring-heralding yellow.

It's as if it's a sign, she thought, unable to withhold a grin of self-mockery.

With a suddenly brisker step, she led the way over to the car.

Then, when she had seen Outhwaite safely installed in it, she moved aside a few yards and took out her mobile.

All very well to freeze off Lady Annabella by suggesting she should get in touch with her solicitor. But, once someone had heard that a senior Maximum Crimes Squad officer was under arrest, what might happen? The news could pass from one person to another, up and down the great ramshackle tower of British society. And, perhaps even inside an hour, it could have reached that two-worlds figure, Reynolds Liebling. Who would, first, take Lord Candover's letter from his safe and then hurry to Heathrow and the first flight on any airline out of the country.

She punched out the number of Persimmon House and asked for the Boxer, allowing herself a moment of ambiguous pleasure at the thought that now the two of them were firmly on the same side.

'Harriet Martens, Commander,' she answered

briskly when the little plastic box in her hand had seemed actually to quiver at his banged-out 'Boxall.'

'Well?'

Equally banged-out.

If I manage this in the right way, she thought at once, it'll be the end of all aggressive answering.

Then a phrase from her girlhood rose up in her mind, something her father had often quoted from Churchill. *In victory magnanimity.* Yes, the not-so dozy northern tart has beaten the Boxer. But not the time crudely to rub it in.

'Commander, I am down in Buckinghamshire where I have just arrested Outhwaite. He's answered our question at last. The letter in Reynolds Liebling's safe was written, not by any officer of the Max, but by – Lord Candover.'

There was a momentary silence at the other end. But it was only momentary. The Boxer was as quick on the uptake as anybody in any police force.

'Candover?' the name came like a cannon shot into the faintly buzzing silence. 'Yes, by God, Lord bloody Candover. That figures. Yes. And you've only just arrested Outhwaite?'

'Five minutes ago, less.'

'Good. Right, I'm on my way round to Liebling's flat. With a couple of my lads. We'll have the cuffs on that bugger before he knows where he is. And, don't you worry, no one's going to lay hands on that letter before I do.'

Then at the far end there was a pause, the shortest of pauses. And . . . 'Well done, Miss Martens. Bloody good work.'

A few minutes later they were on their way back to London, the car explosive with suppressed tension. But it was not until they had to slow down for the solid, grey-faced streams of suburban traffic that Harriet, in the back beside the hunched shape of Jackson Outhwaite, began to think what lay ahead when she had dealt with Outhwaite at the Yard.

Right, what I'm faced with is telling C.A.G.D. Anstruther that the minister he reports to is Pablo Grajales's cat's-paw, and that my inquiries have shown that the only wrongdoing in the élite Maximum Crimes Squad has been Detective Inspector Outhwaite's now unsuccessful attempt to make improper use of the evidence of Lord Candover's crime that he came across in the course of his duties, though I'd better omit the fact that his duties at the time were a piece of gross corner-cutting on the orders of that one-man infantry battalion, the Boxer.

Then Mr Anstruther will have to undertake the task of explaining to the home secretary how far up into the world of high government Grajales's billions have taken him, and the home secretary, in her turn, will have to tell the prime minister and after him the whole Cabinet. What next? The trial, I suppose, of the wretched man beside me here. And, a nice thought, when the news of that comes to light whatever Mrs Althea Raven and Frank Parkins may have had in mind for me in the way of a nasty story in the *Sunday Herald* will be a dead duck.

But soon there'll be a really sensational arrest and trial, Candover's comeuppance.

Or, wait, perhaps not. Perhaps not. Will there be simply a sudden resignation and the often repeated, hollow *to spend more time with his family*? And then will a similar quiet tucking-away be arranged for Outhwaite here? Well, for him perhaps there's already been punishment enough, the years of married misery, the collapse of all his long-cherished hopes.

And I wonder now ... Did C.A.G.D. Anstruther foresee all this, or the possibility of it, when, adroitly outmanoeuvring his political master, he chose out of all the provincial detective superintendents he might have selected the much-hyped Hard Detective to conduct the investigation that Lord Candover intended to fall to the ground?

But, no. I think in fact C.A.G.D. Anstruther, smiling his occasional reticent smile that Sunday morning at his big, bare desk in the Home Office, stroking his nose between thumb and forefinger as if to draw down the right thought, chose someone more fitted for the task than the Hard Detective. He chose— It was what, sitting there opposite him all that time ago, with a flicker of amusement I labelled myself as, a female gentleman. He chose a female gentleman.

And, damn it, he chose rightly.